CHASING DESTINY

Sydney Ashcroft

SYDNEY ASHCROFT
DANI NICHOLS

Dani Nichols

CHASING DESTINY

CITY OWL PRESS
www.cityowlpress.com

Cover Design by Mibl Art and Tina Moss. All stock photos licensed appropriately.

Edited by Amanda Roberts.

For information on subsidiary rights, please contact the publisher at info@cityowlpress.com.

Print Edition ISBN: 978-1-944728-97-7

Digital Edition ISBN: 978-1-944728-98-4

Printed in the United States of America

For the folks of Subreality Cafe and the Dancing Evil Oreo of Chocolaty Goodness.

CHAPTER ONE

BERLIN, GERMANY 1941

Sometimes, the call of angels demanded sacrifice, and this was the second time Akantha was deep within the heart of Germany during a world war. Akantha, now known as Alexis Rowland, had many jobs in the past twenty-four hundred years, but this was by far the worst and her least favorite. Two years as a spy in Nazi Germany wasn't glamorous, but it was necessary if the Allies had a chance of winning the war.

Voices drifted in from the open windows near the ceiling, and Akantha paused in photographing documents containing sensitive information. Other people in the offices at this time of the night was not an uncommon thing, but she recognized both voices and continued to listen. Himmler spoke freely when he thought no one else was around. Not everything was on the classified papers she looked at daily, and every bit of information helped.

"We have a spy problem," Karl Wolff, adjutant to Himmler, said. Thoughts of watching the life pour out of both men always brought a small smile to her face. "Our couriers carrying orders for the commanders for Operation Barbarossa were ambushed. We assume the information is now in the hands of the enemy. "

"Enemy spies are a hazard of war," Himmler responded. What would he think if he knew one sat in the next room listening? She allowed herself the briefest of smiles.

"Yes, but this one is quite concerning. The mission was top secret and very few individuals were aware of the couriers' missions. The whole eastern operation could be in jeopardy."

Akantha's heart raced in her chest and blood thundered in her ears, drowning out the soft whoosh of the fan overhead. As Himmler's secretary, she was allowed access to the most sensitive information, and she passed it along to the resistance and Allied forces. Did they suspect her? The fear of being discovered sat in her stomach like a rock—cold, hard, and immovable.

"This is serious," Himmler agreed. "We need to find this person immediately. This is something that will reach the Führer, and I must answer to him. Who had access to this information?"

"You, me, your secretary, and three others."

Panic welled up, creating a lump in her throat, but she forced herself to remain calm. Panicking never solved anything and usually produced disastrous results. She'd stay calm and find a way to cast suspicion off her. It wouldn't take them long to find out she passed the information on to the Special Operations Executive if she didn't keep it together.

"I want you to ferret out this spy and bring him to me. I will deal with him personally."

"Of course, sir. Will this impact our plans for Russia?"

"I do not believe so."

Akantha looked at the papers and folders on the desk in front of her. She brought the camera up but stopped when she heard them continue.

"Our troops continue to move through Italy," Wolff reported. "A spear is rumored to be in the Vatican. Mussolini is cooperating with our search, though he is not aware of what we are searching for."

"Good. Acquiring the spear is our number one priority at the moment," Himmler replied. "Legends say it holds unimaginable power and can shape the fate of the world. I am confident the *Ahnenerbe* will find it. It's imperative we have it, even if we have to bring every spear we find back to Germany."

She sat down in the wooden chair and gripped the armrests, her knuckles turning white. The last thing the world needed was the Nazis getting their hands on the Spear of Destiny. They couldn't be talking about anything else. Himmler was obsessed with the occult and had sent teams all over the world searching for legendary, even mythical, objects. Others would have to pass information on to the SOE. Akantha had a new mission.

"Understood, sir," Wolff replied. "What about the one from Vienna?"

"I don't believe it's the true spear. Something so powerful, so important, would not be kept in such an obvious place."

"The Führer thinks it is the true spear."

Silence roared and each tick of the clock on the wall lasted an eternity.

"It is not." A chill froze her spine and her stomach twisted into a Gordian knot. Did he know more than he let on?

"Herr Holtz believes it is elsewhere."

Her heart pounded as she waited for Himmler to respond. "Herr Holtz will take as many troops as he needs. I want any rumored to be the true spear brought to Wewelsburg. With the Spear of Destiny in our hands, we will be unstoppable."

"It shall be done."

"How goes the search for the other items?" Himmler asked.

Other items? Fear wrapped icy hands around her heart. A myriad of weapons rumored to have power existed, and the Nazis getting their hands on any of them was unimaginable. It was bad enough bullets, bombs and tanks caused death on a scale unprecedented in history, but now the Nazis were looking for items that could alter the world in unfathomable ways. Millions would die. Tens of millions. Her own immortal existence was threatened as well, along with the existence of people she had known for centuries.

"The search continues, but so far we haven't been able to find any of the other items."

"I had hoped the news would be better. The summer solstice approaches and I would like to have all the items in our possession by then."

"We will have them."

"Good."

Silence settled over the two rooms and she wondered if they had left. The door to the office opened and Himmler's form filled the doorway. His head tilted to the side when he spotted her sitting at his desk. "Alexis? It's late. What are you doing in here?"

She slid her hands into the pockets of her jacket as casually as she could, slipping the small Minox Riga in. "It's only nine. I was going over your schedule for tomorrow and organizing all the paperwork for you to review." Despite the pounding in her chest and thundering in her ears, she kept a calm outward appearance. She placed her hands on the desk, hoping he didn't take notice of how they shook. This wasn't the first time he had walked in on her going through papers, looking for information. The prepared response slipped past her lips as natural as breathing.

Akantha took the position of Himmler's secretary when Hedwig Potthast left. A few months passed before she could get into his bed, but the invaluable information she collected made her personal sacrifices worth something. She played the good little Nazi and was paid in valuable information she then passed along to SOE contacts. Even in the heart of Berlin, people resisted Nazi rule.

"You work too much, my dear." He moved around the desk to stand next to her. Her eyes rose to meet his smiling face.

"Your schedule is complex and takes time to organize. Working odd hours isn't unheard of for either of us."

He nodded. "Yes, we do tend to work around the clock."

"You're too important to the cause for me to allow you to fail." The bitter words came out seamlessly across her tongue. Boosting his ego always worked to take his mind off what she was doing. The last thing she needed was him questioning why she was going through papers containing sensitive information.

"Everyone must contribute to the cause as they can," he said. "I do what I can." Himmler smiled benevolently.

"I left a copy of tomorrow's schedule on your desk."

"Did you put in a few hours in the afternoon tomorrow for me to visit my family?"

"Of course," she answered. His plans presented her with the opportunity to sneak out of Berlin and start looking for the spear. Akantha usually used the time when he went to visit his wife, or his other mistress, to meet her contact in Berlin and pass information along to the Allies. It was dangerous, but she enjoyed the thrill.

He held out a hand to her.

Breathing deeply, she gathered her courage. Tyranny, like hell, was not easily conquered. She remembered reading Thomas Paine's words back in 1776 during the dawn of the American Revolution. A long time had passed, but the words still rang true. Hitler, with the backing of the juggernaut of the German army, was a tyrant and needed to be stopped. Placing her hand in his, she rose from the chair. She forced a smile as he stepped closer. His head lowered and his mouth covered hers.

Her stomach churned from the false intimacy and she fought to keep from pulling away. Revulsion welled up every time he touched her. Screwing her courage to the sticking place, she returned the kiss.

A slight sigh slipped past her lips when the kiss ended. Every moment around him was a test of self-control and every time he touched her she wanted to take a long bath and scrub her skin raw. "It's time we should be out of here and in bed," he whispered. Sex was a useful tool to get information and one she didn't mind using even if it meant cozying up with the enemy. She may regret sleeping with him for a century or two, but if it helped stop the Nazis it would be worth the burden of regret.

"Yes, it is," she agreed while thinking of interesting ways to kill him. One day he would die a slow and painful death by her hand and she would enjoy every second of it.

"Then come," he said as he brought her hand up and placed a kiss on her knuckles.

The door squeaked behind them and hope welled up. With luck he would be pulled away for the evening and she would be able to slip away earlier than planned.

He turned on his heel and faced the source. Akantha looked around Himmler, spotting a low-ranking officer. "I apologize for the interruption. Herr Holtz is downstairs."

"Very well," Himmler said. "I will go down and see him now."

The officer saluted and disappeared from the doorway. Himmler turned back to face her. "It seems our immediate plans are to be postponed."

She feigned disappointment. "Duties always come first."

"Yes, but I would rather keep our plans."

A genuine smile appeared on her face. Let him think it was for their 'plans', but it was more relief. She wouldn't have to tolerate his vile touch tonight. "As would I."

"I must see to Herr Holtz." He turned toward the door, took one step, and stopped. He turned back to her. "Come with me," he said and held out his hand.

"Is there something you require?" She straightened her uniform, looking every inch the loyal Nazi she was supposed to be.

"No, but I would like you by my side."

She regarded him for a long moment and nodded. Did he suspect something? He never had qualms about leaving her alone in his office. Nervously she wiped the palms of her hands on her skirt. She followed him out of the office.

The spacious building in the heart of Berlin functioned as the headquarters of the SS and it housed some of the top officers. Although Himmler had a private house in the suburbs for his family, he rarely stayed there. Instead, he stayed as close to Hitler and the center of power as he could. Despite the late hour, bright lights reflected off the polished marble of the floor. Plush carpet ran down the middle of the hall and stolen works of art adorned the walls. The looted paintings spoke to the art lover in her, and her fingers itched to tear them off the walls and return them to their rightful owners. The thought of the Nazis looting museums and stealing from people was another thing to hold against them. She clenched her hands into fists as she imagined reaching out and strangling the man walking in front of her.

She followed him through the building and ignored the few people they passed. They all gave Himmler a wide berth and looked past her. She preferred it that way. It allowed her to move more freely and gather much-needed information. She followed him and froze in the doorway when she saw the individual standing in the center of the room.

Six hundred years ago, when she had a different life and name, she first saw his face, but it cut through the present and let the past rush back in a torrent. "Matheus," she whispered as her heart skipped a beat.

CHAPTER TWO

Matheus, now going by Herr Holtz, was a Nazi. A whisper of a prayer fell past her lips, praying her eyes were deceiving her; to think otherwise would be unfathomable. Matheus was one of the best men she knew, a Templar at one time, and her lover for over two centuries. Her heart refused to believe he was enmeshed in the evil of the Third Reich and the Nazis.

"Alexis." Himmler motioned for her to join them.

Akantha took a deep breath and stepped into the room. Himmler was pedantic, dull, and dogmatic, but the man had a shrewdness about him, he was ambitious and was unquestioningly loyal to Hitler, which made him very dangerous. She maintained the loyal charade every second of the day.

"This is my assistant, Alexis Rowland. Alexis, this is Herr Holtz."

"A pleasure to see you again." Akantha extended a hand and hoped Himmler didn't see how it shook. Of all people, Matheus was one of the last she expected to see and the least objectionable. She looked up into his warm brown eyes and a smiled. His hair, normally long and wavy, was considerably shorter and his face lacked any trace of stubble. He wore a pair of glasses, making him a striking image in the uniform, but Akantha preferred him with longer hair and some whiskers.

"The pleasure is mine." Matheus took her hand and gave it a fond squeeze.

His hand was warm compared to hers and electricity coursed through her. A hundred years had passed since she saw him, six hundred since she met him, and it was as if she were seeing him for the first time. All the old emotions came rushing back in a flood and her smile grew, becoming more genuine.

"You know each other?" Himmler's forehead wrinkled and his brows drew together in thought.

"We know each other from childhood," Matheus answered without hesitation. Immortals always had a story ready to explain to others how they knew each other. It saved time and warded off unwanted questions. The generic "we knew each other from childhood" was the one they used the most. "We grew up in the same village."

Akantha nodded. "We haven't seen each other since." Her voice wavered as the butterflies grew. This was crazy. She was acting like a love-struck fool. She took a deep breath and tried to shove those emotions aside.

"I'm glad I've been able to reunite two longtime friends. Herr Holtz is undertaking a special mission for me," Himmler explained and relaxed.

"I'm sure he'll complete the mission, whatever it may be." The only thing she wanted was to rush into Matheus's arms. Self-control had to win over impulse. She couldn't afford to act recklessly.

"Your faith in me is reassuring." Matheus smiled and released her hand. Her heart melted a little under his smile and her knees quivered. The memories of centuries together raced around in her head.

"*Reichsführer-SS* Himmler would not have honored you with this mission if he thought you would fail," Akantha said, appealing to Himmler's ego.

"Alexis is correct. I would not trust anyone else."

"What task will Herr Holtz be undertaking?" she asked, doubting he would answer.

"I've been tasked to find an important item," Matheus answered.

Himmler nodded. "The item is very important to our cause and will ensure victory over the enemies of the Reich." Of course, Himmler didn't mention the item in from of her. Trust only went so far.

"There is no one better to find it. Herr Holtz was always good at finding lost items."

"I'll leave the two of you to get reunited. There is something I must see to. Do not keep him long, Alexis. If you'll excuse me?"

Akantha and Matheus nodded. They watched him leave, then Akantha turned to Matheus. "What are you doing here?" she asked in French, keeping her voice low.

He leaned in to kiss her cheek. "It's a pleasure to see you again, Akantha," he replied in kind. His husky voice was low and his breath brushing across her ear sent a shiver through her. A longing to be alone with him grew inside of her and she pushed it down. Such feelings were dangerous.

"Alexis," she corrected in a low voice. Her real name sounded foreign to her own ears, since she hadn't heard it in at least three decades. Here she had to be Alexis, not Akantha.

"Of course. It's good to see you. How long has it been?"

"Since the Crimean War. You're looking well." He didn't look any different than he did when she last saw him a hundred years ago. "Handsome as ever."

"You are as beautiful as ever. You don't look a day over two thousand."

Weak-kneed, heat caressed her cheeks and she bowed her head. So much time had passed and she still loved him. Old feelings didn't die easily and didn't stay buried or controlled. "Flattery, sir..."

He offered an arm. "Shall we go for a walk?"

Akantha blinked, a bit surprised, but then realized he wanted to go somewhere out of Nazi earshot to talk. She took the offered arm and he led her to the main entrance and out the door. It was a cool evening for June, but refreshing, and helped clear her head after Matheus's unexpected presence. The love-struck girl inside was pushed aside.

They descended the steps and he turned her to the right.

He broke the silence first. "I didn't expect to see you working for the Nazis," he said, continuing to speak in French.

"I'm not working for them. I'm gathering any information I can and passing it to the Allies. What are you doing here?" The thought of lying to him didn't cross her mind. He would never betray her to the Nazis.

"I'm doing all I can to impede their efforts."

Relief flooded through Akantha. He was too good of a man to believe in what the Nazis spewed forth. "Does that include finding the Spear of Destiny for them?"

"I'm going to find it, but I'm not going to let them get their hands on it."

Akantha kissed his cheek. The familiar scent brought back memories of long summer evenings together and cold winter nights with limbs entwined. Had it been so long since she last saw him? Why didn't she find him sooner? A hundred years was far too long.

He turned his face and his mouth hovered near hers. She breathlessly pulled back, despite the overwhelming urge to kiss him, and turned her face away. The streets appeared empty, but unseen eyes could be watching. "I'm sorry."

A rueful smile appeared on his face and she knew they shared regrets. "I am too."

It would have been too easy to let all thoughts of war go and spend the next few hours getting reacquainted, but they had a mission to complete. It had been some time since she had slept with someone she cared about, and it would be some time still before she allowed herself the luxury. "Maybe when this war is over we can spend some time together."

"I look forward to it."

"As do I." Seeing him after the war gave her something to look forward to and would keep her going. His presence was a sudden light in the blackness of war. "Where are you going to look for the spear?" she inquired. A different topic was safer and wiser. "The Nazis cannot be allowed to get their hands on it. The world is at risk if they do."

"How so?"

"It's one of the most powerful weapons in existence."

"I thought it was more of a symbol than anything."

She shook her head. "I wish that were the case. Where are you going to look?"

"I'm not sure. There are ten spears rumored to be the Spear of Destiny. The one in Vienna is already in Hitler's possession. I was thinking about starting in Istanbul. Constantine was said to have it in his possession. One was passed around between the European monarchs and lost."

"I may be of some help. I know people who may have a good idea where it could be."

He lifted a dark brow and looked at her. "Any help would be greatly appreciated." He took her hand and squeezed it affectionately. "At all costs, we cannot let it be found by accident. Hitler's luck seems damnable at the worst of times."

"Agreed. We cannot let it fall into his hands and you know I'd do anything for you."

"That makes two of us on both points."

She returned the squeeze, the most daring sign of affection she could risk. "I will find a way to get out of here to go talk to my contacts. Himmler has plans to spend time with his family tomorrow afternoon. I'll leave while he's distracted." Their path brought them around the block and back to the entrance. The few moments of speaking French felt refreshing after the guttural nature of the German language.

"Go, now," he suggested. "Take a truck. I can meet you

somewhere and then we can search for the spear from there. We can handle whatever may be thrown at us."

"I can't," she explained. "If I leave now, he'll have a warrant out for my arrest before I could be out of Berlin. If I leave tomorrow when he goes to see his family, I'll have a few hours' head start. It may be enough to keep ahead of being arrested. They already suspect me of espionage."

She'd been in worse situations in her long life, but none came readily to mind. The sooner she left, the sooner she wouldn't be within his reach when Wolff's hunt for the spy came to an end. Himmler would try to execute her and fail. Then things would get interesting.

"You cannot stay here if they suspect you. They will eventually discover you. It will be better you are nowhere near Berlin."

"I agree." Quickly she calculated the distance and time she would need. "Meet me in Bucharest in two days," she instructed. "That will give me enough time to get out of Berlin, see my contact, and get to Bucharest."

"It's a plan. Bucharest in two days. From there we will find the spear." He squeezed her hand again. "Then when our quest is done, we can spend some time together."

"I like the sound of that." She looked around and then planted a quick kiss on his cheek. "I must go back inside. Himmler will soon notice my absence. Words cannot describe how happy it makes me to see you again." He smiled and once again he was a wounded, young Knight Templar fleeing from the king's men.

"I'm happy we're reunited. When this war is over, we can work on a proper reunion." He dropped a kiss on her cheek. "Two days," he repeated. "Manuc's Inn?"

"Two days at Manuc's Inn," she confirmed

Akantha slipped her hands out of his. Regret flooded her. She hated this war and the Nazis for keeping her from him. She turned and walked toward the building, not looking back.

CHAPTER THREE

BERLIN, GERMANY 1941

Sunrise brought a bundle of nerves along with the normal revulsion after a night in Himmler's bed. Akantha lingered in the clawfoot tub and scrubbed her skin until it was bright red. The scrubbing and scalding hot water didn't take away the memories of his touch. A thousand baths would not take away the feeling.

The morning seemed longer than the twenty-four hundred years she had been alive. No amount of willing made the clock tick faster. Himmler caught her off guard a few times and had to repeat his instructions. It led to questioning her and her lying her way out of it. By the end of the morning her blouse under her jacket was drenched with sweat.

"Is that all for today?"

Akantha blinked and focused her mind on the here and now. Thoughts of reuniting with Matheus ran circles in her mind. She looked up at him, hating when he seemed to loom over her when she sat at her desk. She nodded. "Yes. I had your car brought around for your trip to Dhalem."

"Good."

"I also procured a small gift for Gudrun," Akantha said as she opened a drawer of her desk. She pulled out the small, wrapped item and offered it to him. He never visited his family without a small gift for his daughter.

The faintest of smiles appeared on his face. "Good. It had almost slipped my mind."

"We cannot let that happen."

"No, we cannot." He looked down at her, his eyes narrowing. "Are you feeling okay?"

"Yes," she replied. "I'm perfectly well. Why do you ask?"

"You look as if something is wrong."

A thin layer of sweat formed on her palms. "I'm fine," she assured him.

"Perhaps you should have Herr Gebhardt give you an exam."

"I don't need to bother the good doctor."

"What are your plans for this afternoon and tonight?" he asked.

Akantha blinked, surprised at the question. She couldn't allow herself to be caught off guard like that again. "I have some paperwork to finish up here and then I was going to walk around *Botanischer Garten und Botanisches Museum Berlin-Dahlem*." A genuine smile stretched her mouth. "I love walking among the plants and trees." It almost made her forget the horrors of war, but she would be photographing as many classified papers detailing troop movements as she could before she left today instead of going to the gardens. While she wouldn't be around to continue to pass information along to the SOE, she'd make sure she didn't leave empty handed. The Minox Riga stuffed in her jacket pocket would be put to good use, but right now it seemed like it was as large as a truck. She was sure Himmler would find it any moment.

He nodded. "And this evening?"

Akantha folded her hands on the desk to keep them from shaking. She wondered why he was interested in her plans while he was away. "No plans. I'll be home and probably reading." With any luck, she'd be in Romania by early morning and talking to her contact about the spear.

"Very well. Use the time to relax and don't work."

"We all do what we can." It was a weary, worn out line, but the Nazis ate it up. In a way, it was the only part of what she said to Himmler day in and day out that was even remotely true. Only in her case it was that she did what she could to help stop them.

"I'm going to arrange a driver and car for you," he said.

"It's not necessary," she said dismissively. "I can walk."

"I insist. It never hurts to have an added measure of security."

For the Nazis or for her? Was he assigning a man to follow her to discover if she was the spy? It would make getting out of Berlin harder, but not impossible. She may have to get creative. Her photography plans would have to be scrapped. She couldn't stay in the office if they expected her to go to the gardens.

She nodded. "I understand."

"I will see you in the morning," he said with a nod.

"Have a good afternoon and evening," she said. He left without returning the sentiment.

A sigh of relief rushed out of her when the door closed behind him. Her hand slipped into the pocket and withdrew the camera. She quickly snapped pictures of the papers lying on the desk until the film was used up. Now she just needed to get out of here and away from her shadow. She could pass off the camera and film to another SOE member and then she could get on with her mission.

The camera was slipped back into her pocket and she grabbed her purse. She took a deep breath to help calm and center her. She could do this. She made her face a mask devoid of expression and exited the office. A soldier standing near the door fell into step behind her and Akantha kept walking. At least she didn't have to wonder where her shadow would meet her.

Halfway to the main entrance, Manfred Fischer stopped her. "Fraulein, do you happen to know where *Reichsführer* Himmler is?"

"He is visiting his family," she replied, hoping that was all the man needed to know. She never liked Karl Gebhardt's assistant much. The man had a youthful, innocent look about him, but Akantha suspected something sinister lurked under the surface. The eyes gave him away.

"When he returns, will you please tell him Dr. Gebhardt would like to see him?"

Akantha nodded. "Of course."

He smiled. "Thank you."

"You're welcome." He walked away and no one else stopped her as she exited the building.

The June afternoon was warm and bright, the pleasant weather bringing a smile to her face. It was almost enough to make one forget there was a war raging.

"Your auto is over here, Fräulein," the soldier said.

Akantha turned and gave him a small smile. "Thank you." He walked to the car and Akantha followed like the good little Nazi she was pretending to be. He opened the door and she nodded her thanks before climbing into the back seat. He hurried around the car and slid into the driver's seat. The car started and a moment later they were rolling toward the gardens.

She watched the buildings of Berlin flow by, not wanting to make small talk with the driver. The less contact she had with him, the easier it would be to do what she had to do. She wasn't in the heart of Nazi Germany to make friends. Her mission may have changed, but she still had work to do.

They sped through the city, the driver seeming to know the route with the least amount of traffic. People moved, almost as if there wasn't a war raging on. Berlin had seen some air raid attacks by the RAF, but bombs hadn't dropped since March. The bombings that did strike Berlin didn't cause much damage. She had seen and heard reports about London and couldn't imagine such devastation.

The car pulled up outside the botanical gardens and Akantha waited for the man to open the door. When he did, she climbed out, said her thanks, and walked into the gardens. She followed the gravel path to the Great Pavilion, mostly ignoring the other people and the beauty of the grounds. The soldier followed, but Akantha paid him no mind.

The air inside was humid and made her smile. Memories of the Mediterranean came flooding back and a longing developed in her core. She shook her head, banishing the thoughts of a place she couldn't be for the foreseeable future.

Bright sunlight filtered in through the glass and the tropical flowers made the air thick and heady with perfume. Very few people wandered the pathways that snaked through the greenery. It was exactly what she had been hoping for. A glance over her shoulder confirmed her shadow was still there and she continued to amble.

She purposely wandered over to an area near a corner where the plants were dense. She ducked behind a tree, grabbed a nearby rock, and waited. A whispered prayer slipped past her lips.

"I call to Tyche, friend of the Fates, mistress of fair fortune who holds the rudder of all ships, who bears the shining horn of Amalthea, who wears the mural crown, whose face was graven upon gold, tossed in the air when a choice need be made. In times of old, men named you Eutykhia; they threw the dice with eyes tight shut and trusted in your goodness. I call to you, Eutykhia. I pray to you, O goddess, grant to me the good."

The soldier appeared in her vision and when he was two steps past Akantha, she burst forth from behind the tree and slammed the rock down where the base of the skull met the neck. The man crumbled silently to the ground. She dropped the rock, turned the man over onto his back, and checked his pulse on the side of his neck. It was steady and strong. He'd wake up in a while with a pounding headache, but he would live.

There were risks to leaving people alive behind her, but he was just a low-ranking soldier and not guilty of the horrors of those further up on the chain of command. For some, serving the Reich wasn't a choice. She'd give him the benefit of the doubt. Grunting, she grabbed the collar of the uniform and she pulled the man into a spot thick with plants. By the time she was done, sweat beaded her forehead and her breathing was heavy. She liberated the man's weapon from its holster and grabbed the keys from his pants pocket.

Akantha whistled as she walked back to the waiting car. Tension drained out of her with each step and her mood improved. The familiar sensation of someone watching her prickled the hairs on the back of her neck and she stopped with her hand on the door handle. She scanned the area, looking for the source of her discomfort. It wasn't the soldier she knocked out; he would be out for quite some time. Someone was watching her and she didn't like it.

Out of the corner of her eye, she spotted a familiar face and her heart leaped into her throat while her stomach dropped to her feet. Too many ghosts coming out of her past lately.

A truck rolled by and when it passed, the face was gone. She sagged against the car in relief as her legs turned to rubber. He was the last person she wanted to see or needed in her life right now. She pushed herself up and climbed into the car. The engine turned over and it pulled away from the curb. She steered it in the most direct route to her drop point. From there, it was a short distance out of Berlin.

CHAPTER FOUR

Romania 1941

The liberated truck pulled to stop in front of a country manor house not far outside of Bucharest, Romania. Akantha didn't want to come here, but the woman of the house might hold a clue to the location of the spear. Hopefully Morana was over the events of over a century ago. If she remembered correctly, there was a man involved and a misunderstanding. Maybe it had been enough time for Morana to cool off.

She sat behind the wheel of the car and stared at the front facade. Morana had to know she was here, but no one appeared in the doorway. Akantha hadn't expected a welcoming committee, but she hoped Morana was still in residence. Truth be told, she expected a greeting more along the lines of gunfire. The other immortal was unpredictable and prickly.

Maybe this was a bad idea. There were other sources of information she could tap, but they were not as thorough or reliable. She took a deep breath, swore, and climbed out of the truck.

The manor house wasn't as large or as grand as those in France and England, but it was a considerable size for the region. The old house created a longing inside for her stately old Victorian along the coast of Maine. She had been away for far too long, but home was something that would have to wait.

She walked toward the house when the front door opened and a dark-haired woman appeared in the doorway. Her arms were crossed over her chest and she watched Akantha's every step with increased annoyance. Akantha put her hands up, palms outward to show that she wasn't wielding a weapon.

"Akantha," Morana greeted her coldly. "This is an unexpected pleasure."

"Morana." Akantha nodded, ignoring the woman's sarcasm. "I wouldn't have come if it were not urgent and you were the closest person I knew."

"Urgent enough you're working for the Nazis?" the other immortal asked, eying Akantha's uniform. Morana was beautiful. Centuries had not lessened her dark eyes and hair, nor lined her pale skin. Akantha wished she looked half as good.

"No. I'm not working for the Nazis. They tend to speak freely when they believe they're among other Nazis. In the spy game, we call it camouflage."

Morana was quiet for a long moment as if she was trying to decide if she was going to believe Akantha. "Well aren't you a real Mata Hari." She stepped out of the doorway. "Come in."

"Nice gal, but she got caught." Spying on the Germans was something she did in the first World War, and she had crossed paths with Mata Hari a few times. That was one person she would never forget no matter how many years passed. There were a few of those through her long life and there were some she wanted to forget. "Thank you." She passed through the open door and into a foyer.

"I don't want your thanks," Morana said as she shut the door behind Akantha. "Why are you here?" The woman's frosty tone was not a good sign.

"The Spear of Destiny," Akantha said, getting to the heart of the matter. "What do you know about it?"

Morana's eyes briefly went wide. "The same as everyone else," she answered as she led Akantha deeper into the house and into a large kitchen. Once a staff of four to six would work in the large kitchen, cooking food for the lord and lady of the house, but now the kitchen stood empty. The tiled room seemed cold and unwelcoming, reflecting its owner. "It's the spear used to pierce the side of Christ at the crucifixion. There's some debate, but it's said whoever wields the spear controls the destiny of the world, for good or evil. Legend says it was passed among medieval kings but was eventually lost. There's at least ten spears in existence, all thought to be the Spear of Destiny." She paused for a heartbeat. "Why do you ask?"

"Heinrich Himmler is looking for it for Hitler," Akantha answered. She collapsed into a chair at the table, exhausted from driving through most of the night to reach Morana's in a reasonable amount of time. Thoughts of a soft, warm bed were heavenly.

"Are you sure?"

"Definitely sure. I was sleeping with him and overheard his plans."

A string of curses flowed out of Morana's mouth and Akantha smiled. Morana reached into a cabinet for a bottle of whiskey.

"Exactly. Help me go after it."

"I can't." Morana unscrewed the top to the whiskey and offered the bottle to Akantha.

She never refused liquid courage. Akantha took the offered bottle gratefully and put it to her lips. The whiskey burned as it went down, but it warmed her stomach. She took another long pull and then handed the bottle back, raising a brow. "Can't or won't?"

"A little of both," Morana shrugged.

"Why won't you help? Do you want to see Hitler get the spear and doom the world?"

"No," Morana replied.

"We can't let the Nazis control the world. I've seen what they're doing and it will only get worse. Much worse if they get their hands on the spear."

"I'm not going to get involved in your mission."

"Why not?"

"I have my reasons."

"What would those reasons be?"

"Why should we get involved if the mortals want to destroy each other?" She dismissed them with a small wave. "All humanity has done through the centuries is to find better ways to kill each other. Why should we stop them from wiping themselves out?"

"You're focusing on the bad," Akantha pointed out. "There's a lot of good out there. Art, music, literature, poetry, sculpture—"

"Civilization is just a thin veneer of ice on a deep sea of chaos," Morana interrupted. "Pretty things don't make up for the atrocities humans commit against each other in the name of whatever the cause of the decade, or century. You're worrying too much. Hitler is only a man and the Nazis won't be in power forever. Tyrants die and empires crumble: Caesar and Rome, Attila, Genghis Khan. Even the great British Empire declined. Such is the way of things since the beginning of time. We have both seen it happen enough times over the centuries."

"It's better to stop this now," Akantha insisted.

"What is it with you and these idealistic crusades to save the world?"

"They're not crusades to save the world," Akantha defended. "It's doing what any decent person would do to stop suffering. If Hitler doesn't get the spear, the rest of the world has a chance of stopping him and the slaughter would stop. Fine, tell me the spear is in your personal keeping and I will go."

"The spear is in my personal keeping. Good bye." She turned away from Akantha and stared out a nearby window.

"You have not learned to lie any better than when I first met you."

"Stopping Hitler will only stop the slaughter for a time," Morana pointed out. "It will start up again. Mortals will always kill each other. We should let them have at it. Fewer humans is not a bad thing. Is there anything else you want?"

"A bed for a few hours would be nice along with a hot meal." Stubbornness was a common trait for immortals, and Morana wasn't the exception. "And any piece of information about the location of the spear."

"I have a bed and can provide a hot meal." Morana turned around. "As for any information about the spear, I'm afraid I have very little. I think, and I'm not one hundred percent sure, Zenon had it at one point."

"Do you know what he did with it?" Akantha met Zenon not long after she became immortal. He helped her adjust to immortality and what her life would be like. He had been somewhat of a mentor to both women and had recruited them into the small group dedicated to keeping powerful items out of the hands of people who would use them for ill.

Morana shook her head. "No, I don't. Though knowing him, he probably hid it."

Akantha sighed heavily and slumped in the chair. She knew Zenon well, which made her job harder, but she had a chance of finding it. The upside was it would also be harder for the Nazis to find. "By Zeus's beard, I can't catch a break."

One of Morana's brows lifted in query. "Are you still clinging to those pagan gods?"

"Are you still a member of that cult?" Akantha shot back.

Religion was a minefield between them and they walked right into it. Akantha had been born and raised worshiping the gods and goddesses of the Greek pantheon. She didn't participate in active worship, hadn't for many centuries, but she still held onto invoking the names in her everyday speech. Morana, on the other hand, had been born during the time the Christian church was still outlawed, but gaining popularity. She had been born into a Christian family and still held onto her beliefs. It had made for some interesting and often heated conversations over the years, but both women weren't in the mood to argue about religion.

"Touché."

"Do you have any idea where Zenon may have hidden it?"

Morana shrugged. "I don't know, but he's always been fond of Thessaloniki. You know as well as I do. It may be a good place to start."

Akantha nodded. Had she not been so exhausted from driving and worried about the Nazis getting the spear, she would have thought to go to Zenon himself.

"Come. I'll show you to a room where you can get a few hours of sleep."

Akantha stood, wincing at the stiffness that had settled into her joints. Living forever didn't mean you were exempt from the small complaints of an aging body. Damp days were the worst. "Where's your household staff?" Akantha asked as she followed Morana out of the kitchen.

"I let them go," Morana replied. "Most went to fight in the war. The others went to be with their families."

"So you let your staff go to fight in the war, but you won't." Her tone held more accusation than intended, but her point was valid.

"Let it go," Morana warned.

"I don't get how you can let others get involved and yet you sit here doing nothing."

"Damianos once said you were the most stubborn person in the world. I'm beginning to believe him. Who said I'm doing nothing? Because you see nothing? Perhaps you don't know what to look for. You have your mission and I have my own."

"Did you have to bring his name up?" Akantha asked as they reached a grand staircase leading up to the second floor. Pain, exhaustion and frustration were making her more irritable than normal. Damianos and Akantha had a very long history, of which Akantha hated being reminded. There were parts of her long life she tried to forget and he was the main part. It had to be a coincidence that Morana had mentioned him and Akantha thought she had seen him in Berlin. She didn't need him in her life right now. "What's your mission?"

"I was merely making an observation." Morana shook her head. "It's better I don't say anything."

Akantha knew Morana was trying to push buttons, but she let it go. She understood about keeping tight-lipped about a mission. One person could keep a secret. Not two.

They reached the top of the staircase and turned to the right. The wooden floorboards creaked under their footsteps. Akantha followed Morana down the spacious hallway and into a bedroom. A large canopy bed made of dark hardwood sat in the middle of the room with the heavy drapes pulled back. The antique bed was in perfect condition. The heavy drapes framed the bed and in days long past they would be pulled closed to keep cold air out.

"You can sleep here. There are clothes in the wardrobe that might fit you. You can't continue to wear that horrible uniform."

"Something we both can agree on, but I must to move freely around Nazi occupied territory. Again, thank you."

Morana waved her off. "You'll have a hot meal before you go."

Akantha bit back a sarcastic response. Morana was attempting to be nice and Akantha could make an effort to do the same. The two women would probably never be friends, but they could refrain from outright hostility toward each other.

"Thank you. I'll be gone later in the day."

"Very well."

"Are you sure you won't help?" Akantha had to ask one more time. The gravity of the situation demanded it.

"I'm sure. Rest well." With that Morana turned and left.

Akantha sat down on the edge of the bed and sighed heavily. She fell back across the bed and stared at the canopy overhead as exhaustion settled in. Undressing was suddenly the last thing on her mind. Her eyes closed and a moment later she surrendered to the welcoming arms of sleep.

―――

Akantha knew someone was in the room before she opened her eyes. She felt their presence despite them not making a sound. The talent had gotten her out of impossible situations on numerous occasions, but was this one friend or foe? There was only one way to find out. Akantha opened her eyes and realized she was still lying across the bed with her legs hanging over the side.

She moved into a half sitting position and looked at the person who had entered the room. Her eyes widened and her mouth opened as the identity of the man registered in her tired mind. She bolted up into a full sitting position and glared at him. Dark brown eyes gleamed with mirth and a smirk stretched his mouth.

"Damianos! What are you doing here?" she demanded. Did she just feel her heart skip a beat? Her stomach flipped as her mouth went dry, as it did the first day she met him so long ago. She hadn't been imagining him in Berlin.

He smiled, leaned in and planted a kiss on her mouth. He pulled back and smiled. "I'm glad to see you too, Akantha. It's been far too long." His words were a declaration of war, and the opening salvo had been fired. She slapped him across the face.

CHAPTER FIVE

Ephesus 420 BCE

Akantha walked along Curetes Street in Ephesus, past the brothel, and ignored the building. Thinking of what happened in there made her cheeks burn. She didn't want to look, but she couldn't help glancing over. An elderly man watched her as he loitered in the doorway. She smiled at him and continued on her way from the *agora* to the Temple of Artemis.

Apollo was making his way in his chariot across the clear blue sky and the air was rather warm. No breeze stirred and offered relief. Sweat beaded on her forehead and she wiped it away with the back of her hand. Leather sandals softly thudded against the cobbled street and kicked up little puffs of dust with each step. Dust lingered in the air, coating everything, and she tasted it in her mouth. Concentrating on getting back to the temple with the basket of olives, she didn't notice the small group of men coming toward her. One bumped into her as they passed and she stumbled. The olives spilled onto the street. Strong hands caught her and prevented her from falling to the ground.

"I am sorry," she apologized, though it wasn't her fault.

"I'm the one who is sorry," a male voice said.

Akantha was tall for a woman, but she had to look up to see him. Dark curly hair framed a tanned, boyish face, and dark brown eyes echoed his smile. She felt her heart pounding in her chest. Her mouth went dry.

"Did I hurt you?"

Akantha shook her head. "No." He was handsome, but she could only look. She was *korai*, a virgin dedicated to the temple, and would remain one for the rest of her life.

"My name is Damianos," he said.

"My name is Akantha." The rules of the temple prohibited her from having physical relations with a man, but they didn't forbid her from talking to them.

"It's a pleasure to meet you, Akantha." He grinned, his white teeth contrasting against his tanned skin. "How could one so beautiful be like a thorn?" he mused. Heat grew in her cheeks. She looked away and only then noticed that the basket had spilled. "My olives!" she gasped. She squatted and started picking up the scattered olives. Punishment would be brought upon her if she didn't return with olives, or if they were ruined.

"Let me help," he said and lowered himself down to help her.

"There is no need." She kept her eyes down and focused on her task. He was close enough she could smell the heady, musky scent of sweat and him. The world seemed to narrow down to the two of them. Time stood still.

"I insist. It's my fault you spilled them."

Heart racing, Akantha looked away when his eyes met hers and her fingers fumbled as she tried to pick up some olives. She could drown in the brown depths.

"See how she blushes. Her cheeks rosy as the fingertips of Eos." His words only made her blush more and she dropped what she had in her hand.

"I'm sorry," he apologized and picked up what she had dropped. "I do not mean to make you so flustered."

Akantha focused on picking up the remaining olives. She silently cursed herself for allowing him to distract her so and cause her to be clumsy. He was just a man. A handsome man. Apollo made flesh. She tried to banish such thoughts from her mind, reminding herself she belonged to the temple.

He grabbed the last one as she was reaching for it and his fingers brushed across her skin. He dropped the olive into the basket and enveloped her hand with his.

She jumped. His warm touch shocked her and the shock spread through her body. Was this what it felt like to be hit by one of Zeus's lightning bolts, or Eros's arrows? The air grew warmer and she pulled her hand away from his. "Thank you for your assistance. I must return to the temple. Excuse me."

"Of course, beautiful lady," he said.

She bowed her head to hide her red face. "Thank you," she muttered.

"I would think a beautiful woman such as yourself would be used to compliments. Do you not get many?"

"No."

"A shame. A woman as beautiful as you should be told frequently how beautiful she is."

"I must go," she told him.

He put a hand on her upper arm. "No. Please, stay for a little longer."

"I really must go."

"Please, just a few moments longer."

She looked up at him and a wave of dizziness hit her as she fell into the depths of his dark eyes. He smiled and the world spun a little faster.

"Sir, please."

"Allow me a few moments longer to linger in the presence of such beauty. You are Aphrodite made flesh and one must appreciate it as long as possible."

Such honeyed words fell from his mouth, casting a spell around her.

"Sir, I must go," she insisted, breaking his spell. His hand remained on her arm. "Please let me go."

"Please don't," he said.

"I must deliver these olives."

"I want to see you again."

"I don't think that is a good idea." She took a step and his hand came away from her arm. She hurried off, not daring to look back.

She dominated Damianos's thoughts day and night. No matter what he was doing, thoughts of her intruded and desire to see her again overwhelmed him. He took to lingering outside Artemis's temple in hopes of seeing her again. He watched people entering and leaving the temple, hoping one would be her. His friends thought him out of his mind, but he didn't care. Only she mattered.

There were a few times when he thought he saw her lingering near the entrance to the temple, but they had to be a trick of the mind. On the fifth day since he talked to her, he saw her leave the temple. He followed, keeping his distance to not spook her. When she stopped at a merchant's stall, he found a place nearby to watch her. She went about her business but stopped a few times to look around. Could she feel the weight of his stare? Could she feel him nearby?

She left the stall with her basket filled with olives and walked in the direction of the temple. He hurried to intercept her.

"Hello, Akantha," he said, drawing as close as he dared.

Her head whipped around and her eyes went wide. Her mouth opened into an "o."

"Apologies. I didn't mean to startle you."

"Apologies are not necessary," she assured him. "Hello, Damianos."

"You are even more beautiful than when I saw you a few days ago." The words stumbled past his lips, the sight of her and the sound of her voice rendering him almost speechless.

Red bloomed on her cheeks and she smiled, bowing her head. His chest tightened at the sight. He had to have her and he would make her his own. No matter what it took.

"You flatter me so."

"It's not flattery, only the truth."

"Truth is in the eye of the beholder," she countered.

"Maybe, but I do not lie. You are the most beautiful woman I have ever seen. Even more beautiful than Aphrodite."

"It would not be wise to insult the gods," she warned. "Mortals never fare well."

"I would risk even Zeus's wrath for you, my lady."

"Do not say such things!" she protested.

"There is nothing wrong with telling the truth," he told her. He'd take on anyone, including the gods, for her. There was nothing he wouldn't do for her.

"What brings you to the *agora*?"

"I was hoping to catch sight of you, and Aphrodite blessed me with a glimpse of your beauty." An offering would be made to the goddess as soon as he could manage it. "Are you running errands for the temple?"

She nodded as the red on her cheeks darkened. He smiled; pleased his words had such an effect on her. "Yes. I must go."

"No, please, stay a little longer," he pleaded. He reached out and gently grabbed her wrist. Her skin was cool to the touch and soft as the finest woven silk.

"I'm sorry. I cannot." Yet she didn't pull her hand away.

"Just a few moments more," he begged. "I want to admire your beauty for a little while longer." Just a little more time. That's all he asked for.

"I really must go," she insisted, pulling her hand way. "It was nice to see you."

"The pleasure was all mine," he said. It was more than nice, but these brief moments were a tease. He wanted to get to know her better and spend time talking to her. These moments were not enough. Forever wouldn't be enough. He took her hand and dropped a light kiss on her knuckles.

She trembled under his touch. Was it fear or something else? He prayed it wasn't fear. He didn't want her afraid of him. He wanted to wrap his arms around her and hold her close until the trembling stopped, but wisely didn't do it.

He reached out and tucked an errant strand of hair behind her ear. The ebony hair was as soft as it looked, and he wanted to run his fingers through it.

"I must go," she said and pulled away from him. She walked away.

He sighed heavily. This wasn't over. He would see her again and he would win her over. No other woman would do.

CHAPTER SIX

Romania 1941

"Piss and blood," Akantha swore. "What are you doing here?" She pushed him away, or tried to. He was solid as a brick wall and moved as much as one would. Gods below, why did he have to show up?

He laughed and rubbed the spot on his cheek where she slapped him. "Thorny as always."

"I invited him." Akantha looked past Damianos to see Morana leaning against the door frame. There was a self-satisfied smirk on the immortal's face. Akantha would have hit her had she been closer. She'd swear this was some sort of revenge. "You wanted help finding the spear and Damianos said he'd help you."

"I don't need his help," she insisted. "I just needed information on the spear.

"Stubborn as always," he commented and a sardonic smile adorned his face. "But that's what I love about you."

She looked at him and her eyes narrowed. "I hate you."

"No you don't," he countered. "I know it. You know it. Yet you keep saying it. Don't you get tired of lying to yourself?"

"Help is help." Morana smirked.

"I asked for your help, not his."

Morana just shrugged. "You wanted help. Does it matter where it comes from?"

"I'm not that desperate."

Damianos laughed.

"Shut up," Akantha growled at Damianos. Over two billion people on the planet and the one she couldn't stand showed up. She couldn't get away from him soon enough.

Akantha rolled her eyes and brushed past him toward the closet. She fell asleep as soon as her back hit the mattress and she felt grimier than before. A long soak in a hot bath would be heavenly, but she had to get moving. The Nazis wouldn't take time off from their search and neither would she. Clean clothes would help counter the grimy feeling until she had time for a proper bath.

"I'll leave so the two of you can catch up." Morana smirked when Akantha turned and glared at her. "Food is ready downstairs if you're hungry." She slipped out of the room.

Silence hung in the air as Morana left. "Why are you here?" Akantha demanded as soon as the other immortal was gone.

He sighed. "Morana sent word the Nazis are after the Spear of Destiny and you were asking for help to find it before them. I was in the area, so I'm here to help."

"I don't need your help," she retorted as she pulled a white blouse out of the closet. "Matheus and I will find the Spear." She tossed the clean shirt on the foot of the bed and started removing the soiled one she wore.

"By Zeus's beard," he swore, "you are so..."

Akantha looked over at him when he stopped speaking to find him leering at her. "Do you mind?"

"I don't mind at all. It's not like I haven't seen your body before."

Akantha shook her head and grabbed the clean white blouse. She slipped it on and buttoned it up, trying her best to ignore him. He was a bad penny that kept turning up and she should have never fallen in love with him. Twenty-four hundred years later and she was still kicking herself for it. One of these days he would be out of her life for good and it couldn't come soon enough.

"How are you?"

She paused in her task of fastening the buttons. "Why do you ask?"

"Forgive me for caring." He snorted. "Can't I ask how you're doing after not seeing you for thirty years?"

Her fingers worked on fastening the buttons. "I'm fine." She finished with the buttons and then shoved the shirt into her skirt.

"So, Matheus again?"

"Yes, Matheus," she said. "Why? Are you jealous?"

"Of course not," he replied.

Liar, she thought, but didn't call him out. Calling him out would lead to an argument and arguing with him was the last thing she wanted right now.

"So where do we start?" he inquired.

"*We*...don't start anywhere," Akantha snapped. Gods above, why did he have to be so damn stubborn? "I don't need your help. Matheus and I will be fine on our own."

"Yes, you do," he countered. "Otherwise you would haven't asked Morana for help. I know the history you two have. It's not as interesting as ours, but you wouldn't have asked her if you didn't need the help."

"I'm trying to forget our history," she shot back.

"Your words wound me." He put his hand on his heart.

"You look wounded." She slipped her feet into the sturdy pair of shoes and grabbed the jacket for her uniform. She wanted to rid herself of the uniform and what it represented, but traveling was easier when she was one of the enemy. She slipped it on and buttoned it.

"I am. Down to my soul. Not even the arrows of Eros have wounded me like this."

Akantha ignored him and walked out of the room.

"Akantha!" he called after her.

She kept walking and a moment later she heard his footsteps following. "You're not coming with me. I don't need your help."

"By Dis, stop being so stubborn for once in your life." He grabbed her wrist and spun her around. His brown eyes bore into her and it was as if he were looking into her soul. Her mouth went dry and her heart beat faster. Butterflies fluttered in her stomach. Damn him for still having an effect on her. "Let me watch that beautiful backside for you."

Akantha could feel her resolve fading in the light of his argument.

He drew her in for a kiss. His lips ground down on hers and she tried to push him away, but he didn't budge an inch. She could feel her resistance melting away under his searing kiss and her toes curled up. That small moan couldn't have come from her. Breathless, she gripped the handrail for support.

He released her and she quickly pulled away, putting some distance between the two of them. She turned on her heel and headed down the stairs.

"I want to help you and Matheus," he called to her as they descended the stairs.

She stopped halfway down the stairs, turned, and looked at him. "Why?" The last thing she needed was to deal with him and Matheus at the same time. Nothing good could come from it.

"Because I do care about you even though you don't want to see it. I don't want anything to happen to you," he explained.

"You're just concerned that your own immortal existence would be cut short if someone managed to kill me."

"That's not entirely true. Though I do admit that the thought had crossed my mind. The main reason why I want to help is because I do care."

"I knew it! You were always selfish."

"And you only hear what you want to hear," he countered. "Let me help you, Akantha. Please." He reached out and took her hands. "Your hands are cold."

Her first thought was to yank them away, but something kept her from doing so. His hands were so warm, she just wanted to soak up the heat and slip into him. She shook her head and pulled her hands away. His touch was trouble and it was wise to keep some space between them. Matheus was waiting for her and they had a possibility of being reunited when this was over.

"Matheus would never let me come to harm," she insisted. She turned and continued down the stairs.

"You put too much faith in your knight."

"You're jealous and don't want me spending time with him."

"Hardly," he snorted. "I know what he means to you and he makes you happy. I don't want anything to happen to you. I love you too much."

Akantha rolled her eyes. "You could say that a million times and I still won't believe it." She reached the bottom of the stairs and kept walking. Stopping and looking at him would melt her resistance. She had to keep as many walls up as possible. It was the safest way. She'd never let him hurt her again. Love would never make her a fool again.

"Then I'll say it a million and one or as many times as I need to make you believe me," he said.

"You'd have more luck with a deaf person," she called back. She didn't love him. The feelings she once held for him were buried deep, never to resurface. No. They weren't buried. They were dead and had been for a long time.

"By Dis, stop being so stubborn for once in your life. Let me help you."

She spun on a heel to face him. "No," she tossed in his face.

"What do I have to do to make you believe that I love you?" he asked.

"Go away and leave me alone."

He shook his head. "No, that's not it."

Akantha growled in frustration and continued toward the kitchen. His mocking laughter followed her. She entered the kitchen to find Morana enjoying a cup of coffee. "Coffee is fresh," Morana said over the rim of her cup. "And real. I have my sources."

Akantha went straight for the coffee. Maybe with a little caffeine in her she wouldn't want to gravely injure Damianos.

He shook his head and followed her to the kitchen. four hundred years and change, and one would think she would have let go of some of the anger and resentment she had toward him. There were brief truces throughout the long years, but they were as fleeting as the dew on grass on a summer's morning. One day she would let go of the anger for good and she'd let him love her like he wanted. Until then, all he could do was try to get her to forgive him. It was easier to stop breathing.

"Thank you," Damianos said and sat at the table next to Morana.

Akantha leaned against the stove and drank her coffee, keeping the table between them. He knew she was trying to keep them physically apart, but she wouldn't succeed. He'd work his way back into her good graces. She shot him glares over the rim of her coffee mug and he smiled.

Her temper and irritability had always endeared her to him. He loved that part about her, but he also knew from first-hand experience that she could be warm and loving. The brief truces they had over the centuries were the best times of his life. He loved her from the first moment he saw her. She had been young, naive, and blushed easily. Now she was wiser, experienced, and fierce, and those qualities made him love her more. She grew more beautiful with the passage of time. He didn't fall in love with her once, he fell in love with her each time he saw her.

"So, do we have any idea where the spear could be?" he asked. He took a sip of his coffee and savored the taste. Good coffee, like everything else in times of war, was scarce. He'd kill someone for a glass of good beer.

"Maybe," Akantha answered, her voice laced with a blast of arctic cold.

"I guess it's better than nothing," he said. "Let me finish my coffee and then we can get going."

"We? We are not going anywhere. I'm going to meet Matheus and go after the spear."

He sighed and prepared himself for another battle in their long war. "I'm going with you," he told her, even if it meant dealing with one of her former lovers.

"No you're not. You can drop dead for all I care."

Her words always injured him more than the bullets and knives she had physically wounded him with in the past. These words cut to the bone. He let them slide off of him as he always did. He loved her despite all of the harsh words, bullets, and knives. Her temper just made him love her more. It didn't make sense, but love rarely did.

Still, it would be a nice change of pace if he didn't have to verbally spar with her.

"Such honeyed words falling from your lips." He put on his best innocent face and smiled at her. Gods, he loved her and loved getting a rise out of her. It had been too long since he last saw her. Why hadn't he tracked her down sooner?

"Oh, will you two stop flirting? Go upstairs and get to it."

"I'm not flirting. I wish he would drop dead."

"And your life would become immensely boring without me in it." He smirked, masking the wounds her words inflicted.

"I think the word you meant to use was peaceful." Akantha drained the last of the coffee from her cup and placed it in the sink. "Thank you for everything," she said to Morana.

"You're welcome. Do you want anything to eat?"

"No, thanks. I need to get going."

Damianos gulped down his coffee and stood. Standing earned him a hard, gray-eyed look. "I'm ready." He placed his cup on the table and walked around to stand in front of her. He braced himself for whatever was coming.

"I told you, you're not going."

"Yes I am, and you're not going to stop me." He moved around the table.

"Move," she growled.

"No." He smirked and closed the distance between them. "Akantha, stop being so damned stubborn and let me help you. Please."

Face to face, inches apart, the light perfume she wore tickled his nose. He reached out and took a strand of hair, rubbing it between his fingers. Soft as he remembered it. He held her eyes, letting himself get lost in the gray depths.

The blow came without warning. Her knee came up and connected with his groin. Pain spread out from the point of impact and he doubled over. His eyes watered and he cursed himself for not expecting the strike. He held onto the counter to keep him from falling on the floor.

She laughed as she stepped around him and headed for the door. Behind him Morana gasped. He hobbled after her, the pain slowly lessening as he walked. He reached the front door in time to see her slam shut the car door.

"Akantha!" he yelled. She didn't even look back. The engine turned over and the rear tires kicked up gravel from the driveway. The truck rumbled down the drive and he swore. Damned woman. Just once he'd like her to cooperate with him. Was it too much to ask for?

"You let your guard down," Morana said from behind him.

And his favorite body part paid the price. "I did," he admitted. It was a mistake, one he wouldn't make again. Even with Akantha. Especially with Akantha. The woman was capable of anything. "Where is she headed?" He turned around and faced the other immortal.

"Thessaloniki. Zenon last had possession of the spear. It's likely he hid it somewhere there." Her eyes glanced down to his crotch. "Do you want some ice?"

He shook his head. "No, thanks." He kissed a soft, pale cheek. "Thank you."

"You're welcome. I'll reach out to him and see if I can get an exact location. I'll get word to you."

"I owe you," he told her.

She smiled. "Yes you will."

He smiled. "I look forward to repaying you one day."

"I look forward to collecting."

He kissed her cheek again. "Take care of yourself and we'll see each other on the other side of this war."

"Take care of yourself and good luck. The spear may be powerful enough to kill an immortal."

He nodded. "Good to know." All the more reason to chase after Akantha. He didn't want anything to happen to her. He left Morana standing in the doorway and made his way to the liberated German army truck he stole in Berlin. The engine turned over and he put it into gear. Now to chase down the love of his life.

CHAPTER SEVEN

BUCHAREST, ROMANIA 1941

Akantha knocked twice on the hotel room door, ignoring the two uniformed soldiers standing on either side. They didn't stop her and she assumed they had been told to expect her. "Hello?" she called through the door. She shivered from the cool night air and from anticipation of being reunited with Matheus. She took a quick glance at the courtyard below. The hour was late enough that not many lingered. Those that did linger were wearing the swastika.

Manuc's Inn was one of the oldest hotels in Bucharest, and Akantha and Matheus had stayed here in the early 1800s. It seemed a fitting place to meet to start their quest. Things had a habit of coming full circle.

"Come in." His voice drifted through the door, making her heart race.

Akantha pushed open the door and smiled when she saw Matheus, her eyes drinking in the sight of him. He stood in the middle of the room. His half-unbuttoned shirt was pulled out of his trousers and he looked as if he had slept in his uniform. He returned the smile and Akantha closed the door behind her.

The rooms in the hotel hadn't changed much in the past hundred years. A double four poster bed dominated the room and a small table with two chairs sat near the window. It was as close to a homecoming Akantha'd had in a long time. Worry and tension drained out of her the further she moved into the room.

"I thought it would take you longer," Matheus admitted. He closed the distance between them, wood floorboards creaking under his weight, and wrapped his arms around her. He lowered his head and covered her mouth with his.

A soft moan escaped her as his mouth claimed hers and she leaned into him without thought. The rest of the stress and tension drained out of her. Her body pressed against his and her arms wound around his neck. He deepened the kiss and Akantha melted. The past hundred years of being apart were erased with the kiss and embrace. The ugliness of war was temporarily gone from her thoughts and left outside the four walls. All that mattered right now was him.

His mouth released hers and moved down to her neck, searing her skin.

"I couldn't wait to see you," she whispered.

As he kissed her neck, gentle hands worked their way up from her hips to her breasts. The feel of his strong fingers and the material rubbing across her sensitive nipples caused her to moan and her head to swim.

"Matheus." His name was a plea as his hands continued their exploration of her body. She moaned again. She felt his mouth curve in a smile against her skin as he unfastened the buttons of her blouse.

In response, her hands started working on the buttons of his shirt. Her clumsy frustration made it take longer than necessary and he laughed softly. Just as she had the last button undone, his mouth left her neck and he lifted her in his arms. Warmth and security flooded through her as he cradled her against his chest. It was a feeling she hadn't experienced in a long time and exactly what she needed to replenish her soul. He carried her over to the bed and gently placed her on top of the blankets. She looked up at him and reached out a hand.

Grinning, he placed his hands in hers as she pulled him toward her, covering her body with his. Her hands slid along the hard muscles of his back, tracing intricate patterns as his mouth came down on hers. The kiss was firm, gentle, just the way she remembered him.

His hands moved to her breasts, fingertips traveling lightly over her skin. Akantha shivered and arched against his touch as fingertips brushed across a sensitive nipple. His mouth left hers and dropped light kisses along her jaw, moving to the tender skin of her neck. She tried to bring him to her and satisfy both their needs, but he would have none of it. His lips leisurely trailed down her neck, alternating between kissing and licking. She loved that he was gentle, sweet and caring, but right now it was driving her crazy. Wherever his hands and lips touched, flames leapt to the surface of her skin and the ache inside of her grew. She traced the trail of coarse hair down to his groin and he moaned as he strained against her touch. If he was determined to taunt her, she would give him the same treatment.

He replaced his fingertips with his mouth, and Akantha gasped at the feel of his hot mouth on her sensitive skin and her nails dug into his skin. His lips found their way to a pert nipple and began teasing and sucking on it. One hand cupped the other breast while he caressed down the curve of her side to her hips with his left.

A deep heartfelt groan escaped her and she hoped it encouraged him. His hungry lips left her breast and blazed a trail down past her stomach. Her hips instinctively arched against his mouth as his tongue parted her soft folds and began to explore.

All thoughts flew away. She couldn't think, only feel—the hard muscles of his back and arms, the softness of his skin under coarse hair, the feel of the linen sheets under her back, his lips on her, his calloused hands running over her skin, and the building pressure inside her.

"Matheus, please!" she begged. She teetered on the edge and she didn't want to be there alone.

His mouth traveled up the length of her body. Placing a single kiss on each hard nipple, he didn't linger, his lips trailing up to her neck. He entered her as his lips pressed down on hers.

Akantha gasped into his mouth. Her head swam at the feel of him filling her and making her complete. The rhythm he set was sure and slow, his thrusts deep inside of her. Her body responded, the pressure inside of her building quickly, threatening to take her over the edge. Her nails dug into his back as her hips moved to match his thrusts.

His kisses turned demanding and fierce as she teetered on the edge. His rhythm didn't change, and Akantha felt the pressure sharpen and then come undone. Her muscles tightened around him as waves of ecstasy rolled through her.

A few more thrusts and he followed her over the edge. "Akantha," he moaned, collapsing to rest on her body. She held him tight, brushing her lips against his sweat-slicked skin. She licked her lips, savoring the salty taste. Thoughts of the war, the spear, and memories of Himmler's touch faded away.

After a moment, he eased himself away and rolled to the side to wrap his arms around her. Akantha settled in next to him and soaked up the heat his body radiated. She found safety and warmth in his arms, the things she needed at the moment.

A shroud of silence blanketed the room and Akantha lay with her head on his chest. She listened to the steady rhythm of his heart as it slowed along with his breathing. He had fallen asleep, as he had been wont to do when they had regularly shared a bed. She was covered with only a sheet, but his body kept her warm in the cool air.

Her fingers lightly traced patterns across his chest as she allowed her mind free rein. It raced past their reunion and on to their quest. She knew she should sleep, but she could no more help it than she could change her immortal existence. Thoughts of their quest ran circles in her mind and occasionally the thought of that bastard Damianos crept in.

She didn't want to think of him, unless it was about the harm she wanted to inflict upon him. The thought of causing the man pain brought a small sensation of pleasure. She made a silent vow to shoot him next time she saw him. Maybe twice for good measure. His favorite body part made a tempting target.

She turned her thoughts to the here and now. She focused on the feel of flesh against flesh. Her body was warm where it was against his, cool where it wasn't. She played with the hair on his chest and pressed a kiss to a pectoral. Given the chance, she'd stay here forever and never leave his bed.

"Are you awake?" Matheus asked as he shifted to hold her closer.

"Yes," she replied and raised her head to look at him. "I'm surprised you are, though."

He leaned forward to kiss her. "And miss even a second of your company?"

"Still the flatterer."

"Only truth, my lady. Is something wrong?"

The 'my lady' brought back memories of the two hundred years she spent with her Knight Templar. One of her fondest memories was the day she saved him as he fled from Philip's men. She showed him the world and helped him adjust to life as an immortal. It was a period in her life she would always remember fondly. She shook her head. "No. Just can't sleep," she lied. How could she tell him she was thinking of another man when lying next to him?

A hand went to her chin and he tilted her face so she was looking him in the eye. "Are you sure?" he asked. His sable brown eyes looked into hers and Akantha had a sudden fear that he could see past the lie.

"I can't help but to think about this war and all the horrors it's creating. I'm so weary of war."

He slid her hand along her jaw to cradle her cheek. "War is a horrible thing," he murmured. "Unfortunately, it's in human nature to destroy each other. We have both seen our fair share of violence through the centuries."

She sighed deeply and placed her head in the hollow of his shoulder. "I know. I would like to see one century without a major war. It hasn't even been thirty years since the last."

"They don't live long enough to see the effects of several wars as we have. They see fortune and glory, and sacrifice their future to get it."

"Someday, it will change. This war can't last much longer."

His arms tightened around her. "This will end soon enough," he assured her. "Order will be restored and life will move on."

Something about his tone gave her pause. She couldn't say what it was exactly, but it bothered her on a level she couldn't put into words. "I know it will, but how many will die this time?" She had seen some of the Nazis' plans and they made her sick to her stomach. Millions would die if the Nazis had their way. In her long life, she had seen such wanton destruction of life only a handful of times. Daily she woke from nightmares, spawned by what she had witnessed while with Himmler on his tours of the concentration camps.

"Too many," he replied. He turned his head and dropped a kiss on her forehead. "Don't think about it right now. Let the weight of the world slide off your shoulders for tonight. Tomorrow is another day to worry about the war. Before I get distracted again, were you able to find out any information on the location of the spear?"

"Not anything definite, but it's a lead. My source thinks it may be in Greece."

"Greece? Is your source reliable?"

"She is. She believes a colleague may have hidden it in Thessaloniki."

"Someone in your little group?" he asked.

Akantha had almost forgotten he knew about the Guardians. Six hundred years had passed since she told him about the *Custodes Thesauri*, the Guardians of the Treasure, as they called themselves. She had forgotten a lot of things in her very long life. That shouldn't have been one of them. The Guardians worked in the background of history and tried to keep their existence a secret. The fewer people who knew, the better the chances of the secret of being kept. Yet, she had told him in the passion of a new love, enticing his imagination with stories of how some immortals spent their lives for the good of mankind.

"Yes," she admitted. There was no use in denying it.

"I'm glad you were able to get some information," he said, dropping another kiss on her mouth.

"Me too. We could spend a decade, or a century, looking for it without any help."

"We'll find it."

"I hope so. I don't want to see the Nazis get their hands on it."

"I know. How will we know if it's the real spear?"

Akantha shrugged. "I don't know. Unfortunately, not much is known. Legend says it has the power to determine the fate of the world, but that's about it. Legends were created to either exaggerate the truth or spread a blatant lie. There's nothing in terms of description or if it has any other power. I assume it's a pilum, which would have been used by Roman soldiers of the time."

"You'd be able to recognize one, correct?"

"Yes," she replied. She smiled sadly. "Roman soldiers were everywhere during the years of the empire."

"Do you think it could kill an immortal?"

It was a strange question, she thought, but she'd have to admit she was asking herself the same thing. "I...I don't know. It's possible, I guess. It's rumored to be one of the most powerful weapons in history."

He gave her a comforting squeeze. "What are you planning on doing after the war?" he asked, changing the subject to a more pleasant one.

"I haven't decided," she admitted. "Though spending some time in the States is a possibility. I may take a decade or two and just relax. Are we going to continue wasting moonlight with talk? I can think of better ways to spend our time," she purred.

"That makes two of us." He kissed her.

The kiss was long, deep, and consuming. Akantha melted and her toes curled. In a world full of troubles, they had seen enough in their long lives and they would still be there when the sun came up. Tonight was theirs, and Akantha was going to take advantage of every second.

CHAPTER EIGHT

THESSALONIKI, GREECE 1941

Akantha and Matheus pulled into Thessaloniki as the sun was sinking below the western horizon. The peaceful eight-hour drive made the time pass quickly. Akantha and Matheus talked about the adventures they shared during the century they had been together and the times when they were apart. After a while, she realized she was doing all the talking. Matheus told her a bit, but there were gaps. She assumed he was either with another woman during those times or had passed them in peaceful existence. She didn't judge or get jealous. She had a few lovers in the hundred years since she had last seen him.

A part of their route took them along the shore and Akantha looked out over the Aegean. Across the water and on the other side lay Turkey and the place where her journeys started. Surprisingly, homesickness welled up. Akantha wondered where it came from. She hadn't thought of Turkey as being home for a very long time, long before it was ever called Turkey, even before the Ottomans called it their empire. Home was an old house on the rocky coast of Maine.

"You okay?" Matheus asked as they entered the city.

"I'm fine," she assured him. "It's strange, but I'm experiencing a little homesickness."

"Strange indeed, but it proves you are human."

"I suppose. Old memories are coming to the surface quite often as of late." The business of life was the acquisition of memories, and while some faded away, others never died. They lived on and echoed in the present.

He nodded. "I can understand. It happens quite often."

"It does," she agreed, but it didn't happen to her. She never felt any longing for the town where she had grown up. Until now. The past was invading the present too much lately. "I've been thinking about where the spear could be."

"And?"

"If I remember correctly, there's a statute of Alexander in the middle of the city. Zenon said it was the best representation of Alexander he had seen. If he hid it in the city, it's a good bet it's there."

"Do you think it could be the one? That's really out in the open."

"It would be the best place to look," she said. "Zenon was a firm believer of hiding things in plain sight and the least obvious place. He was quite the Alexander worshiper and this is his home territory. He would tell stories of marching with Alexander all night if you let him."

"Have you heard from him?" Matheus asked.

Akantha shook her head. "No. Not since the Crimean War." In order to make Matheus immortal, Akantha turned to Zenon for help. He was one of the few, if not the only one, who knew how to do so. Zenon still had some plants growing somewhere, but he would never say where, nor had he ever divulged the secrets to making Soma.

"Shame," Matheus commented. "I've always enjoyed talking to him."

Akantha smiled. "I remember. The two of you would talk for hours."

His smile echoed hers. "Those were some great conversations. I learned so much from him."

She did too. He had taught her to survive on her own in a world where women's survival depended on men. When this war was over, she was going to visit him. It had been far too long since she had last seen him.

"What if it's not there?" he asked.

"Then we go find him. If he did possess it at some point, there's a good chance he still has it."

"It would be good to see him again."

Akantha nodded. "Yes, it would be."

"If I may ask, what are we going to do with the spear once we find it?"

"Lock it away in a vault. Keep it away from anyone who wanted to use it," she replied without hesitation.

"You and your group always want to hide things away from the world. We could use it and restore order to the world. The Nazis would be defeated."

Akantha shook her head. "Our place is to live in the world and keep things like the spear out of it. Humans do enough damage on their own. They don't need powerful weapons helping them." Akantha glanced at him and he looked away.

Silence dominated the cab of the truck and the nagging feeling from the previous night wouldn't leave her alone. Something was not right, but she couldn't put a finger on it. "You're quiet."

"Just thinking about this war."

"Such as?" she prompted. Conversations with him were never this one-sided.

"I'm not sure there will truly be a victor and order be restored." Now he turned and looked at her. The nagging feeling grew stronger and she wished she knew why. Her gut was trying to tell her something, but she wasn't understanding the message.

"There will be a victor and hopefully it will be the side of the angels."

"Where's this statue?"

"It's close," Akantha replied. "I think. It's been awhile since I've been here. The statue of Alexander is in the middle of Aristotelous Square."

The truck rolled down the nearly empty Egnatia Street. The Nazi occupation had deterred people from the streets and those who did venture out didn't loiter. They performed their errands quickly and returned to their homes as soon as possible. Akantha missed the normal hustle and bustle of a city.

She remembered this city from Roman times as she made her way west to Athens with Damianos. The place she knew was long gone, but if she looked closely she could see the ancient city peeking out from behind the more modern one. Most cities held echoes of the past and she found herself missing the old and not looking favorably upon the new.

They reached the end of the street and rolled into a large square. The road curved off to the left and to the right, forming a horseshoe around the square. In the middle of the expansive square the statue of Alexander stood looking out over the harbor to the Aegean.

"There." Akantha pointed to the statue. "If anyone was paying attention they would have realized Alexander is holding a Roman pilum. Something that wouldn't have been used until the later days of the Republic, long after Alexander died. Pull the truck over there and we can see if we can remove the spear from the statue." Scholars probably thought the artist took the liberty because it looked good. Historical inaccuracies were a personal pet peeve of hers.

He nodded and pulled the truck off the road and shifted it into park. He looked at her and grinned. "Ready?"

"Ready."

They climbed out of the truck and walked over to the statue. The pedestal stood as high as Akantha's head, adding a little challenge to their quest. "Give me a boost," she instructed.

He bent over and cupped his hands together. Akantha placed a foot in his hands and jumped with his efforts, making it to the top of the pedestal. She climbed around to stand in front of Alexander and looked up. The statue did closely resemble Alexander, or at least how she remembered him. She had seen him from afar a few times, but never up close. A plaster-like substance covered the spear, making it look like the statue. It was a small miracle the *Einsatzstab Reichsleiter Rosenberg*, Hitler's own cultural looting organization, hadn't taken the statue like they had so many others across Europe.

She grabbed the shaft and gave it an experimental push. It held firm in the statue's grasp. Zenon had done his work well. It would take a great deal of force to separate the spear from the statue. "By Dis," she swore.

"Something wrong?" he called up.

"It won't move. Do you see any rocks or anything I can use to hit it out of place?"

"Hold on," he said. A few moments later he returned with a fist-sized rock. He offered it up to her. "Vandalizing art work is not like you."

She looked down at him, taking the rock. "Desperate times call for desperate measures. Besides, it's not like this is Michelangelo's David or his Pietà. Thank you." The thought of destroying a piece of art, even one by an unknown artist, made her queasy.

"You're welcome."

Taking a deep breath, she smashed the rock against the statue's fingers. Pieces of marble flew off as she kept hammering away, and it didn't take long to demolish the fingers. Destroying this piece of art was for a good cause. At least that's what she told herself each time she smashed the rock into the statue. Finally, the plaster on the bottom of the shaft flew away in pieces.

Once the plaster from the bottom was cleared, she set the rock down on the pedestal and tried moving the spear again. It shifted a little. She got a better grip on the spear and tried moving it again. It lifted and Akantha kept pushing it up. It cleared the remaining fingers and came free.

Sweaty and dirty, she looked down at Matheus. "You did it." He grinned as he held out a hand. "Hand me the spear and climb down."

"We did it," she clarified and placed the spear in his hand. Akantha carefully climbed down off the statue. "It was a team effort. Let's get that thing where it won't see the light of day. If it is the true spear, it'll be far from the hands of the Nazis."

"Wait." He motioned with his free hand and armed German soldiers came toward them from all directions and a heavy truck emblazoned with swastikas rolled into the square. "There's been a change of plans."

"What?" Her mouth fell open and she couldn't move as the soldiers approached them. They closed in ranks and pointed weapons at Akantha. It would have been kinder if he just shot her or knocked her out. "Matheus, what's going on?"

"It's rather simple, my dear," he said as he took two steps away from her. "The spear is too important to be hidden away where it can't be used. It was meant to be used. Humanity needs guidance and control."

His words slammed into her and kicked her in the gut. She struggled to draw breath. The sharp pain of betrayal hurt more than a hundred bullets. She refused to believe Matheus could be doing this. It just wasn't possible. Not her Matheus. "You—you can't do this!"

"I can and I am." His strange smile never wavered. There wasn't an ounce of warmth behind it or in his brown eyes. A stranger stood before her.

"You cannot do this, Matheus. The Nazis are horrible. What they're planning, by the gods, it's just not right."

Just when she had been the happiest in a long time, the dark machineries of Fate stepped in to rip away happiness and replace it with fear, dread, and shock. The world grew a little darker.

"Who said this has anything to do with the Nazis?"

"Then why are you doing this?" she demanded. She couldn't wrap her head around what was happening. What would ever cause Matheus to do something like this?

"You are in no place to demand answers, but since you were so helpful I'll give you one. I'm going to restore order and right the wrongs that have been done. I will make this world clean again. Something you should have done centuries ago. "

"What?" Akantha shook her head. Did rediscovered love blind her? The nagging feeling she had now made sense. She should have listened to her gut. "What are you talking about?"

"Restrain her," he ordered the two soldiers next to him and they moved toward Akantha. She plastered herself against the pedestal. Before they could reach her, shots rang out and the square erupted into chaos.

The rooftop of a nearby building provided the perfect vantage point to view what was happening in the square below. He had been lying on the rooftop with the rifle, watching, and waiting for the past few hours. He had even managed to take a short nap while waiting, knowing the rumble of the German vehicles would wake him. He woke before the trucks arrived and watched the people moving below to pass the time.

He lined Akantha up in the rifle's sights and followed her as she moved toward the statue of Alexander in the middle of the square. He shifted and put Matheus in the middle of the sights. His gut told him something wasn't right about all of this and that trouble would come. He was as sure of it as he was sure of the sun rising in the morning. What that trouble was, he couldn't say, but he was prepared.

Akantha removed the spear from the statue and climbed down. Then things went to hell. German soldiers appeared like cockroaches and two restrained Akantha. It was time for a rescue and some thrilling heroics.

He took aim at the soldier to Akantha's left and fired. He shifted his sights and shot the soldier on her right. They both fell to the ground. The few civilians in the square dashed for cover. His next shot hit Matheus and the man jerked when the bullet slammed into him. He yelled and Akantha lunged for the spear. Matheus's grip didn't slip and Damianos put another bullet into him. The soldiers started firing in all directions, hoping to hit the person who just shot their commander.

Soldiers continued to appear in the square and Damianos methodically aimed and fired as they arrived. He didn't feel anything as each man died from a simple squeeze of the trigger. War and death were old friends of his. He had been fighting and killing for far too long to be affected. He had learned to compartmentalize feelings from taking a life a long time ago. The enemy soldiers were obstacles to be removed, nothing more.

He watched Matheus yank the spear away from Akantha and saw her jerk backward. He growled and took aim on Matheus again. This time the bullet slammed into his forehead and Matheus crumpled to the ground. Damianos put another two bullets into the man. Knowing Matheus wouldn't die didn't lessen the small sense of satisfaction that shooting the man brought him. Two soldiers grabbed Matheus's inert body and dragged him toward a waiting a truck. Two more closed in on Akantha and she put her hands in the air. He took aim and shot the two men in succession.

Damianos dropped the rifle and ran to the roof door. He charged head first down the stairs until he finally reached the ground floor. He burst out into the square, drawing a pistol as he exited the building. He fired as he ran toward Akantha, soldiers already replacing the two he had just shot. One soldier went down and Akantha struggled to grab the weapon of the remaining soldier. Damianos didn't have a clear shot and ran faster across the square. The soldier pushed Akantha backward and aimed. Damianos fired two rapid shots. One grazed the soldier and distracted him enough to allow Akantha to grab the weapon from him. She turned the gun on him and fired. He went down in a heap at her feet. Damianos fired at another soldier while Akantha shot at yet another. They both fell to the ground, one clutching a wound in his stomach, the other dead with blood pouring out onto the cobblestones.

The truck carrying Matheus rumbled out of the square. "Piss and blood," she swore.

"My thoughts exactly," he said as he shot the soldier with the stomach wound, putting the man out of his misery. She whipped her head around and her eyes went wide. "What are you doing here?"

"Saving your beautiful behind," he said as he watched her eyes roll back. His arms darted out and he caught her before she fell to the ground.

He scooped her up in his arms, cradling her against his chest. A quick scan of the area revealed no more enemy soldiers and he made for a nearby truck. He placed her in the passenger seat and climbed in behind the wheel. The engine rumbled to life and he stomped on the accelerator. Lingering would only attract unwanted attention and he needed to get Akantha to a safe place so he could remove the bullet from her chest.

He weaved in and out of traffic, trying to go as fast as possible but not attract any unwanted attention. Sometimes Nazis didn't ask questions before sending folks off to the camps. He had been in one or two of the camps and what he saw there was stuff of nightmares. He had been in too many wars to count and had seen more than his fair share of carnage, but the scenes in the camps gave him nightmares.

He glanced over. Akantha was still unconscious and blood seeped out of her wounds. The crimson spread across her clothing. He'd have to stop soon and put temporary bandages on her wounds. She wouldn't die, but too much blood loss would make her recovery slower. She had to be on her feet and functioning if they were to recover the spear from her former lover. His only regret was not putting more bullets into the man.

CHAPTER NINE

Pain registered as Akantha clawed her way back to consciousness. Her shoulder throbbed, like someone was trying to drive a stake through her, as did her side. She forced her eyes open and struggled to keep them that way. A dry sob escaped her as she breathed in the blood-scented air. The ache in her chest hurt more than the wounds.

"Sleeping Beauty is awake," a male voice said and Akantha's stomach sank. Damianos. She was in agony, emotionally and physically, and didn't have the energy to deal with him. She only wanted to hide away in a safe place, but she knew he would give her no quarter. The man re-entered her life at the damnedest of times. He was the tide, turning and always coming back around. A first love changed you forever, and no matter how hard she tried, the feelings never went away. Not even after twenty-four hundred years.

"What are you doing here?" she demanded, looking at him. His dark hair was slightly mussed and stubble created shadows on his jaw. Dark brown eyes locked with hers, looking down into her soul, making her feel naked and exposed. Her heart raced. She shivered and realized she was almost naked beneath the covers. Her jacket, blouse, skirt, and shoes had been removed, leaving her in her bra and underwear.

He leaned in and planted a kiss on her mouth, then pulled back and grinned.

She weakly slapped him across the face.

He rubbed the spot where she slapped him and laughed. "There's the Akantha I love."

Akantha looked away. He was the last person she expected to see and the one she didn't want to ever see again. She didn't have the energy or desire to partake in another battle in their own private war.

"Do you always have to slap me? Would it be easier for you if you could throw something at me? I have a knife on me somewhere—"

She looked at him just long enough to glare. "Go away."

"And leave you wounded? Hate me all you want, but I'm not leaving. I rescued you, remember? Do you think the Nazis would have bothered to dig the slug from your shoulder and side, and treat your wounds? That I took the time to do both should count for something."

Of course he would want acknowledgment. It was just like him. He had an ego the size of the world. "Fine. You rescued me. Thank you. Now leave. I can take care of myself." She moved to sit up and grimaced as her wounds protested with sharp spikes of pain.

"I don't know if I should be insulted or amused that you think it's that easy to be rid of me." He picked up the thin spare pillow and moved to help her sit up. "I'm not leaving, so get over that idea now. How do you feel?"

"How do you think I feel? I'm in pain," she growled. Telling him the truth would open a conversation she didn't want to have. The wall she had erected around her heart against him had to remain in place.

"You need me. Now stop being your usual self and let me help." He reached for her uninjured shoulder to pull her toward him, tucking the pillow in behind. "The more you fight me, the more it's going to hurt. And if you're good, I have a little something that'll help with the pain."

"I don't need you," she growled as she reluctantly let him put the pillow behind her and help her sit. "Not now. Not ever." Why couldn't he just leave and let her heal her heart and soul in peace?

"I have always loved your independent streak, but even I know that's the pain talking now." He helped her ease back against the pillows and smirked. "But I have morphine and you will love me again. It came with the medical kit. Not as much as I'd like, but enough to take the edge off and let you rest."

"I will never love you again," she told him as she looked away. She didn't want to see his smile. It was dangerous and would wear down any resistance, and she needed to keep the walls around her now more than ever. Despite herself, she looked at him. Sadness bled into his dark eyes and she knew her words had cut deep.

"Maybe you should wait to make that decision ." He reached over her for the small bag containing the rest of the first aid supplies. "You should never make decisions in pain."

Or because of love, she thought as the wounds throbbed more. Love spurred decisions she came to regret. Her heart led her astray many times and she failed to learn the lessons. Even as old as she was.

Damianos withdrew one of the morphine syrettes. "I was making light of the situation and suggesting that the fact that I have morphine in my possession might possibly make you look kindly at me. At least with less hostility. I am, after all, considered to be a powerful ally in some circles."

She glared at him, trying to ignore the small amount of guilt she held for hurting him with her words. "I don't need morphine and I don't need your help." Why couldn't he just let her be? She just wanted to be left alone to lick the deep wounds Matheus's betrayal cut into her soul. She quickly looked away as the thought of her former lover brought tears to her eyes.

"You need it to rest and begin healing, and you know it. A bargain then. I give you a shot and then I will leave. Long enough for you to fall asleep. I'll use the time to reconnoiter and find what there is to know. Agreed? Make it your choice and not your downfall."

"I don't need it," she insisted as she blinked back the tears. "What I need is for you to leave me alone." The last bit came out as a half-growl. Her temper and patience were wearing thin.

"For once in your life, stop being so damn stubborn!" he snarled. "Gods save me from your stubbornness." He sighed. "Please, Akantha. Let me give you some morphine."

Oddly enough, it was the please he snarled that made her relent. It was only when he was angry enough to let go of his placating attitude that she could believe his intentions. She tried to ignore the shiver racing through her. "Fine."

Damianos kept his face frozen at his small victory. A smile would antagonize her and make this harder than it had to be. Right now he needed her to cooperate and she could try the patience of a saint. Their little war could continue at a later time. He never missed a chance to go a few rounds with her.

"Where are we?" she asked as she watched him break the seal on the syrette with the needle.

"Scupi—Skopje," he answered. His movements were efficient enough to make an outside observer think he had medical training. Sometimes he slipped and thought in terms of ancient names. Akantha did the same more often than not. It was a common habit among immortals, one they tried to break with little success. There were times he found himself switching to his native language in the middle of a conversation with someone who didn't understand it. "I stole a truck and drove us here. This is an old place of mine. Once I got you here, I dug the bullets out, and sewed you up." He gave her a small smile. "I thought about giving up this place quite a few times, but it's a good thing I didn't."

Frowning, she looked away.

He'd give the world to see her smile at him again and see the light return to her eyes, just like the moment when he first met her and she ruined him for other women. Instead, he shook his head, clearing his thoughts and focusing on the here and now. "You know I'll always watch out for you," he told her as he gently tucked her wrist between his torso and upper arm to hold it firm. He rubbed a spot on her arm and slipped the needle in.

Akantha remained quiet. He knew if she believed him, it would alter the way she looked at her past life and they both had too much to look back upon. He was the living embodiment of her long past and he tried to overcome that mountain each time he saw her.

She hissed as the morphine went in. Damianos set the spent syrette aside and tenderly rubbed the injection spot. He released her arm and took her hand. "It shouldn't take long."

"How did you find me?"

"Morana told me you were heading here," he explained. "I also remembered Zenon's fascination with Alexander and the statue here. When you weren't going to emerge from the room at Manuc's, I left Bucharest and waited here for you. Kept my distance and watched. I knew you would need me."

"Bastard," she grumbled and pulled her hand from his. "Why didn't you just take the spear?"

He chuckled, amused at her disgruntlement. "It wasn't my place to take it."

"How'd you know?"

He shrugged, his heavy shoulders rolling easy with the motion. He could tell her he followed from Berlin to Morana's because he loved her and wanted to protect her, but she wouldn't believe it. She never did, no matter how many times he told her. "A gut feeling. I couldn't let you walk into danger alone." A lie was easier. She'd just get angry if she knew he had been following her and keeping an eye on her for the past year. "Tell me what happened," he urged in a soft and gentle tone. He put two fingers under her chin and lifted her head so he could see her face. His heart ached when he saw the pain etched in the gray depths of her eyes. It was said the eyes were the window to the soul and right now he could see the recent wounds inflicted upon hers. If he looked hard enough maybe he would see the wounds he inflicted.

"I don't want to talk about it."

"Talk to me." He kept his voice even and calm. She needed to stay still for the time being and not engage in their usual war. With a lot of luck, she'd cooperate.

"I. Don't. Want. To. Talk. About. It."

"I can help you better if I know what happened," he insisted. He reached out and tucked a strand of ebony hair behind her ear. "I need to know what he's planning so we can stop him." It was the truth. He could plan better if he knew his adversary and she knew Matheus better than anyone. Getting her to talk about him in her current state would be difficult, but Damianos was always up for a challenge.

"I don't need or want your help," she countered. "I'll fix this."

"No? You'd be a guest of the Reich if I hadn't been there to get you away from them. Fixing it on your own should be the last thing you'd consider as a next step."

She opened her mouth to argue but immediately closed it. She glared at him for being right, and any other time he'd be tickled. Now he just wanted to help her get past the wounds her knight inflicted upon her, both physical and emotional. He resisted pointing out that he was right. He didn't want to antagonize her.

"I don't need you or your help."

Her words always injured him more than any weapon. He loved her despite all of the harsh words, and her temper just made him love her more. It didn't make sense, but love rarely made sense. He was a simple man in love with a very complicated woman. He sighed and ran a hand through his hair, further messing it up. "Look, you're injured and the German army is probably looking for you, possibly both of us. I put quite a few rounds in your knight, so we have time for you to heal."

"He's not my knight."

He heard the unspoken "anymore" and his heart ached for her. He hated seeing her hurt, but he hated seeing another man in her life. The next time he ran across Matheus he'd make the man paid for hurting her. He couldn't kill the man, but he did know quite a few interesting ways to torture someone.

"Get some rest," he told her.

"I don't need—"

"Get some rest. You'll heal faster if you do." He stood and grabbed the medical supplies. He carried them back to return them to the medical kit sitting on a small table. "I'm going to go out. I don't exactly keep my safe houses stocked with food." He turned and looked at her. "Please rest."

Her eyes held his for a long moment and she nodded. He smiled and left the bedroom, closing the door behind him.

CHAPTER TEN

Skopje, Yugoslavia 1941

Akantha woke to pain for the second time. Her shoulder and side protested the slightest movement, but she had to move. Her bladder would not let her stay in the bed. She threw back the covers and slid her legs over the edge. She took a deep breath and pulled herself up to a sitting position. Barely. Pain raced through her abdomen and her shoulder. Curses fell from her lips.

The door opened and Damianos stepped into the room. "What are you doing?" He reached her side and put an arm around her, helping her to her feet.

"I need to use the toilet," she answered. "I don't need any help."

He sighed. "Of course you don't, but you're going to get some anyway. Are you hungry?"

His arm remained around her as they slowly made their way across the bedroom toward the small bathroom. "No."

"Are you sure? I managed to find a few pieces of fruit and some bread."

"I'm sure," she insisted.

He released her once they reached the door to the bathroom. The door slammed shut behind her and a chuckle floated through the door. She glared at the door for a moment. Tired, heartbroken, and wounded, she still had enough energy to be mad and irritated with him.

She sat on the toilet, enjoying the few moments of solitude and was more thankful he was quiet. A few moments of peace were golden. It wouldn't last. If she stayed here too long, he would burst in to see if she was all right. She stood and washed her hands. A heavy sigh left her and she grasped the door knob and froze, gathering her courage and strength to deal with him.

"This brings back old times," Damianos mused when she opened the door. Of course he was standing right by the door, waiting for her. "You, me, a war, one of us injured, and holed up somewhere."

"It does. The good and the bad," she admitted.

"They weren't all bad," he said in a soft voice. "I think the good outweighs the bad." He slipped his arm around her and started them in the direction of the bedroom.

The going was slow and all she wanted was to crawl into the bed and go to sleep, the one place he couldn't bother her. "I think we remember things differently," she shot back.

"I think our daughter was a good point."

They stopped. Akantha sighed. "She was." The grief over her daughter's death bubbled to the surface. Her breath caught in her chest and she clutched the silver star at her neck. The necklace was a gift they gave Eleni on her wedding day and Akantha had worn it since the day Eleni died. Eleni had been a bright spot in their lives, and Akantha and Damianos had been together for almost four decades. Four good decades.

Silence loomed. The memory of their daughter and the mention of her was the closest thing they could come to a truce over in the long, bitter war between them. The ticking of the clock on the wall and passing autos on the street below broke the silence growing between them.

"Are you okay?" His voice seemed loud in the quiet room.

The brief truce evaporated like mist. "Tired," she lied to get past the awkward moment.

"Then you'll rest," he said and urged her with his arm to walk.

She walked toward the bed, hoping he wouldn't talk. He helped her in, despite the fact she didn't need his help or want it. Saying so would have brought another round of arguing and she was too exhausted to argue.

"How are they?" he asked. He pulled the blanket up to her waist.

He didn't need to specify who they were. She had kept track of Eleni's descendants through the years. Some still lived in the small Maine town where they had raised their daughter and then their granddaughter. He asked about them every time they saw each other. "They're good."

He smiled. "I'm glad. I've been meaning to go back and check on them myself."

"They're fine. The boys are in their late teens."

He briefly frowned. "If the United States gets involved in this mess, they'll be going off to war."

She nodded. The thought had crossed her mind frequently and always caused a pit to form in her stomach. Even though they were several generations removed from her, she still worried about her family coming to harm.

"Tell me what happened," he urged. "From the beginning."

She saw the stubborn look in his dark eyes. To think, he called *her* stubborn. She grabbed the edge of the blanket and pulled it up to her chest. "I was spying for the Allies. I was posing as *Reichsführer-SS* Himmler's secretary and overheard plans to go after the spear. I was going to sneak out of there and go after it myself, but I ran into Matheus. He was undercover as well and we decided to work together."

He frowned when she mentioned the other man's name. It tickled her a bit to know that being with Matheus bothered him. "You found it," he said and she gave him a hard look. "Not that I would doubt your abilities. Continue."

"I don't know. I can't explain it. We had it and he took it out of my hands. He said something about restoring order and righting wrongs."

"What wrongs is he talking about?"

"I don't know. I can't even begin to guess what they are. Something happened to him. He's not a bad person and would never do something like this. At least, I didn't think he would. He said we should have made the world clean centuries ago." Each word sharpened the pain of Matheus's betrayal and it was hard to say the words. Tears formed in her eyes.

She was a fool to think Matheus was the same man he once was. A lot had to change in six hundred years. She shouldn't have expected out of him what he embodied in the past. That part of him no longer existed. It was an error in judgment and one that she would never make again.

The tears spilled from her eyes and he wiped them away with a thumb. "I'm sorry it happened, and I'm sorry he hurt you," he whispered.

Akantha looked at him and nodded. "Thank you."

"Did you sleep with him?" Damianos asked.

"Of course I slept with Matheus," she snorted.

"I wasn't talking about Matheus. I know all about you and Matheus. I've heard of him through the years."

"You're jealous," she accused.

"My dear, I've never been jealous of Matheus." He cupped her cheek with a hand and gave her a rueful smile. "You were happy with him and all I've ever wanted was your happiness. He was not a rival to me."

Akantha snorted. She knew him well enough to know when he was lying, but she wasn't going to say anything. It would lead to an argument and she didn't have the fight in her right now.

The minute facial expressions betraying his thoughts and feelings didn't go unnoticed when she mentioned another lover's name.

"I was talking about *Reichsführer-SS* Himmler," he clarified.

"What if I did?"

"I'm just asking. I figured you did in order to get closer to him," he said. "It's a sound tactic."

"Sometimes we need to do repulsive things." She shrugged and the movement made the wounds in her shoulder and side throb despite the morphine. "It wasn't any worse than sleeping with you."

He removed his hand from her cheek. "You don't mean that."

She could feel his eyes on her and she didn't dare look over at him. She'd admit he was right if she did. Ignoring him was usually the best policy and sometimes he even stopped talking if she didn't respond.

"Your silence confirms it."

"Shut up."

He laughed. "I love you, thorns and all."

Akantha remained silent. A yawn slipped out and she knew the morphine was working its way through her system. Drowsiness settled over her and her eyelids were lead weights.

Movement caught her attention and she forced her eyes open wider. Damianos splashed his face with water from the basin and used wet hands to comb his thick black hair back from his face. The hard planes of his face were thrown into relief in the fading light. As much as she hated him, she had to admit he was a handsome man.

"Where are you going?" she asked.

"To find some more food. What we have won't last us. And see if there is any news of Nazi movements in the area. Get some rest so you can heal. I'll be back before you wake." He slipped out the door and it closed quietly behind him.

Sighing with relief, she sank deeper into the pillows. Regret washed over her. Her mind still didn't want to believe that Matheus had betrayed her, and the thought of him made her heart ache more. Betrayal was the intentional murder of trust.

The dam holding her emotions in check burst and tears followed. Anguish gripped her heart and squeezed. It was more than she could bear. Never again would she trust someone so completely or fall so deeply in love. Love made her do rash things and follow her heart instead of her head. It only brought trouble. It had proved true with Matheus, and with Damianos long before him.

The pillow became wet with tears and she was glad Damianos wasn't here to see her cry.

The hunt for food had taken longer than Damianos wanted to be away from Akantha, but in wartime everything was scarce. Food. Clothes. Beer. The three basic necessities. Not to mention soldiers were everywhere. Not Nazis, but Bulgarians. The Nazis handed over control to Bulgaria back in April. Every time he turned around, there was a man wearing a uniform. Most had no idea what they were involved in and some didn't have a choice. He was all too familiar with tactics used to get young men to sign up to be cannon fodder.

One day he hoped mankind would evolve past war, but he doubted it would ever happen. He had spent more than two thousand years going from one war to another. Killing people and making others die for their cause were the only things he was good at. The last regular run-of-the-mill job he held was working on fishing boats back in Athens. When he had Akantha. He held onto those days as if they were precious gems and would give up his immortality for the chance to go back and do things differently.

This brief time away from her allowed him the chance to smooth over the most recent wounds to his heart and soul she delivered. It would have hurt less had he been the one shot. The woman's words were sharper than any knife or sword and she knew how to wield them with proficiency. He loved the woman beyond words, but gods be damned, he didn't know how many more wounds he could take.

Shaking his head, he crossed the street and was greeted with the blaring of a car horn. The car swerved out of the way and he continued across the street. Leave it to her to distract him when she wasn't even around. One of these days she would be the death of him. He crossed the Stone Bridge and glanced up at Mount Vodno. Mountains and the stars were the constants in an immortal's life.

Everything else changed. Ottoman ruins, Roman ruins, and medieval ruins could be found all through the city, but the mountain remained the same. He remembered scaling the Kale Fortress during his life, but he had been in the city before that had even been built.

The small bakery he spotted earlier was open and he prayed to any god listening they still had some bread. He had already managed to find a cheese shop with some meager blocks of cheese. The cost of a small hunk was enough to buy four during normal times. Luck was with him when he spotted a few bottles of homemade beer for sale. Along with the cheese, they took most of what little money he had. He wasn't poor by any means—Akantha wasn't the only one to acquire a substantial amount of wealth through the long years—but he didn't have access to any of his wealth.

The bakery was warm and welcoming, something rare at the moment. Despite the late hour, the smell of freshly baked bread assaulted him and it made his stomach rumble. An elderly man stepped out from a back room and Damianos offered him a smile.

"Hello," the man greeted him in Bulgarian.

"Greetings. How much for a loaf of bread?"

"One dinar," he replied.

Before the war it probably cost between ten and twenty para. Damianos nodded and pulled out what little money he had left. "Reichsmark?" he asked, holding the currency up. He didn't have any dinara.

The old man frowned.

"All I have," Damianos said.

The old man sighed and nodded. He grabbed a loaf of bread and held it out along with his other hand. Damianos placed the Reichsmark in the man's hand and took the loaf of bread.

"Thank you."

"You're welcome."

Damianos shoved it in the bag with the cheese and beer. He left the shop and headed back toward his apartment. He had hoped to purchase more food, silently cursing the Nazis and this war. He casually walked through the streets of Skopje, not wanting to hurry and attract unwanted attention. He could handle anything that came his way, but the purpose was to not have to fight. Akantha was already injured; he didn't need both of them wounded.

He glanced down an alley and noticed laundry strung out between two buildings. Akantha would need clothes. The uniform he removed from her possessed two bullet holes and bloodstains. It wouldn't do; she needed clothes that would attract less attention. He ducked into the alley and grabbed a long skirt and a white blouse. They were as nondescript as clothes could be. He bunched them up into a ball and shoved them under an arm. He hurried out of the alley and toward Akantha.

The door creaked as he entered and he hoped it wasn't enough to wake Akantha if she were sleeping. Even though they couldn't die, healing took time and rest was the best prescription. He sat the bag down on the small wooden table in the kitchen area and headed to the bedroom. The door didn't squeak as he opened it and he poked his head around. Relief washed through him. She slept and he had some time to rest. Crawling in next to her would wake her, so that wasn't an option, and sleeping on the couch in the small living room was too far from her. He didn't need her trying to move about on her own. The chair by the bed it was.

He closed the door behind him and crossed the room, trying to be as silent as possible. The last thing he wanted to do was wake her. He eased himself into the chair and settled into a position that wasn't too uncomfortable. A sigh escaped him and he looked at the woman asleep in the bed.

Asleep she was nineteen again. Young, innocent, and full of life. Beautiful beyond words. It wasn't strange he fell in love with her at first sight. Any man would. If he knew then what he knew now, things would be different. He would have loved her better and fought for her, not walk away in the face of betrayal. He had been young and stupid, too hurt to go after the one thing that mattered most.

She was the only thing in the world that mattered. What happened in the past, centuries of mistakes, were of no consequence.

He had a mission. Get Akantha to love him again or die trying. If he had to take on the whole of the German army, he'd do it. He didn't try to find the wisdom in loving her so much and not wanting to let her go—he would never find any. Time couldn't change the hopeless ways of fools and he was one of the biggest fools out there.

Exhaustion caught up to him and his head fell backward. His eyelids grew heavy and a half-yawn, half-sigh escaped him. He wanted to crawl into bed next to her and wrap his arms around her but didn't dare. Her injuries and the need for rest kept him in the chair. He closed his eyes and fell asleep to thoughts of the woman sleeping in the bed across from him.

CHAPTER ELEVEN

Ephesus 420 BCE

"Come away with me," Damianos whispered as he dropped kisses along the edge of her jaw.

"I can't," she said. "I belong to the temple." She wanted to go, but she knew her place. The temple had purchased her from her parents years ago and she could not simply run away. The gods would curse her and she would live her life in misery until she died.

"I love you, Akantha," he whispered in her ear. His warm breath brushing across her ear tickled, sending a shiver down her spine. "I want you to come to Athens with me. We'll get married and have a family."

She pulled away and looked at him. "How would we do that? You have very little money and I cannot leave the temple."

"You can leave the temple," he insisted. "We'll leave and not look back. The money is just a small problem. Tyche and Aphrodite will smile upon us and we won't have to worry about money."

"You are a fool," she accused.

"Then I am a fool in love with a beautiful woman. Even one with thorns."

Heat flared on her cheeks and she smiled as she turned her face away from his. It was a familiar reaction to his flowery words and compliments. She knew she shouldn't listen to his words, but it was as if she were under a spell when he spoke and kissed her.

"See how she blushes," he chuckled. "Eros has wounded me with his golden arrows and I cannot bear to live without you. You are my moon, my stars, my sun. My world would be dark, cold, and empty without you." He threw the apple in his hands to her.

She caught it and her cheeks burned hotter. She stared down at the apple for a few moments. She looked back up at him. "Such honeyed words fall from your lips and you urge me to take advice from a fool."

"Yet, they do not sway you to come with me. What can I say to convince you that I love you and cannot live without you? Maybe it is not words I need to use." He put a hand on her chin and turned her face to his. His lips pressed against hers briefly and then he deepened the kiss, drawing her into his arms.

Akantha melted under his searing kiss and the feel of his body pressed against hers. It made her head swim and her blood race in her veins. She returned the kiss, ignoring the persistent voice in the back of her mind that she shouldn't be doing this. Her life was not her own and she could not be with a man. The path of her life had been set.

Casting fortune to the wind, she wrapped her arms around his neck and let herself get lost in the moment.

"Come with me," he whispered when his mouth finally left hers.

She heard herself answer without thought. "I will."

Two nights later she crept through the temple toward the altar. She avoided the small circles of yellow light cast by the oil lamps, staying in the dark recesses of the shadows. Sandals dangled from her hand and the marble floor chilled her feet. She didn't want to risk attracting attention.

The hour was late and only a few slaves remained to sweep the floors. Akantha moved as quiet as a spirit among the columns until she reached the wooden statue of the goddess. Artemis, wearing a mural crown, looked outward, surveying her temple from the pedestal. Amber gourd-shaped drops adorned her chest and her legs tapered into a decorated term. One arm reached out, and nestled in the palm of the hand was a pearl. It reminded Akantha of the full moon. It beckoned to her as the light from a nearby lamp swirled in a rainbow of color along the surface.

"Forgive me," she whispered to the goddess. Akantha swallowed past the lump in her throat and reached out. Her fingertips brushed over the smooth, polished wood and the cool surface of the pearl. Her fingers curled and lifted the pearl from its resting place and dropped it into a small pouch fastened at her waist.

A eunuch priest appeared out of the shadows near the altar and Akantha ducked behind the statue. She held her breath and her heart raced. Surely she would be caught and punished. Akantha peeked out and watched the eunuch priest pass by.

The breath she held left her chest with explosive force. Normally she would send a silent prayer to the gods to get her through this, but none would look favorably upon what she was about to do. Akantha took a deep breath and then moved to the front of the statue.

She looked at the baskets of offerings spread out in front of the statue. Akantha crouched down next to a basket and removed the purse from her belt. She loosened the strings and grabbed a handful of coins, quickly shoving them inside the leather pouch, before standing up. She looked around for any signs that she had been noticed. Not seeing any, she continued with her mission.

The next basket held jewelry, so she grabbed a few of the smaller pieces. She stuffed them in her bag and stood. With as much grace and control she could muster, she walked slowly toward the temple exit. The walk seemed endless, and Akantha swore that with each step someone would cry out an alarm and she would be discovered. The cool night air greeted her as she neared the exit and her steps quickened. Once clear of the columns, she jogged down the marble steps and out into the night.

"A curse upon you," a female voice called from behind. Akantha dared a glance back. A priestess stood on the top step. "A curse upon you until you return what you have stolen! A curse on both of you!" she cried out into the night.

Akantha ran fast, as if she were trying to outrun the priestess's words.

CHAPTER TWELVE

Skopje, Yugoslavia 1941

Akantha woke to pain and the priestess's words echoing in her head. She shook her head to chase away the echoing words. Her shoulder and side throbbed and she looked up to see Damianos sitting next to the bed in the room's only chair. The only other item in the room other than the bed and chair was a small table. The spartan furnishings weren't a surprise, since he wasn't the type to decorate. He watched her with genuine concern in the dark depth of his eyes.

"How long was I asleep?" she asked.

His face softened a bit and briefly she saw the young man she had fallen in love with. Her resolve to hate him weakened and she silently cursed herself. She couldn't soften toward him. He was the reason why she was cursed and doomed to live forever and he would only end up hurting her again. She promised herself to never fall for his charms again.

"About six hours," he answered. "Are you hungry? I have some fresh bread and some cheese. I even managed a few bottles of beer. I found some clothes for you too."

"We have to keep moving," she said as she tried to sit. Her shoulder and side flared with pain and she immediately regretted trying to move.

He rose from the chair and sat down on the edge of the bed. He put his hand under her uninjured arm to give her leverage to pull herself up. "You're going to eat and then rest more. A few more hours will do you wonders."

Akantha shook her head. "No. I need to find Matheus and get the spear."

"No, you need a few more hours of rest," he told her. "We can't die, but we do need some time to heal. A few hours more and you'll be able to take on the whole German army."

Akantha remained silent but settled for glaring at him. He smirked. She hated that smirk, and the urge to hit him was almost too great to resist. "Why are you doing this?"

A dark brow rose, surprised she questioned his motives. "Doing what? Taking care of you?"

"You should be going after the spear. I'm only going to slow you down."

"I don't know Matheus," he explained. "I can't predict what he's going to do or where he'll take it. You know him, and as soon as you're healed enough, we'll go after him." He shrugged. "Besides, I like taking care of you."

"I don't need you taking care of me," she countered. "I'll heal just fine on my own. I always have."

"And miss the chance to share this war with you? Never."

Akantha wanted to wipe that grin off his face, but it would cause too much pain. "I'd rather spend time with the Nazis."

He laughed. "You never were a good liar, my dear. Perhaps I should have left you with Matheus. I'm sure the Nazis would have taken very good care of you."

It was the laugh that spiked her anger. "By Dis, shut up!"

"Speaking of the Nazis, your photo and description are being spread around. Apparently, Himmler has noticed your absence."

"This will complicate things."

"As if we'd have them any other way." He gave her a smile, fond memories bubbling to the surface.

"It'd be a nice change of pace if things weren't so complicated."

"It would," he agreed. "It's not the worst situation we've been in. We can do this. Now tell me about Matheus."

Akantha wished he could give her a little of his confidence. "What do you want to know?" she asked.

"I only know you love him," he replied. "Never once have I asked anything about him. I need to know what kind of person we're facing. I cannot plan if I do not know the person I'm dealing with."

Akantha opened her mouth to disagree, but she couldn't. He was a soldier at heart, and his tactical planning had been honed by over two thousand years of war. She didn't want to talk about Matheus but she couldn't deny that Damianos needed whatever she could tell him. The wounds on her heart were deep and fresh, but she had no right to wallow in her grief when so much was at stake.

"Please, Akantha." He moved the chair closer to the bed.

She nodded and gathered her courage. Talking about Matheus just made the sharp knife of betrayal go deeper into her soul. "I saved him from Philip IV's soldiers," she explained. "Matheus was a Templar, fleeing from the king's soldiers." Talking to him added to the burden of guilt she carried. Tears formed in her eyes. "He was a deeply honorable man. Reminded me a lot of Philip of Cognac. I saved him and took him to England. I fell in love with a good man and I begged Zenon to make him immortal until he did so. Two hundred years passed before our lives took different paths. I was tired and he still wanted to see the world. We parted ways and he traveled on. I don't know what happened to him during those years, but something did. Whatever his personal mission is, I made it easier for him to complete it. It's my fault the Nazis have the spear." Akantha paused and took a deep breath, thankful for Damianos's silence. "I never thought he would do this. It's not like him."

He reached out and gave her hand a gentle squeeze. "Don't feel guilty. How could you have known?"

"I should have known," she countered. "I should have seen it. I was with him for years before I made him immortal. Now he's helping the Nazis and I'm the reason why."

"You're wrong," he insisted. "You didn't make him help the Nazis. He's over six hundred years old and he made the choice, not you. You're not responsible for his actions any more than you're responsible for my actions."

"I'm responsible for him being alive," she snapped. "He wouldn't be alive to help the Nazis do gods only know what if I hadn't made him immortal."

"You can't blame yourself, Akantha. You are immortal, not a seer. There was no way you could predict what he would do. All we have is hindsight and its 20/20 wisdom. What we know is that Matheus is no longer the man you loved."

Damianos was right on occasion, but Akantha wasn't sure if this was one of those moments. Matheus's immortality had been her doing, but she didn't control the man's actions. She hadn't seen him for at least a hundred years. It was enough time for a person to change.

"Where do you think Matheus will take the Spear?" he asked, changing the topic.

Akantha shrugged and immediately regretted the movement. "Himmler wants all the spears brought to Wewelsburg."

"Where's that?" Damianos asked.

"About four hours southwest of Berlin. Himmler has been using it for a school for the SS, but mainly for their research into Germanic pre- and early history, medieval history, folklore, and *Sippenforschung.*"

"That's about—"

"Seventeen or eighteen hours from here," Akantha finished. "We need to get the spear before Matheus gets it to Wewelsburg. Once it's there, it'll be almost impossible to get into the castle."

"You've been there?"

Akantha nodded. "A few times with Himmler. Now you see why I don't want to delay."

"I do, but you do need to heal a little more. No castle is

impenetrable. I have found ways into castles before. Remember when John installed that sewage chute into Richard's castle?"

Worry twisted her gut too much for even a small laugh at the memory of him covered in filth after having to climb that chute. "I can rest and heal after we get the spear back. Go find us some transportation. I'll rest while you do that."

He shook his head. "I can do that tomorrow. Today you rest. Matheus isn't going anywhere for a few days."

"Why are you being so damned stubborn?" she snapped angrily. "Every moment we delay, the worse our chances of getting the spear." Gods save her from this man's stubbornness.

———

Damianos brought her hand up and pressed a kiss to her knuckles. "Because one of us is concerned about your well-being." Stubborn, thy name is Akantha. "Your wounds are fresh and too much movement will tear your stitches out. If we have to assault Wewelsburg, we'll both need to be at our best, or as humanly close to it. Another day or two will not hamper our efforts to retrieve the spear."

"But—"

"Akantha, you will rest," he said, an edge to his voice. "I'm tired of fighting and arguing with you. You will listen to me and rest." Just because she came across as strong didn't mean she didn't cry herself asleep. The puffiness and red lining of her eyes betrayed the facade. She needed time to heal the wounds to her soul as well as the physical wounds.

She blinked and opened her mouth to protest, but immediately closed it. He knew in that instant he had won this round of the battle of wills. Victories were rare, but he'd take them when they came. "Fine."

He refrained from smiling. The victory would turn on a dime into a defeat. "What were you doing in the few decades of relative peace?" She probably wouldn't answer, but he wanted to get her thinking about something else rather than getting out of bed.

She blinked, clearly surprised by the change of topic. It tickled him that he could still surprise her even after knowing each other for so long. Sometimes she needed to be kept off balance and he was the perfect man to do it. "I was home enjoying peace and quiet."

"Which house?" he asked. He knew she had a few properties around the world.

"Maine."

Now he smiled. He watched her eyes narrow. "What's that look for?"

"What look?"

"That smile. Makes me think you're planning something."

He laughed and shook his head. "I'm not planning anything. I was just remembering how fond you are of that house."

"What were you doing before this war?"

"I was in Spain, advising Franco."

"Of course you were," she grumbled.

"Everyone has to make a living," he said with a shrug. Fighting was the only thing he knew how to do and he did it really well. He never did have the temperament to sit and collect things like Akantha did. He had to be moving and doing things. The quiet life wasn't him and never would be. "Are you hungry?"

She shook her head. "No."

She had to be hungry and was saying no just to be contrary. If he left some food on the small nightstand, she would eventually eat. Just once he'd like to have her cooperate and do something without an argument.

"How about a beer?"

"No."

"Would you like some morphine?"

"What I'd like is for you to go away and leave me alone."

"I'm not going to do that."

"Why not? It'd be a nice change of pace if you did something I asked you to do."

"I love you," he answered simply. "I've never stopped, not once in the long years. A million years could pass, the mountains could crumble to dust, the seas could turn to sand, and you could hate me forever, but I will still love you and I will take care of you."

She yanked her hand free. "How many times have I heard that? Why waste the words? They've already been said and I still don't believe them."

"A million times doesn't make it any less true." He reached over and took her hand again. A thumb lightly stroked the soft skin on the back of her hand and silk felt rough in comparison. "I'd say it a million and one times if it makes you believe."

"You can say them until the end of time, but I'll never believe them."

"There was a time you did," he pointed out. He wanted nothing more than to be able to go back to the time where she did love him, but he couldn't. Instead, he would fight until she loved him again. No. Until she admitted she still loved him. Her love for him hadn't died. It existed behind the fortress she had built around her heart. Thankfully, he excelled at storming battlements and setting them on fire.

"I wouldn't bring that up if I were you."

"Is admitting that you still love me such a bad thing?"

"No," she said. "That part of my life is over. I don't love you."

"You know I don't believe that. What is so distasteful?" he inquired. "What makes you hate me?"

"As if you didn't know."

"The fiercest anger of all, the most incurable, is that which rages in the place of dearest love."

"Good. You know your Euripides." Her voice was thick with sarcasm. "You were never my dearest love."

"Maybe not, but you did love me. And still do."

She shook her head. "No. I don't."

"Tell me," he urged. He pressed her hand against his whiskery cheek. "Tell me why you hate me," he coaxed. "Tell me and let us be done with all of this bad blood between us. Let us end this old war."

"You left me!" she yelled and jerked her hand away from his. "You abandoned me in Athens! I was nineteen years old and you left me alone!"

CHAPTER THIRTEEN

Akantha woke to sunlight pouring in through the window of the small rented room. It was as if Apollo himself was looking down and smiling upon her. Today, Damianos would be returning home from spending a week on a fishing boat. Akantha trembled with excitement and anticipation. It had been a long week.

Akantha rose and washed herself with a cloth and tepid water from a nearby pitcher. Humming, she fastened the *strophion* around her chest and the slipped on her *chiton*. Not once had she regretted leaving the temple to be with Damianos. He was her life. Money was tight and sometimes they went a day or two without eating, but they were happy. One day they would have money and have a family. She couldn't wait to give him children.

She finished dressing and looked at herself in the polished bronze mirror Damianos had given her. She wanted to look her best for him after not seeing him for a week. Satisfied with her appearance, she left the small room and jogged down the stairs. The blinding sun made her pause as she stepped out into the street. People going about their daily lives passed by and she waved to familiar faces. Her step was light as she walked toward the main gates of the city. Damianos would be coming along the road from Piraeus and she was too impatient to not meet him at the gates.

Akantha weaved her way through the bustling marketplace. Confectioners sold pastries and sweets while fishmongers, vintners, cloth merchants, dressmakers, slave traders, and shoemakers hawked their wares. Men gathered in the center of the space and discussed politics and the younger men gathered around to listen to a man named Socrates.

Akantha stopped briefly to admire a dress but continued when the seller approached her. She didn't have money for the dress and didn't want to get yelled at or chased off. She only lingered when she had money to spend, which wasn't very often. Smiles greeted her as she walked and she returned them. Some even received a hello.

She made it across the square and headed down the street leading to the main gates. The sun was warm and sweat beaded on her forehead, but she paid it no mind. It was a minor annoyance.

Akantha reached the gates and found a spot in the shade of a tree to stand and wait. She watched people moving in and out of the city as the sun made his journey across the sky, but Damianos did not come through the gates. It slipped below the horizon and Akantha walked back to the small room with heavy footsteps.

She spent the next five days waiting at the gate whenever she didn't have to work. Whatever little money she made as a laundress supplemented what Damianos earned on the fishing boats. They were together. It was everything she had hoped when they left Ephesus.

Her hopes sank with each passing day replaced by fears he died at sea. It happened sometimes. A boat would leave and never be seen again, Poseidon claiming it for himself. People would say it was attacked by sea creatures or captured. The men were forgotten.

Her hopes soared on the sixth day when she saw Androkles, a

good friend of Damianos's, come through the gates. He usually worked the same fishing boats.

"Androkles!" she called out to get his attention and waved. His cheerful smile widened when he saw her and then disappeared. He made to walk past her but relented at the last moment and approached her.

"Where is Damianos?" she asked, craning her neck to look past him. "Did he sail again so soon? He has not been home for so long."

Androkles looked at her and then looked away. "He is not coming."

Her stomach sank. "You mean he's..."

Androkles shook his head and looked at her with compassion. The expression softened the lines of his face. "No. He is not dead."

Relief flooded her and her knees weakened. "Then where is he?" Dread quickly replaced relief when he wouldn't look at her. Androkles had always treated her like a little sister. "Androkles? Where is he?"

"He is not returning to Athens," he said as he reluctantly met her eyes. "He left the ship in Aegina."

She bent at the waist as if someone had hit her in the stomach and she stumbled, leaning against a tree for support. Her legs wobbled, unable to support her. "What do you mean he left the ship?"

"He's not returning to Athens," Androkles repeated. "The last time I saw him he was with some woman he met." He sighed. "I should have told you he died. It would have been kinder."

In the wake of his words teared welled up in her eyes and spilled onto her cheeks. Her chest tightened and she started to shake. The bitter taste of losing him and everything she held so dear filled her.

"Akantha?"

She stared dumbly up at him through the tears, unable to move or speak. The sharp knife of betrayal cut into her very soul, tearing her heart out and leaving behind a deep hole.

"Come." Androkles put a gentle hand on her elbow. "Come home with me. I will take care of you."

Akantha looked at him blankly, but eventually nodded. Akantha stumbled on the first step, her feet feeling as if they had turned to lead. Her whole world had crashed down around her and the only thing she could do was numbly follow the man at her elbow.

CHAPTER FOURTEEN

Skopje, Yugoslavia 1941

"I did," he confessed. "I've never denied it. I left you for another woman. The only thing I can say in my defense is that I was young and stupid."

Akantha turned away from him, hiding the angry tears. Why was he so intent on making her hurt more? The emotional wounds never fully healed, and now he wanted to reopen them on top of Matheus's wounds. It would hurt less if he poured salt into the bullet wounds. The hardest part about losing someone wasn't saying goodbye, it was learning to live without them. She spent a long time trying to fill the void in her heart when he left. It would take a long time to learn to live without Matheus.

"I've apologized a thousand times and will apologize a thousand more if that's what it would take for you to forgive me." His voice was low, tender, and Akantha listened to him against her better judgment. "All that I've ever wanted was your forgiveness."

Her head bowed and her words were thick with emotion. "I'll never forgive you." The nineteen-year-old girl inside of her, still madly in love with him, wanted to forgive him and run into his arms, but time didn't heal all wounds. Some wounds were so deep the passage of time couldn't erase the pain. Instead, it layered more years over it until it was an ache she could only remember during her darkest moments. She could close her eyes and be taken back to that day so long ago and feel her heart shatter again into a million pieces.

"Never is a very long time," he observed. "I regret it every single day. Surely you can understand doing something you regret and wanting to go back and undo it."

Akantha remained silent. She carried twenty-four hundred years of regrets and the burden never grew lighter. She regretted falling so deeply in love with him. She regretted making Matheus an immortal. Those were just two among many and the ones she regretted the most.

He reached over and took her hand. "I love you." He dropped a soft kiss on her knuckles.

She pulled her hand away and turned over on her side, away from him. Her injured side screamed with pain, but she refused to face him. Tears landed on the pillow as a sob racked her body. She felt his hand on her shoulder.

"Akantha," he whispered.

"Leave me alone," she begged as tears flowed freely, drenching the pillow. He gently pulled on her shoulder to get her to roll over to her back, but she refused to budge.

"I need to change your bandages," he explained.

"You can do it later."

"Akantha," he sighed. "We don't know when later will be. Please, let me change your bandages while I can."

She remained immobile and his hand left her shoulder. She listened to him move around the room and was surprised when he didn't come to the side of the bed she was facing. She turned and tearfully watched him. He stood, with his back toward her, at the small table. Akantha couldn't see what he was doing.

A moment later he turned around and approached the bed. She looked away and hoped it would dissuade him from talking to her.

Instead, he sat down on the edge of the bed and offered her a chunk of cheese and a slice of bread.

"Hungry?" he asked. "The bread is fresh."

About to protest, her stomach rumbled, despite what her heart wanted. She reached for the bread. With his free hand, he wiped away the tears on her cheeks with the back of two fingers. "I'm sorry the men you loved betrayed you," he whispered. "I'm sorry I left you. I'm sorry Matheus wasn't the knight you needed. I know you loved him."

Mutely, she tore off a piece of bread and forced it into her dry mouth, chewing it until she could swallow. The lump in her throat rebelled at the idea of food. She set the rest of the bread on the nightstand.

"You need to eat," he urged.

She shook her head. "I can't." More tears slid down her cheeks. He wiped them away again.

"You didn't deserve what I did to you, and you don't deserve this," he told her. "If I could change the past I would, but I can't. What I can do is help you get the spear back and stop your ex-lover. I'll even hold him down while you make him suffer."

Akantha looked at him through shiny tears. His dark eyes were hard and Akantha knew he meant every word he said. Eventually she nodded. He cupped her cheek and his thumb gently caressed the smooth skin. His eyes held hers and she found she couldn't look away.

"I'm sorry," he whispered, his lips pressed against her forehead.

Her resolve was slipping away, and words of forgiveness would fall past her lips if she weren't careful. The past twenty-four hundred years hating him would be for naught if she forgave him. She looked at a point past his shoulder and wiped her face with the back of her hand. "Are you done?" she asked, an edge to her voice.

He sighed and his hand released her cheek. "You make steel seem soft and ice seem warm. What can I do for you?" He placed the chunk of cheese on the nightstand next to the bread.

She bit back a reply, not having have the heart or desire to argue with him. "Nothing. I just want to rest. You're right, another day won't delay us much." She was exhausted down to her soul. Tomorrow was another day to spar with him and get out of this place.

He nodded. "I need to change your bandage." He stood and walked over to the table. He grabbed the rolls of bandages from the medkit and returned to the bed. As he moved to the buttons on her blouse, she batted him away. "You won't die of infection, but it will take you longer to heal. Do you really hate me so much that you'll do yourself harm?"

Staring defiantly at him, her hands moved to unbutton her blouse. All buttons undone, she moved enough to slip her blouse off her injured shoulder.

"This may hurt a little." Taking a firm grasp on the edge of the adhesive surgical plaster, he gave it a hard yank, ripping it off in one motion.

Akantha growled and glared at him.

"Sorry," he apologized as he removed the bandage. He started cleaning the wound. Scar tissue had already formed and the raw edges were closed. "You know as well as I do that any slower would make it hurt more."

He didn't look sorry in the least. She took the opportunity to inspect his work. "Your needlework is improving."

His mouth twitched. "Is that a compliment? I learned from the best."

Akantha snorted. "Hardly."

"You were always better at patching people up."

"All those years of boring needlework had to pay off somehow." Akantha didn't look up at him.

"I have skills other than fighting," he remarked as he covered the wound with a fresh bandage. "Although this particular one is related to war. It's a difficult skill until you need to apply a needle to living flesh. Then it simply becomes life and death. People I cared about would have died if I couldn't put this skill to use."

Fighting was one thing he excelled at. He had seen countless conflicts and wars and had mastered nearly every weapon imaginable. He had been by the side of some great generals. Julius Caesar, Wellington, Tran Hung Dao, and Hannibal Barca all called him adviser. There were others that history had forgotten. He had even been a great general himself when he carried the name Scipio Africanus Minor. The thought made her involuntarily frown.

"What's the face for?" he asked as he finished replacing the one bandage. He ripped the other one off of her side without warning.

Akantha came out of her reverie. "Bastard," she growled. "Just thinking."

"About?" he prompted.

"Carthage," she answered and looked up at his face. The unexpected surprised look on his face pleased her.

"Why are you thinking about Carthage?"

"I just was. That's another thing I'll never forgive you for."

"For Carthage? Are you serious? That was over two thousand years ago." He shook his head and put a clean bandage on the wound in her side.

"Yes, for Carthage. I loved that city, and you burned and razed it to the ground. You wiped it off the map!"

CHAPTER FIFTEEN

CARTHAGE 146 BCE

Akantha stood on the Byrsa hill, looking down at the harbor. Proud Carthaginian ships burned in the sapphire water while Roman troops marched ashore. Black smoke billowed up and orange flames consumed the wooden triremes. The wind shifted and the smell of smoke filled her nose, making her cough. Terror-filled screams drifted up from the lower city. War was never pretty or kind to the innocents.

Roman soldiers slowly made their way through the city streets. They went house to house, grabbing the residents and setting the buildings aflame. "*Carthago delenda est!*" they yelled, their shouts reaching her on the hill. She wept as beautiful Carthage, the shining jewel on the Mediterranean, was being destroyed. She had lived in the city for fifteen years and had grown to love her adopted home.

Anger filled her. She wanted to take up a sword and cut her way through the Roman troops. As much as it would satisfy her blood lust, it would do no good. Rome was an unstoppable juggernaut. Carthage wouldn't be the last city Rome destroyed, but it was her favorite. Her heart ached and she wanted to scream, but she remained silent.

"Goodbye, beautiful Carthage," she whispered, her words taken by the wind. Fires flared up and the screams continued. She wished she could save them all, but she knew she couldn't. Those who did survive the onslaught would be taken as slaves, forced to work for their new Roman masters.

Akantha gathered the heavy cloak around her against the sudden chill, despite the warm sun. As much as she wanted to mourn the destruction of her beloved city, she had to make her way out of the city before the Romans captured her. Slavery wasn't something she wanted to experience.

"My lady, we must go," a voice said from behind her.

Akantha took a last look at the burning ships in the harbor and turned around. She nodded to the old woman standing there. A small group of women, young and old, along with children had gathered in the gardens, looking to her for guidance. Responsibility weighed heavily on her shoulders.

"Is everyone ready?" If she could get them out of the city, they would be spared rape and torture now, a life of slavery later.

"Yes. We are waiting for you, my lady," replied a woman holding an infant.

Akantha nodded. "May Tanit protect us and see us through." Though Akantha worshiped the Greek gods in her heart, it never hurt to respect the religion of the region. They echoed the prayer as they huddled together in fear. She hoped she could deliver on her promise to get them out of the city. "Let us go. Stay close and move quickly. Stay quiet. Do not look back. Never look back," she ordered. They nodded and clutched their few possessions. "Have knives ready. We will surely run into Roman soldiers. It will be better to die than to be taken."

Akantha started walking, a knife in her hand. She followed the path through the lush gardens, her stomach twisting at the thought of them being set aflame. They were a balm to the soul, the heart of Carthage, and they would soon be razed by fire. The

Romans wouldn't let the city stand after Carthage had dared to stand up against Rome, and Hannibal had razed the Italian countryside.

Soon enough the group entered a narrow alley. Carthage, like any other city, contained a maze of narrow alleys. It was this maze that would give them a chance at escaping. The cool shade created by the buildings made the women pull their cloaks tighter around them. Silence settled over the small group, the only noise coming from the few infants and small children. The older children did their best to quiet the younger ones.

They moved quickly, but Akantha slowed down at intersections. She didn't want to turn a corner and stumble upon Roman soldiers. Only a fool rushed blindly ahead and Akantha wasn't a fool. The maze-like pattern of the alleys would allow them to take a different route if they ran across soldiers.

They made it past four intersections before the sound of heavy footsteps greeted them. She motioned for her little group to stop with a raised hand. "Stay here and keep quiet," she ordered, then moved ahead with slow, careful steps. The smallest noise could bring the attention of whoever was ahead and the soft thud of her sandals on the stones echoed loudly in her ears. The alley came to an intersection and she stopped.

The approaching footsteps grew louder and Akantha risked a glance around a corner. She came face to face with a Roman general. Her eyes went wide in surprise and he smirked. Of all the people to run into, it had to be him.

"Damianos," she hissed.

"*Carthago delenda est,*" he said.

She did the only thing she could, she slapped him across the face.

He laughed as one of his soldiers grabbed her, pinning her arms to her sides and digging his fingers into her flesh. They yanked the knife out of her hand. "I will cut off your hands for daring to strike the general," the soldier snarled.

"Why are you doing this?" she demanded, ignoring the soldier holding her. Hands moved roughly over her body, searching for any hidden weapons. The soldier removed the knife she kept strapped to her calf.

"For the glory of Rome," he answered, twisting the words for his own sarcastic amusement. He waved the soldier off and the man released her.

Akantha eyed the soldiers around him, glaring at the one who had held her. She rubbed the spot where his fingers dug into her and she focused her attention toward Damianos. "I am leading women and children out of the city," she said in Greek. The soldiers around them wouldn't have bothered to learn a civilized language, or so she hoped. "They are mine. I have sworn to help them. Let us go in peace. Spare the women and children from slavery. Please."

The world slowed around them and time seemed to stand still.

He was still and Akantha's heart sank along with her stomach. He wasn't going to let them go. She held onto a small glimmer of hope he still loved her. Hope for some kindness from this bastard dimmed as the moments passed. The women and children were going to be taken as slaves where they would be beaten, abused, and worse. Akantha was no stranger to how soldiers treated captive women.

He nodded, and she sagged under the weight of relief. "You surrender to me and I'll let them go," he demanded in Greek.

Eyes wide, her mouth dropped open, not believing what she heard. He smirked and anger replaced relief. Her hand curled into a fist but remained at her side. The soldiers around her would not tolerate her striking him a second time.

"Well?" he asked with a brow raised in inquiry, and he leered.

Her eyes narrowed. The bastard would enjoy this and enjoy having her at his mercy. "Fine. They leave unmolested and they are left alone after they're out. Agreed?" She'd surrender herself if it meant that the women and children would go free and not be taken as slaves. She knew he was doing this to torment her, but a little dignity was a small price to pay to help innocents.

A brief look of surprise crossed his face and Akantha was a little pleased. He nodded.

"They are two alleys over. Lead your men away from them and I will surrender to you."

He motioned to one of his men. "This one is mine," he said. "Take her to my *praetorium* and I'll deal with her later." The soldier nodded and grabbed Akantha's upper arm. "No one touches her. I will kill you and the man that tries. You." He motioned for him to draw closer. Damianos spoke softly in the man's ear. He nodded and headed off in the direction of the women and children. "The rest of you, come with me. Burn everything you see."

"Thank you," Akantha said to him in Greek.

"You can thank me later." He grinned. "I will insist on it."

"I hate you," she growled as a soldier led her away, his laughter echoing in her ears. She glanced over her shoulder to see him leading his men away from where the women and children were hiding. She was thankful they would leave the city unmolested and it was worth anything he would put her through.

What she would put him through would be every bit what he deserved.

The soldiers led her through the burning city to the large hole that had been created in the walls. The citizens had gathered every piece of metal, including the jewelry, and used it to forge swords, shields and projectiles to keep the Romans at bay. Now the city would be razed and Carthage and her people would cease to exist. Akantha kept her chin up as she walked, ignoring the soldiers next to her.

They reached the Roman camp outside the walls and she was escorted to a large tent. Someone shoved her into the *praetorium* and she went willingly. Having one of the general's bodyguards to watch her and see to her safety was an honor, but she didn't feel so honored at the moment.

Sweat beaded on her forehead from the oppressive heat inside as it took her eyes a few moments to adjust. The decor was spartan; a simple wooden *kline,* with a few pillows and a blanket, was off to one side. A mahogany *abacus,* covered with maps and scrolls, dominated the center and a single, plain *solium* sat next it. It wasn't the most welcoming place and she knew it was intentional. He wouldn't want anyone to feel comfortable inside.

She didn't sit in the *solium* or stretch out on the *kline*, instead she paced back and forth apprehensively. A quick peek outside revealed a guard at the entrance and she quickly closed the flap. She wrung her hands as she paced. The tent was spacious, but not big enough to keep her from reversing direction after a few strides.

The tent flap opened and she spun on her heels, ready to give him a verbal lashing, but saw it was only a soldier carrying a tray of fruit. He placed it on the table and left as quickly as he entered. Akantha eyed the plate but didn't touch it. She knew he wouldn't try to poison her, but she wouldn't give him the satisfaction of knowing she ate.

She dominated his thoughts like only she could since he had first seen her. Damianos wanted nothing more than to rush to his tent and collect her thanks. He knew what kind of payment he wanted, and she would resist. He loved a good challenge and she was a challenge made flesh. She would be completely his by the time darkness fell. If he managed to get back before dark fell.

He stood outside the walls near the main gate and watched the smoke plumes rise into the air. Carthage lay destroyed, as Rome wanted it. No longer would it be a thorn in Rome's side. Now he could take a much-needed break from fighting and enjoy the spoils of war. He turned and headed for his tent and Akantha.

Two steps later, a soldier stepped into his path and saluted. He glared at the man, saluted, and listened to the report. Given orders, the man disappeared and Damianos continued walking.

After a dozen stops to issue orders to soldiers or take a report, his patience grew thin. All he had wanted was to return to his tent and see the dark-haired, gray-eyed beauty that haunted his dreams every night. He knew she was in Carthage and had hoped to find her.

He sent a silent prayer to the gods thanking them she hadn't left the city before he arrived.

One side of his mouth pulled up into a smile as he walked, thinking of her and what awaited. She asked him for a favor and the opportunity had been too good to pass up. He would have given his soul for something like this, and she gifted it to him. Her scathing and vicious tongue wouldn't deter him. He'd enjoy every second of this.

He finally reached his tent and the two guards posted at the entrance saluted him. Damianos put a fist to his heart and nodded.

"I do not wish to be disturbed." The guards nodded and he entered the tent.

She froze and stared at him. Time stopped for a moment and then stuttered into motion. Her eyes darted around the room, looking for something.

"You will find no weapon here save the one I am carrying."

She straightened up and defiance flashed in her gray eyes. "I wasn't looking for a weapon."

"Of course not." He smirked. "The women and children are safe," he said while he removed his helm and sat it on a map of Carthage. The black crest was made of horsehair and there was even some gilding on the cheek guards. "My man took them out of the city and they are on their way to Alexandria."

She nodded once. "Thank you."

"I keep my word."

She looked away. "Why?"

"Why what?"

She turned and pinned a look on him. "Why did you destroy Carthage?"

He unbuckled the fastener on his shoulder and removed the red wool cloak, tossing it over the back of the lone chair. "Rome wanted Carthage destroyed," he answered with a gleam in his dark eyes. "I knew you were in Carthage, so I worked at getting the command to lead the attack." It was a lie, but it would get her riled up. He removed his armor and piled it in a heap. A slave would clean it and put it in its proper place.

Her eyes narrowed and if she could kill him, he knew she would. "I hate you," she growled.

She rewarded him with the reaction he had been hoping for. He grinned. "That may be, but now you owe me for saving those women and children." He sat down and leaned back, exhaustion settling over him. It had been a long few days, today being the longest of all. A two-year siege ended with a day of fighting house-to-house through the city. By the time he reached the top of the Byrsa hill and the fortress, he could barely lift his sword.

"I owe you nothing," she countered. "It was the decent thing to do."

"It was the decent thing to do, but a deal was struck and you are going to honor your part." He wouldn't let her wiggle her way out of this. She was his for the foreseeable future and he planned to enjoy every second of it. Just as soon as he found some energy.

The tent flap opened and two slaves entered carrying a large metal bath. They placed it in the middle of the tent and other slaves followed carrying jars of water. One by one they emptied the water into the basin and exited the tent. They returned and left, repeating the process until the bath was full. He stripped and lowered himself into the hot water. A sigh escaped him. It wasn't a real bath, but it would do for now.

"What do you intend to do with me?"

He looked over at her. "I'm going to enjoy my bath and share a meal with you. Afterward, I intend to enjoy your company."

Her chin went up, but she remained silent. Defiance flashed in her gray eyes.

He let her stew while he enjoyed the bath. The heat of the water soaked into sore muscles and the dirt and sweat from fighting washed away. Slaves entered carrying trays of food and placed them on the table. They left without a word and he rose from the water. He stepped out of the bath and grabbed a clean white tunic. He glanced over at her and smiled when she quickly looked away. His nakedness wasn't easily ignored and it thrilled him.

He took his time slipping on the tunic. Once it was settled on his shoulders, he walked over to the table and stretched out on a couch. She hadn't moved.

"Come eat, Akantha. You have been in here all day and have not eaten. Surely you must be hungry."

"I'm not hungry," she snapped.

He sighed. "Must everything be a battle?"

She remained silent.

"Akantha, please eat something." He selected an olive and popped it in his mouth. "Would you care for some wine?"

No answer.

He climbed to his feet with a sigh and looked at her. She glared at him and he closed the small distance between them. He grabbed her arms. He lowered his head and his mouth ground down on hers. She bit down on his lip and he pulled away, blood covering his mouth and running down his chin.

"So it's going to be like that?" He grinned as he wiped away the blood with the back of his hand. She was all fire and resistance, pure Akantha.

"Gods damn you," she swore.

His laugh was a thundercloud in the small space. She made all the years of fighting for Rome worth it in that moment. "Oh Akantha. I am going to enjoy this."

CHAPTER SIXTEEN

Skopje, Yugoslavia 1941

Damianos laughed. "Oh Akantha. Those thorns have grown long over the years. I love you despite them."

She turned away from him as he said those words. He would never know the doubts she carried as long as she had breath in her body. He would use them against her if he knew. "Are you done?"

"I'm done," he said as he placed the adhesive over the bandage on her side. "Do you want some more morphine?"

"No." She looked back at him.

He lifted a heavy brow. "Are you sure?"

She nodded.

"Very well then," he said and stood. He placed the extra bandages and adhesive on the table with the other supplies. He walked around to the empty side of the bed.

"What do you think you're doing?"

"I'm going to lie down and get some sleep," he said.

"You can sleep in the chair."

"No. I'm going to sleep in the bed next to you. I need real rest, and to do that, I'm going to sleep in the bed."

"You can't sleep here," she insisted.

"Why not? Do you think I'm going to try something? How low your opinion of me must be." His laugh was tired. "You're wounded and I'm exhausted. The most I'm going to do is snore and dream of you in my arms."

"I know you."

He sighed and his shoulders slumped with sudden exhaustion. "I give you my word that you will sleep unmolested." He removed his shirt.

She regarded his back for a moment as he removed his shirt and admired how the muscles moved under his skin. Scars, history written in flesh, crisscrossed his back. She thought of all the wars they had seen together and all the battles he had fought. Her armor weakened a little. "Fine," she relented.

He grinned as he turned to face her and Akantha rolled her eyes. She eyed him as he crawled onto the bed and stretched out next to her. He turned to her and put his arm across her and she stiffened. "By Dis, what are you doing?" she demanded. "You gave me your word."

"Going to sleep," he replied, closing his eyes. "I'm not trying anything. I'm getting comfortable and you're wounded. I would not cause you any pain if I could help it. I just want to hold you."

"Damianos—"

"Shut up," he ordered. "Get some sleep."

"I hate you." She turned over, giving him her back.

He chuckled and dropped a kiss in her dark hair. "No you don't."

She didn't, but he could never know. Akantha didn't try to pull away from him. If she fussed any longer, neither of them would sleep and he would be insufferable. Warmth and security were two things she needed, but she didn't want them from him. Allowing him to get close was dangerous. His breathing quickly fell into a regular rhythm and he snored softly. Confident he was asleep, Akantha relaxed. He rolled onto his back and she turned over to lie against him.

She allowed herself a moment to enjoy the feeling of a warm body sleeping against hers. Her head was on his chest and she listened to the steady beating of his heart. The craziness and frantic pace of the past few days melted away in the steady sound of his heart. His nearness calmed her thoughts and the world became less dark. The maelstrom of thoughts swirling in her mind settled and calmed.

Hours later, Akantha woke to a dark room and she immediately cursed herself for sleeping so long. Her eyelids were heavy and she was still tired, but they had to get moving. She couldn't let Matheus reach Wewelsburg with the spear.

Carefully she rolled out of his arms and swung her legs over the edge of the bed. Movement was painful, but it wasn't debilitating. She sat up and reached for the lamp on the nightstand next to the bed. Her fingers fumbled to find the switch and she turned it, but the room remained dark. Power outages were to be expected, but she had hoped to catch a break.

She opened the drawer felt around for a candle and matches. Finding what she was searching for, she removed them from the drawer and closed it. She removed a match and swiped it against the side of the box. It flared to life, pushing back the darkness. The flame touched the wick and for a brief moment the two flames pushed the darkness back further.

Akantha extinguished the match and she tossed it on the nightstand. She turned toward Damianos and admired him in the golden light. It illuminated his face and softened his stark features. He looked younger in the candlelight, the long centuries erased in the warm glow. She smiled.

It was in the quiet moments where she could set aside the anger and admire how handsome he was and remember how much she once loved him. Still loved him, but she would never admit it. His dark hair was medium length and curled a little. She loved running her fingers through the dark locks when they lay together in bed. His cheeks were shadowed with stubble, and she wanted to lightly run a fingertip over the coarse hair. The sheet came to his waist and his chest was exposed. Dark curly hair covered his pectorals and shadows outlined his abdominals.

His eyes snapped open, and Akantha jumped, causing hot wax from the candle to land on her hand. His mouth stretched into a lazy smile and her stomach did a somersault. She looked away.

"Beautiful Psyche stealing a look at Eros?" he asked.

"Hardly," she snorted and returned her gaze to his face. "You are certainly not Eros."

"You are as beautiful as Psyche. More beautiful, I would say."

Akantha rolled her eyes and set the candle in a holder on the nightstand. "Flattery will get you nowhere."

"I need to check your bandages. Then we can get moving."

"The bandages are fine. We need to get moving." Akantha wasn't going to argue and waste valuable time. They were already behind when she wanted to leave. The extra time spent still helped. Her shoulder and sides were sore, but bearable. She could move, albeit stiffly, and would be in better shape by the time they confronted Matheus.

He pulled himself up into a sitting position. She turned and he saw her wince. "Do you want morphine?" he asked.

"No. I need my wits about me. Maybe later."

"I'll make sure we take the medical kit," he told her and held her uninjured arm just above the elbow. He pulled her toward him and blew out the candle. His kissed her before she could utter a word of protest. Her eyes closed and she savored the feel of her lips against his.

Her brain told her to pull away, insisting she make him understand what she wanted with the flat of her hand against his face if necessary, but the rest of her wavered. The aura of danger he carried about him wrapped itself around her. His mouth seared hers with a kiss that melted her resistance by reminding her of the old days when they were happy and she had been safe.

She made a last effort to say something, demand he release her, but he took the advantage to plunder her mouth.

All at once she was his.

His hand slid along her cheek to cradle her head and she leaned into his touch.

This is wrong, she told herself as her toes curled. Her blood rushed like the first time they touched. Her heart thundered in her chest. Akantha gave into passion as desire drowned the little voice of reason. One touch from him could kill and one kiss could do her in.

His strong hands moved over her body, thick, calloused fingers now awakening remembered places. Her mind reeled at the feel of his bare chest under her hands. Too many emotional blows in recent days had left her dangerously vulnerable, and his warmth and protection soothed her heartache. She moaned again.

Her moan encouraged him on and his other hand traced the curve of her shoulder to gently push her shirt away. His fingers traced a patch to cup her breast. Kissing and touching erased the distance and time they spent apart. His mouth left hers and moved down along her jaw to her neck.

Her head fell back, giving him better access to her neck. His mouth seared her skin with every kiss. She wanted to feel that mouth on other parts of her body.

The sound of trucks rumbling outside and shouts echoed through the room and broke the spell he had cast.

Akantha's eyes snapped open and she pulled away from him. "We have to go. Is there a back way out of here?" The intimate attention left her breathless and she struggled to regain her composure. She licked her lips and tasted him. She didn't wait for a response but pushed herself to her feet. She went to the window and stole a glance outside. Two stories down, she watched uniformed soldiers moving about in the faint light. They separated into groups of three and went to nearby buildings, starting a search. It was just a matter of moments until they were discovered. "They're about to enter the building."

"Of course there's a way out." He was a bit offended that she would think he'd stay in a place where he didn't have an exit strategy. "They may not be here for us, but better to not take the chance." Thousands of years spent as a soldier had taught him to go from idle to full speed, whether it was from a surprise attack in the middle of the night, or diving from a cannonball or bullet. As a soldier, when it was time to get moving, you moved.

Now was one of those times.

He climbed out of bed and reached for his boots. He wanted nothing more than to crawl back into bed with Akantha. If he had his way, the next time he was in bed with her she'd be naked and moaning his name. Despite the urgency of their situation, he smiled as he slipped his boots on.

"What are you smiling at?"

"Just thinking," he answered as he pulled his shirt on.

"Let's go."

"Not going to ask me what I was thinking about?" He stood and headed for the small table. He grabbed the small medical kit and the food. She may want more morphine and they had to eat. He would have preferred to stay another day or two so she could heal more.

"No," she replied. "I don't want to know what's going on in your head." She handed him the second Walther P38 that had been lying on the table next to the other items.

"Scotland," he informed her as he checked the ammunition in the pistol. Six shells left. "Right after Flodden and I showed up at your place. Then the English arrived and we had to make a quick exit."

CHAPTER SEVENTEEN

SCOTLAND 1513

"Akantha!" a booming voice yelled from outside. Akantha, now going by the name Lady Isabel Montfort, stood and walked over to the window. A large furry dog followed. Not many knew the name she had been born with and the unexpected visitor could mean trouble. She unfastened the lock and pushed the widow open. A large tawny colored stallion reared and pawed the air. "Akantha!" the man on the horse bellowed and the horse reared again.

"Stop yelling," she scowled. Dramatics were so tiresome. She took a closer look at the rider. His long hair was dark and his dark beard was peppered with a little gray, but there was a familiarity to the face. He was wearing a green plaid kilt, worn leather boots, and a dirty white highland shirt. She was right. It was trouble.

"Open the door," he called. The horse pawed the ground and snorted.

"Damianos? By Dis, what are you doing here?"

He laughed and dismounted. "Grant me entrance. I am weary from battle, wounded, and have missed your loving arms."

"Gods have mercy on me," she muttered as she pulled the window shut. If she had known he was in Scotland, she would have moved to India or China. She could have gone another century or two without seeing him. She sighed and went to the door, not bothering to ring one of her servants.

She opened the door and strong arms wrapped around her, picking her off of her feet. Low menacing growls came from the dog and sharp teeth were bared. Akantha waved him off. Damianos's mouth came down hard on hers in a kiss that threatened to consume her. Her toes curled up in her slippers as his tongue invaded her mouth and her head swirled. She did her best to resist, but her resolve disappeared in the searing kiss and his overwhelming manliness.

The kiss ended and she wobbled a little, his strong hold keeping her steady as he set her on her feet. Breathless, she looked at his face. He wore the smirk she hated so much. Irritated, she slapped him hard across the face.

His head fell back and he laughed, a booming thunderclap.

"What are you doing here?" she demanded, his arms still around her. The dog continued to growl.

"I am weary from battle. King James was killed and the Scots were routed at Flodden. I need some time to rest and I wanted to see your beautiful face." He looked at the dog. "Stop it." The growls didn't stop.

"You can't—"

He cut her words off with another deep kiss and her body flushed. Her arms wrapped around his neck and her body pressed against his. Her mind told her to resist him, push him away, and not give in to into her desires. Her traitorous heart and body had other ideas. He wobbled and Akantha pulled away, looking up at him. She placed a hand on the dog's head and the growling stopped.

"Something wrong?"

"I am in need of some needlework," he said, looking down. Only then did she notice the swath of red across his stomach. She had been so put off guard by his unexpected appearance she hadn't noticed the wound.

She sighed heavily and knew she couldn't turn him away now. She wasn't heartless. "Come with me." She closed the heavy door behind him and walked toward the solar, not looking back to see if he followed. The clicking of dog nails and heavy footsteps followed. She wondered how much grief he was going to give her this time. His reappearance into her life always brought a whirlwind of emotions and a mountain of issues, things she didn't need at the moment while she was nursing a broken heart.

She crossed the room and pulled a silk rope. Damianos entered and fell onto one of many Roman style couches.

Akantha looked out the window, resisting the urge to look and the urge to go to his side. The dog sat next to her, in a protective pose and ready to defend her against the man on the couch. She didn't want to get close, physically or emotionally, again. The man had hurt her too many times in the past and her heart was still aching from losing Matheus.

A maid materialized in the doorway.

"What can I do for you, milady?" a doe-faced maid asked.

Akantha turned away from the window. "Bring hot water, needle, thread, and bandages," Akantha ordered. The maid nodded and disappeared. She steeled herself, turned, and crossed the room to where he lay. "Remove your shirt."

One side of his mouth pulled back and light twinkled in his dark eyes. "I love it when you try to get me out of my clothes."

"I'm only doing this because you're wounded. Do not mistake this for me having any feelings for you."

He sat up, groaning as he did, and slipped his shirt off. Akantha winced when she saw the long gash across his stomach. Had he not been immortal, he would have died by now. The part of her he hurt so badly in the past wished he had, while the nineteen-year-old girl still in love with him felt sorry for him and was concerned he was injured. She pushed both parts down and focused on the task at hand.

The wound ran from his navel across his abdomen to his side under his ribs. Blood seeped out of the wound and collected on his flat stomach. The edges of the wound contained dirt and grime. He'd had worse wounds, but she couldn't remember when. The fact he was still conscious was a testament to his fortitude and willpower.

Akantha grabbed the garment after he had removed it. It had been white at some point, but now it was stained red and brown from blood and mud. She dropped it on the floor and would deal with it later. The metallic smell of blood lingered in the air along with the smell of sweat and his distinctive scent. It tugged at old memories.

"Where is that blasted—" She stopped when the maid appeared in the doorway. The woman gasped when she saw the wound across Damianos's stomach.

"Don't be a fool, woman," Akantha instructed when the maid almost dropped the basin of hot water she was carrying. "Bring that over here." The maid placed the basin on a small table near the couch. "Hurry and get me the other items," she snapped at the maid.

The maid practically ran from the room.

"You never treat your maids this harshly," he pointed out. "What has gotten under your skin?"

Akantha scowled. He was right. Damn him. This was his fault. "Nothing."

He laughed and then groaned from the pain.

"Serves you right," she smirked. She looked at the wound. It didn't appear to be too deep, but she had to check. "This is going to hurt."

"It will hurt less than your words," Damianos said. Her tongue, always sharper than knives or swords, hadn't dulled in the time since he last saw her. Gods, he had missed her in the past century. Even exhausted as he was, her temper was welcomed. Just seeing her made everything worth it. Nothing healed him like she did.

Akantha ignored the bait and probed the wound with two fingers. He stiffened and held his breath. Wounds were nothing new, but having someone put fingers into them was a whole different level of pain. After a few moments she removed her fingers from the wound and wiped them on her dress. "Tyche must have been watching over you. The wound is deep, but it doesn't appear any of your organs are damaged."

"I'd rather have you watching over me." He grinned. "An up-close and personal supervision of my recovery."

Akantha rolled her eyes. The maid returned with bandages, cloth, needle, and thread. Her eyes went wide when she saw the blood on Akantha's dress and her fingers, but she kept quiet. Akantha took the needle and thread, placing them in her lap. She dipped the cloth in the water.

"Please go tell the cook to have a tray prepared," she instructed as she squeezed out the excess water. "The gentleman will need food to regain his strength. Have the groom see to his horse. Prepare a room for him, and have Maria bring a clean shirt." Well at least she wasn't going to patch his wounds and kick him out right away. He'd have clean clothing and a bed to sleep in. With a hot meal and some rest, he'd be as good as new in no time.

"Of course, milady." The maid nodded and left.

Akantha dabbed the wound with the wet cloth. He inhaled sharply. "I'm not staying in your room with you?"

"No," she growled and pressed the wet cloth against the wound.

"You could try being a little more gentle."

"You could try being a little tougher," she countered. She cleaned the wound and wiped most of the blood away, focusing on the task at hand and avoided making eye contact with him.

"Those thorns have not gotten dull over the years," he said.

"I sharpen them for every time I see you," she replied, setting the bandage in the basin. The water turned pink from the blood.

"I suspected as much." Nothing surprised him when it came to her.

She snorted and picked up the needle and thread. She threaded the needle and didn't warn him before she started sewing his skin together.

"Dammit, Akantha," he swore. "You could have given some warning."

"Oh shush and don't be a baby," she said. The needle and thread moved in and out of skin, slowly bringing the two sides together. Her movements were efficient, making short work of the task. "There. Unfortunately, you're going to live," she said as she tied off the thread. She bit it off close to him and then stood, tossing the extra thread and needling on the table next to the basin.

Maria appeared in the doorway carrying a man's shirt. He wondered why she had men's clothing on hand. Was there a man in her life?

"Bring it here," Akantha ordered. Maria crossed the room and offered the shirt to Damianos.

"Thank you," he said with a charming smile. The maid blushed and out of the corner of his eye he watched Akantha roll her eyes. "I can't imagine the Lord of the Manor being pleased to find a stranger wearing his clothes." He held up the shirt in front of him for a moment and then slowly slipped it on. Maria hastily left the room.

"There is no Lord of the Manor," she half-growled.

The fact there wasn't a man in her life pleased him. He hated seeing her with other men, but he tolerated it if it meant she was happy. But something told him she wasn't happy, and it wasn't just because of his presence. He had to know what caused the sadness in her eyes and her short temper.

"Are you all right?" he asked.

"I was fine until you showed up," she shot back.

"Liar. What happened?"

"Nothing."

"I can tell when you're lying. Who do I need to kill for hurting you?"

"You," she said.

"What is his name?" She looked away and confirmed his suspicions. "What did he do to you?"

"Nothing."

"Akantha, a blind man would see that you're hurting inside. Tell me what happened." Despite the vitriol, he could see sadness in her eyes.

She walked toward the door, the dog following her. "Follow me."

He looked at her and then stood, grunting as he did. "Wait up," he called.

"Are you getting too old to keep up?"

"Hardly," he said as he followed. "I can always keep up with you. Even when wounded."

Akantha snorted. She reached the foot of the stair and waited for him. The dog looked up at her. "I know what I'm doing," she told the dog. "I do."

Damianos caught up and she offered him a hand. He put his hand in hers. She turned away and led him up the stairs. The dog padded quietly after them.

"Not going to talk?"

"No."

"Tell me who hurt you," he urged.

"His name was Matheus. He was a Templar. We spent over two hundred years together. He wanted to continue to travel and see the world. I grew tired and wanted to settle down in one place for a little while."

He hadn't expected her to be involved with another immortal, one he knew nothing about. That had to change. Killing the man for hurting her was no longer an option, but he could make the man suffer a bit. No, a lot. "I'm sorry."

"Not as much as I am," she said, barely above a whisper.

Clearly, she hadn't meant for him to hear that. His heart ached for her and he wanted to reach out and take her in his arms, but he knew she wouldn't tolerate it.

"Milady!" Maria yelled as she ran toward the two of them. "Riders approaching! They're English!"

"Piss and blood," Akantha swore. "Go and grab the bloodied bandages, and all other traces of our guest, and toss them in the fire. Now!" Maria nodded and ran toward the solar.

Akantha squeezed his hand and pulled him with her. "Just don't pass out or I leave you where you fall."

"And step on me a few times for good measure," he added.

"Of course. Would you expect less of me?"

He chuckled. "I'm surprised you're not turning me over to the English."

"Don't think the thought hasn't crossed my mind at least dozen times since you arrived."

"It's nice to see you still care."

"I don't." They descended the stairs, him leaning on her for support. "Meet us in the barn," she said to the dog and he padded off. "Why are they after you?"

"I killed a few of their nobles in the battle."

"I should hand you over to them for bringing them to my door."

He knew she would never do such a thing, despite all the threats.

They made their way down the hall and came to the kitchens. Heat from the two large fireplaces greeted them when they stepped into the room. The two cooks and their assistant froze when they saw Akantha entering.

"The trap door! Hurry!"

The cooks and their assistants ran through the doorway leading to the dining hall. They lined up on one side of the heavy table and started pushing. The heavy oak table didn't move at first, but it eventually moved and slid across the floor, taking the ornate rug with it. A wooden trap door appeared from under the rug, and one of the cooks grabbed the handle, yanking the door open.

"Come on," Akantha said and pulled Damianos along with her. She grabbed the oil lamp from the mantle over the fireplace before descending the small wooden stairs. Damianos was on her heels. "Don't make a sound."

The trap door closed above them and the sound of the table

sliding across the floor echoed over their heads. "Come on," she urged.

"Where are we going?" he whispered in her ear.

"Out to the stables."

"Good thing you have this tunnel."

"I always have a way out."

"That's my girl."

Akantha ignored him and continued to lead him through the tunnel toward the stables. The air was heavy and damp, and once they were out from under the main house, roots pushed through the earthen walls. Akantha tripped on an exposed root and fell forward. Damianos caught her before she could fall and pulled her back in against his chest.

For a brief second, she was in his arms, then she pulled away. He wanted nothing more than to pull her back in and keep her there.

The trip seemed to take forever, but eventually they came to the end of the tunnel. A ladder led up to another door.

"Wait here," she instructed and climbed the ladder. She pushed up against the trap door, opening just enough to peer out. The dog greeted her with a lick of his slobbery tongue. She pushed the door all the way open and climbed out. Damianos blew out the lamp and set it on the ground before climbing up the ladder to join her. Akantha closed the door and then turned toward him.

"I'll saddle the horses. Sit."

"I'm fine. Let me help," he insisted.

"No. You'll pull your stitches. Let's not do that until we're at least on our way. Now stay still and let me do this. If he moves, bite him." The dog woofed.

"Whatever milady wants," he smirked. He eyed the large dog but remained still. The dog wouldn't hesitate to bite him if he moved. And to think he saved the dog's life over two hundred years ago.

"For you to go away," she muttered as she opened a stall door. His eyes never left her while she saddled two horses. When she was done, she handed him the reins to a horse and she sprang up into her saddle. "Let's go. Head north. Hopefully they won't follow us further into Scotland."

He nodded and slowly climbed up into the saddle. "After you."

Akantha nodded and kicked her mare into motion. They left the stable at a gallop with the clatter of hooves on stone and the large dog running along next to the horses.

CHAPTER EIGHTEEN

"I said I didn't want to know," she snapped.

He sighed. "Is there ever a chance of you being nice to me?"

"Not as long as you mistake civility for nice," she answered as she went to the door to the room. She opened it a crack and listened for sounds. The hall was quiet. "Come on," she whispered.

Damianos came up behind her and dropped a kiss on her cheek. "For luck," he whispered.

Akantha ignored him and opened the door wider. She stepped out into the hall with Damianos on her heels. Two steps into the hall she heard the inn's doors open and the thud of heavy boots below. She froze.

"The back stairs," Damianos whispered in her ear, sending a shiver through her. She wondered if the man was doing it on purpose. Knowing him, he was. "This used to be an inn and there's a back stair leading down to what used to be the kitchens."

Akantha slowly started walking toward the back stairs and the well-worn floors creaked with each step.

Damianos put his hand on her uninjured arm for support. Distracted, she tripped.

"You okay?"

"Little lightheaded," she answered, touched that he cared. Then she remembered she hated him.

"Just don't pass out. I'll have to carry you out if you do and it won't be an easy trip over my shoulder."

"I won't."

The progress down the hall was slow out of fear of discovery, but they reached the stairs. Akantha glanced over a shoulder at him and put her foot on the first one. It creaked under her weight and she froze in place. She held her breath and listened. Voices drifted up, but it didn't sound like they were coming closer. The apartments on the first floor kept them busy.

"We have to risk it."

Akantha hated to admit he was right, but they couldn't move at a snail's pace. "Ready?"

"Go," he urged.

Akantha took a deep breath and started down. The sound of her shoes on the wood was thunder in her ears and Damianos's footsteps added to the impression. His grip tightened on her arm as they descended. She moved fast as she dared, running would attract attention and she couldn't risk falling.

They reached the bottom and entered a small hallway. What used to be kitchens had been partly used for the first-floor apartments and a small hallway leading to a door.

"The back door," Akantha told Damianos.

"Right behind you, beautiful."

Akantha sighed and she headed for the back door. The sound of boots on the hard wood floor caught her attention and she turned to see a German officer appear in the doorway leading to the downstairs hallway.

"Halt!" the man yelled in German.

Akantha and Damianos stopped, but they didn't turn toward the officer.

"Identify yourselves," he ordered.

Damianos's grip on her shoulder tightened and relaxed. Akantha gave him the slightest of nods.

"Come with me," he ordered. "We will ask you both questions."

She turned toward the officer, using her body to shield Damianos's movements. She took a step toward the officer.

Damianos grabbed a knife from a boot and sent it hurtling through the air at the officer. The knife struck the officer in the chest. He staggered back and Damianos was immediately on him. He rammed the heel of his hand into the soldier's throat and lowered the gagging man to the floor to avoid collateral noise.

"Go," Damianos urged.

Akantha didn't need any urging and bolted for the door. Luck was with them. The alley was empty.

"We need to find a vehicle," Damianos said when he joined her seconds later.

"I agree. Let's head a few streets over and see what we can find."

"I'm right behind you."

Despite her feelings about the man, there was no one better to have watching her back. She just wished the man wasn't so damn infuriating. "Tyche favor us."

"From your mouth to her ears," Damianos told her.

They made it half way down the alley when a truck slowed to a stop at the one end. Two soldiers exited the truck and Akantha wrapped her arm around Damianos's waist. She pushed him up against the wall and kissed him.

Damianos pulled away for a second. "You picked a bad time, beautiful."

"Shut up and kiss me," she muttered.

He pressed his mouth to hers and wrapped his arms around her. Akantha turned her head so she could keep an eye on the soldiers and still keep up the act of kissing Damianos. The men looked down the alley, but none of them moved toward the two immortals. Akantha broke the kiss and nudged him to move. Damianos slipped an arm around her waist and Akantha leaned into him. He bent his head to put his face close to hers and they started walking down the alley toward the soldiers.

Akantha kept an eye on the two soldiers and tried to ignore the man next to her. The whispered endearments in her ear reminded her of their years together when they were still mortal. Akantha pushed the memories back to the dark corner of her mind and concentrated on their current situation, trying to ignore the man next to her.

"This is rather nice," he said, barely above a whisper as he nuzzled her ear.

"Sure. If you like trying to avoid Nazis with one of us being injured," she mumbled.

"You're looking at it wrong. The weather's rather pleasant, the stars are shining overhead, and I'm next to a beautiful woman. What more can a guy ask for?"

"You'll never change." Her voice was thick with exasperation. "Right now, the only thing I'm asking for is to get out of here without any more bullet holes in either of us."

"The Germans were kind enough to provide a truck for us. Head for them."

Slowly they made their way to the end of the alley. So far, the soldiers didn't give them so much as a glance. They stepped out of the alley in front of the soldiers and caught their attention.

"Halt!" one of the soldiers yelled.

They stopped. "Identify yourselves," one soldier ordered in German as they pointed their rifles at Damianos and Akantha.

"We do not understand," Damianos said in Bulgarian as he put his hands in the air. Next to him Akantha did the same.

"Identify yourself," the soldier repeated and thrust the end of his rifle in Damianos's face.

"We do not understand," Damianos repeated. He looked over at Akantha and gave her a wink. With a quick movement, he grabbed the rifle out of the hands of the soldier and smashed the butt end into the man's face. The crack of the man's nose breaking filled the air and blood gushed out. Damianos didn't give the man time to recover, he threw a right hook and the soldier crumpled to the ground.

Akantha moved with Damianos. She lunged for the other soldier and yanked the weapon away from him. The rifle went to the ground and the soldier threw a punch, catching Akantha in the jaw. White spots of pain danced in front of her eyes as she stumbled a few steps from the blow. She tried to shake it off.

Damianos moved to the other soldier and wrapped his arms around the guy's head and neck. He applied pressure as the guard struggled to break free. The soldier's struggling lessened and eventually he went still. Damianos released him and he unceremoniously fell to the ground.

"You okay?" he asked.

Akantha nodded. Her shoulder and side were on fire, but she had to keep going. Now was not the time to allow weakness to stop her. "Let's get these two into the alley before we're noticed."

Damianos nodded and put his hands under the man's armpits and dragged him into the alley. Akantha would have done the same, but she probably would have passed out from the pain. Damianos returned and pulled the second soldier into the alley.

Once the soldiers were in the alley, Akantha and Damianos quickly removed the soldiers' uniforms and slipped them on. Just when she thought she was done posing as a Nazi she was putting on another uniform. Akantha used her blouse to bind her breasts before putting on the shirt. "I thought I was done pretending to be a man," she complained as she put on the jacket.

"I'll help you remember you're a woman later, but right now I suggest we get out of here."

She ignored the first part, refusing to take the bait. "Let's go," she ordered as she fastened the buttons. Thankfully, the jacket helped to hide the slight bulge of her bound breasts. She pulled her hair up and tucked it under the helmet. From a distance she'd be able to pass for a man.

Damianos shoved the helmet on his head and picked up the two rifles. Akantha climbed into the driver's seat and Damianos shoved the weapons on the floor of the passenger's side before climbing in. The truck's engine rumbled to life and Akantha put it into gear. She pulled out slowly to not attract attention since the last thing they needed was to be chased.

"Where are we going?" he asked as he watched the side mirror for signs of pursuit.

"Towards Wewelsburg," she answered. "Tyche favor us, we'll find Matheus."

"Hermes smile upon us as well," he added.

"We could use all of the help we can get." Akantha glanced over at him. "Get some rest. You may have to drive later."

"You were always so bossy," he said with a fond smile on his face.

"You were always a pain in the ass," she countered and refocused on the road ahead. "Some things will never change."

"If I weren't a pain in the ass, you might confuse me for someone else."

"No, I wouldn't. I would know you if I were blind and deaf."

He laughed. "It's nice knowing I've gotten so far under your skin."

Responding would just encourage him to continue, so she remained quiet. If she were lucky, he'd fall asleep and she would have blessed silence to think and plan, but she had a feeling her luck wouldn't be that good. They couldn't find the spear quick enough for her tastes. It would be out of the hands of the Nazis and he would be out of her life. Again.

"Maybe after this war we can find a nice quiet spot somewhere and spend a few decades catching up," he mused. "It's been far too long since we've spent any time together. Maybe the Caribbean. You've always been fond of sun and water."

"We are not going to do anything and there's a reason why we don't spent time together." She jerked the wheel to avoid a dog in the road. "I'm going to go home and catch up on some reading. Maybe I'll take a trip with Munchkin."

"You *still* have that dog?" he asked.

"Why wouldn't I still have him?"

He shrugged. "Thought maybe you would grow tired of his orneriness after seven hundred years."

"He's not ornery. He just doesn't like you."

"The feeling's mutual," he grumbled.

Akantha laughed. "You're the one who let him drink from the Cup of Jamshid and made him immortal. Maybe he resents you for it."

"In my defense, I was drunk and didn't realize Artemisia handed me the cup. He looked thirsty so I offered him something to drink." He shrugged. "I say he's just ornery. He bit me twice after I saved his life. Where did you put him while you're spying in the heart of the Reich?"

"He's safe until I go home."

"I hope so. I know how much you love him. And yes, I may be a little envious of all the attention you lavish on that walking rug."

Akantha just let it go. Munchkin loved everyone except Damianos, and she couldn't blame him. She didn't like the man next to her much either.

"I'm serious though. We could find a nice, quiet, very remote place and catch up on the past three or four decades. Bring Munchkin if you wish. I've missed you. If I had a flower for every time I thought of you, I could walk through my garden forever."

She looked over at him. "Quoting Tennyson will not put you in my good graces," she stated. Tennyson was one of her favorite poets and he knew it. The audacity the man possessed at times.

"It doesn't make it any less true. I think of you every day, Akantha, and miss you more than I can put into words."

She turned her attention back to the road. "Get some rest," she ordered.

Damianos sighed and leaned his head back against the corner of the cab. He knew the fortress and walls around her heart had been his own creation, but he wouldn't give up until he reduced them all to rubble. The fact that they were still together searching for the spear was proof she still held feelings for him. If she really hated him, she would have left him behind. It would take time to rekindle the fire between them and burn clean his sins.

He studied her from half-open eyelids. She would always be the most beautiful woman in the world to him. He'd put her up against the fabled Helen of Troy and still swear she was more beautiful. Even the sun paled when compared to her. Beneath the beauty lay a strength unmatched. There wasn't anything she couldn't handle.

She'd been broken, defeated, and felt pain most couldn't handle. She looked fear in the face, year after year, century after century, but she never ran and never hid. She always found a way to get back up and fight. She was a warrior and unbreakable.

Anger welled up and replaced admiration. Matheus hurt and betrayed her, and Damianos would make him pay. He made a silent vow to help end Matheus's existence for her sake. Damianos knew he hurt Akantha so long ago, but he hadn't been there to see the effects of his actions. He saw what Matheus did to her and could just imagine how much worse she would have been so long ago. Matheus betrayed a capable woman who would make him pay. Damianos betrayed a naive young girl.

Matheus was more dangerous than he thought. The man would cause disaster, more than the current war was causing, on a global scale. With the spear in his hands, there would be no stopping him. He should have taken care of the man centuries ago when he broke Akantha's heart. He silently promised to make the man hurt for this and if it were possible to kill him, Damianos would do it.

She looked over and he smiled. She quickly looked away.

Knowing the Nazis were after the Spear of Destiny unsettled him. He had seen countless wars and killed too many men to count, but he never held any concern for his own existence. Until now. It was a strange feeling and he didn't like it. He hadn't thought about dying in over twenty-four hundred years and now he had to face the possibility that he could be killed. Worst yet, Akantha could be killed. Her safety was paramount, and if he died keeping the spear out of the Nazis' hands, then so be it. As long as Akantha survived.

CHAPTER NINETEEN

Belgrade, Yugoslavia 1941

"You should have woken me," Damianos said, his voice loud in the quiet of the truck cab.

Akantha glanced over. She had let him sleep. It was much more peaceful when he wasn't speaking, and the quiet gave her time to think and deal with the turbulent emotions inside of her. Her head was a jumble of thoughts and she was trying to make heads and tails of all of it. "You needed the sleep."

"And you don't?"

She shook her head and focused on the road ahead. "No. Not yet."

"You push yourself too hard," he observed. "One of these days it will catch up to you."

"You need to mind your own business."

"Can't I be concerned about you?" he asked.

"No," she snapped.

"Where are we?" He sat up and looked at the buildings on the horizon.

"Just outside of Belgrade," she answered.

"What's the plan? Do you think we're ahead of Matheus?"

"Depends. How many bullets did you put into him?"

"Three or four," Damianos answered. "One was a head shot."

"Then we're probably ahead of him," Akantha reasoned. "It'll take him longer to get on the road." While they healed from wounds faster than a mortal, it wasn't extremely fast. A head injury would take even longer to heal.

"So are we going to sit tight and wait for him?"

"I don't know. I hate waiting."

"I know all too well, but you should take the time and heal a little more."

"I don't want to waste any more time," she told him. "We need to get the spear back before Matheus gets anywhere near Wewelsburg."

"I know, but we have to be smart about this. We can't blindly search for him, we don't have the time or the resources. What we can do is take a day, plan out what we're going to do, and pick a place to intercept them."

She opened her mouth to argue but stopped. Damn him for making sense. He usually made sense and it was one more reason to hate him. "Okay, fine," she growled. She hated it when he was right and she couldn't argue.

He laughed at her disgruntlement. "Let's find a place to stay."

She didn't know if she could survive another day in a room with him. Three decades had passed since she last had to deal with him and she wanted it to be another few dozen decades. She was getting too old to play this game with him. "I haven't been to Belgrade in ages. Know any good places?"

"Some," he said. "But not sure how safe we'll be. The Germans control the city. Do you know who's in charge here?"

"B...Bone...no. Bohme. General Frantz Bohme."

"Do you know anything about him?"

"No. I just remember the name from some reports."

"All right. Let's find a place to stay for the night."

"If I may ask, what are you going to do with the spear once we find it?" he asked after a moment.

She kept her eyes focused on the road ahead. This was German territory and there were patrols to avoid. "I don't know. Probably lock it away in a vault."

"You and your group always want to hide things away from the world. Are there other options?"

His words almost echoed Matheus's, but the difference was important. He'd be the last person to want to keep it. She had been wrong about Matheus's intentions, but she wasn't wrong about Damianos. If he wanted power, he would have taken it centuries ago. "Give it to the Allies to help their cause, but then how do we get it back once the war is over? Whoever has it won't want to give it back."

"You never know. Mortals may just surprise you one of these days."

"They haven't yet."

"Don't you ever get tired of thinking the worst of things and everyone?"

Akantha didn't justify that question with an answer. It was hard to be optimistic in a world where humans spent more time at war than they did at peace. The only saving grace in the past was that the wars had mostly been contained to a certain geographical area. Advances in warfare and technology had changed all of that, and now most of the world was involved in a war again. When would it ever end?

"I guess not, judging by your lack of an answer."

She wanted nothing more than to hit him, but her hands stayed on the steering wheel. She couldn't let him get to her. They, no, *she* had a mission to accomplish. She knew letting him come along had been a bad idea and now she was proven right.

"I was just thinking that in all of my life I've never seen any group as evil as the Nazis."

"That's something we can agree on"

"I saw some of their plans. Being where I was—"

"In Himmler's bed?" he interrupted.

"Yes, in Himmler's bed, but also as his secretary. As his secretary, I saw what they are planning and have already carried out. When this war is over and the world sees what they are doing, the true horrors will shock everyone. Himmler set up special camps for any political prisoners, Jews, Romany, and anyone else they deem inferior. Places where they are worked to death or outright exterminated. Dachau, Auschwitz, to name a few. I accompanied Himmler to one of these camps, Mauthausen-Gusen, and saw what they were doing. It was horrendous. People worked until they died. They were nothing more than skin covered skeletons by the end." The images haunted her dreams at night and whenever she closed her eyes for more than a second. The frail walking skeletons were horrible, but the piles of bodies in a mass grave or the piles waiting to be put in the ovens more so. "The *Einsatzgruppen* are nothing more than death squads created for the slaughter of Jews and other people. Before I left there was talk of an invasion of Russia and plans to reduce the population by thirty million."

"Thirty million?"

Akantha nodded.

"Piss and blood," he swore. "It took the Mongol conquests a hundred years to kill so many and the Nazis are planning to do it in less than a tenth of that time. *Hannibal antes portas*."

"Yes, Hannibal is at the gates. Which is why it's important they don't get their hands on the spear. They will be unstoppable with it and more than thirty million will die." Thinking what the Nazis could do with the spear made her stomach twist into a knot.

"Then we won't rest until we get it. I should probably contact Morrow and tell him of the situation. There could be a lot of people affected, and he could have agents help."

She had almost forgotten about the policing organization he belonged to. If she remembered correctly, he was there when it was founded and helped Morrow build up the organization. She personally wasn't fond of Morrow, a Green Man, but they had professional respect for each other and that allowed them to work together when the situation called for it. She glanced over at him and smiled. "Thank you."

"You're welcome. You know there's nothing I wouldn't do for you. Morrow told me to say hello the next time I saw you."

"I don't want you to do this for me. You should do it for humanity and the non-humans in the world." He would just hold it over her for the next hundred years or so and she couldn't have that happening. He was insufferable enough. "How long ago was that?"

"I am, but I'm also doing it for you." He shrugged. "About twenty years ago."

She wanted to roll her eyes at his blatant attempt to get in her good graces, but she didn't. For whatever the reason, he was helping, and that was the important part. No matter her personal feelings toward him, she knew he'd do the right thing. "Did he actually say that, or are you just saying he did?"

"He asked about you."

Immortals made Morrow nervous, and she knew the less he had to deal with them, the happier he was. It tickled her that he always found a reason to leave not long after seeing or talking to her. "Tell him I said hello the next time you see him."

"I will."

Movement ahead caught her eye.

"Checkpoint," he said. A truck sat to one side of the road and armed soldiers stood in front of a barricade blocking the road.

"This isn't going to go well."

"Relax," he said. "You always think the worst of things. We'll get through this."

"Famous last words," Akantha said, "are still last words. I'm blaming you if something goes wrong." A soldier put up a hand and Akantha slowed the truck until it came to a stop. "Let me do the talking."

"Nag, nag, nag," he said in a droll voice. "You'd blame me no matter what."

"Shut up." This was one moment she didn't need the distraction his presence always offered.

A soldier appeared at each door a moment after they stopped. "Can we help you, *Oberleutnant*?" Akantha asked the one at Damianos's door. He was the one wearing the rank of an officer. The one on her side was nothing more than a soldier. She prayed to the gods that they would get out of this without a problem.

"Where are you going?" the officer asked.

"We are heading to Berlin," Akantha responded. Her hands had a death hold on the steering wheel.

"Where are you coming from?" he asked.

"Thessaloniki."

"What business do you have in Belgrade?"

"Just stopping for some rest and some food," Damianos replied.

"Move on."

"Thank you," Akantha said and put the truck into gear. The barricade was moved and the truck rolled past the small group of soldiers.

"That wasn't so bad," Damianos commented as the truck rolled past the checkpoint.

Akantha didn't comment. The rug was usually pulled out from under a person when things were going well. She wouldn't say this was going as planned, but it was better than she hoped.

"I think the route we took from Thessaloniki is the most direct back to Germany. Do you think he'll take it?"

"He won't waste any time in taking the spear to Wewelsburg, provided that's what he intends to do with it."

"Do you think he'll do that?"

"I don't know," Akantha admitted. "At this point all bets are off the table. I'm not sure what he'll do."

"What's your best guess?"

"I think he'll go to Wewelsburg. If the spear we recovered isn't the real Spear of Destiny, he'll be within arm's reach of the others."

"It's the soundest strategy."

"I suppose."

"You suppose? Would it kill you to admit that I'm right?" he asked. Gods save him from her stubbornness. Just once he'd like her to say he was right.

She didn't answer.

He chuckled and she glanced over. Her expression had forced weaker men to back down, but it had no effect on him. There was nothing like a strong woman. Especially this one. "You've always been too stubborn for your own good"

"You think you know me so well," she told him.

"I do," he said, his voice confident.

"You always were delusional."

"Akantha, my thorny beauty, I know you better than you know yourself. For instance," he shifted his position to lean into the corner of the seat, "you're blaming yourself for Matheus. While you are the source of his immortality because you loved him, you know you're not responsible for his actions. Yet, you'll keep blaming yourself."

She kept her eyes focused on the road, not daring to look over at him.

"Just like I know that you don't hate me as much as you claim. There's a part of you that still cares and, dare I say, still loves me. I can see it in your eyes and in your face. Somewhere deep inside of you is that girl I first met. You're stubborn to a fault and will never admit when you're wrong about something. Shall I go on?"

Her hands tightened around the steering wheel, her knuckles turning white. His words hit too close to the mark and she hated it.

"Your silence tells me I'm right," he said, quite satisfied with himself. The cracks in her armor were getting wider.

The skyline of Belgrade loomed on the horizon and Akantha increased the speed of the truck.

"I haven't asked, but what can the spear do?" he asked.

"Nothing concrete, but it's said that whoever possesses the spear controls the fate of the world."

Damianos gave a low whistle.

"It could be powerful enough to kill an immortal. There are a few weapons out there capable of such a feat and this could be one of them.

"What are the other weapons?" he asked.

"Durendal. Kusanagi-no-Tsurugi. Excalibur. Gram. Fragarach. Tyrfig. Dainsleif. Shamshir-e Zomorrodnegār. And others."

"That's quite a few. Do they actually all exist? Most are only mentioned in myths and legends."

Akantha nodded.

"So where are all these weapons?" he asked.

"Afraid someone's going to use one on you?" she countered.

"No, but I'd like to know where they are in an effort to keep away from them."

"Most we have in our possession, but there are some hidden in plain sight."

"Like the spear?"

"Yeah. The problem is the ERR has been looting conquered lands and we don't know what they have and don't have."

"ERR?"

"*Einsatzstab Reichsleiter Rosenberg*. Hitler's official art and cultural property looting organization. Hitler's creating the Führer Museum, a place for him to show off all the stolen art. I thought one of the tenets of warfare was to know your enemy."

"It is," he replied. "Have I said how much I hate the Nazis?"

"You don't need to," she said. "Anyone with half a brain hates the Nazis. How is it you don't know what the Nazis are doing?"

"I've been in the States until a month ago. Once we get to a hotel, I can plan out our strategy."

"Here's where you tell me how many famous generals you have known and how many you have been."

"Are you implying I brag?" he asked.

"No, just that you mention it quite often."

"I do not."

"I'm not going to argue with you," she said. "Do you know a place to stay?"

"I do. There's a hotel I've stayed at a few times. It's been here for a very long time. It'll do for one night."

"Just tell me how to get there."

"Just drive. I'll get you there."

CHAPTER TWENTY

They reached the hotel and Akantha killed the engine. Keeping a low profile and planning to intercept Matheus were the goals for the evening. They checked in, took possession of the key, and headed upstairs to their room. Akantha would have preferred separate rooms, but it was the only room available. Luck was not with her. Spending another night with him in a hotel room was the last thing she wanted. "I'm going to go find us food," he said as soon as they were in the room.

Her stomach rumbled at the mention of food and she realized she was hungry. The bread and cheese he had found for them in Skopje hadn't lasted long and they hadn't eaten anything in the past six hours. "Be careful."

"That almost makes me believe you care."

"I don't," she assured him.

He laughed and left the room.

Akantha glared daggers at the door for a few moments and then slumped with relief. He was gone, and she could have a few moments of peace and quiet. She entered the small common bathroom down the hall and used the time alone to wash up. A bath would have been heavenly, but she didn't want to risk lingering in one. She wanted to be prepared to make a quick exit.

She took a moment to look at her reflection in the dim mirror. Dark smudges made her eyes look bruised and exhausted and stood out against her paler-than-normal skin. It had been several of the longest days of her life, and it didn't look like it would slow down anytime soon. With luck, they would retrieve the spear quickly and she could put some distance between her and Damianos. She needed some time to deal with the heartache of Matheus's betrayal without Damianos driving her to distraction.

Akantha turned on the water and splashed some on her face. It gave her a small shock and she felt refreshed and more awake. She splashed more water on her face. It helped, but a good stiff drink would help more and she regretted not having any alcohol on hand. Though maybe it was for the best she lacked alcohol. It usually got her into trouble and with the bastard around, she needed her wits about her.

She dried her face and hands. Slightly refreshed, she felt ready to go another few rounds with the infuriating man.

An empty room greeted her when she returned. She took advantage of the time alone and went to the window to look at the street below. Cars and trucks went by, though not as many as there should be. The occupation and war curbed activity.

She watched the outside world and paid no mind to the passage of time. The sound of the door opening roused her out of her reverie. She turned to see Damianos entering the room and the temporary peace she had found shattered. The room seemed smaller with him in it. The gods help her get through this night.

"I could only find some basic foodstuffs," he said and placed a bag on the small table. "Bread, cheese, and some small apples."

"It's good enough. We've both had worse. Thank you."

He smiled. "That we have. Do you remember that trek through central Asia?"

Akantha turned back toward the window. "I do. I remember we had to eat insects for a while. It was a long time before I could look at another cricket." It was one of the few times she had set aside her anger and the two of them had gotten along rather well. She couldn't remember why they were in central Asia, but she didn't forget eating insects. They weren't the worst things she ever ate, but she didn't care to do it again.

She heard his footsteps behind her and turned to look. He was standing next to her and too close for comfort. He put a hand on her shoulder and she looked at it. "Damianos," she warned. She turned to face him and then realized it was a mistake. She tried to take a step backward, but his hand on her shoulder prevented her from moving. Akantha tried to pull away from him, but his hand tightened.

"Akantha," he whispered. He cupped her cheek with his other hand before leaning in to kiss her.

Akantha knew what he was doing and tried to pull away, but his lips met hers in a light kiss. It didn't stop there. He deepened the kiss and her toes curled in her shoes. She gasped, or started to, at his audacity, but his tongue entered her mouth at the slightest parting of her lips and her gasp was swallowed along with any protest. Her hands went to his chest and she tried to push him away. Her efforts were wasted when he didn't move. She could feel the danger in the kiss. She shouldn't be doing this, but his kiss overwhelmed her senses and his touch unraveled her.

Her resistance encouraged him and he wrapped his arms around her, crushing her body against his. His lips ground down on hers, bruising hers while his tongue invaded her mouth.

As before, warmth and urgency melted her resolve. Deep in that place said to house her soul, she knew that if she really didn't want this, he would stop. He would step away because he did care and she felt it. She called him a bastard, but in reality, a gentleman lurked inside. There was still time, mere seconds that she could stop him and return to her cold thoughts of betrayal and hurt.

The seconds were gone in the blink of an eye and she returned his kisses, silencing the voice of objection.

He groaned against her mouth when she returned the kiss. The hunger inside of her intensified and her blood hummed his name. He pulled at the stolen uniform she wore and he carefully undressed her. His hands moved lightly over her exposed skin and occasional bump of a scar. Her long history was written in scars that marred her skin, but the ones that hurt her the most couldn't be seen and were the hardest to heal.

She watched his eyes travel up her body and they met her gaze, half-hidden by dark lashes. Akantha was breathing heavy and she blinked when he pulled away. She looked into his brown eyes and they reminded her of a predator who had spotted prey and was ready to consume the meal. The look and the kiss left her with her insides swirling. Her mind told her this was a bad choice, but her body had other ideas. She was a live wire and something inside of her snapped. She rushed toward him and her mouth captured his in a fierce kiss as her hands went to his cheeks.

He didn't move for a long moment and then he returned her kiss with equal passion. He scooped her up in his arms. She groaned against his mouth and the pain from wounds spiked, but she continued to kiss him. He carried her to the bed and he gently set her down.

Akantha reached up and grabbed his shirt to pull him down on top of her. This wasn't like it was with Matheus. That was tender and gentle, but this was all passion and all-consuming. She was starving and he was the only thing that could satisfy her. He kissed the tender flesh of her neck and his body pinned hers to the mattress. She groaned and her body arched into his in response to the feel of the searing kisses along her neck. She hissed when he clamped down on an earlobe with his teeth. A shiver raced over her skin as warm breath drifted over her ear.

He smiled when her hands scrambled to push his shirt off. He pulled back and watched as she tried to unbutton his shirt. "Let me help," he urged. Akantha growled her frustration and he smiled. He brushed her hands away and quickly unfastened the buttons. Once he undid the last one, her hands grabbed the sides of his shirt and pulled it off him.

He didn't give her the opportunity to unfasten his trousers—he did it himself.

Akantha wished his hands would move faster. She knew he was doing this on purpose to push her buttons and it was working. She didn't want to just lie here and wait, she wanted him and she wanted him now. Her hands batted his away and she unfastened the buttons of his trousers. Once they were undone, she slid his trousers and underwear past his hips. He pulled back for a moment and when he returned, he was naked, his hot body pressed against her.

For a long moment, it was all skin and warmth.

His mouth burned a path across her collarbone, while his hands explored bare skin. He branded her with his mouth and hands, reclaiming her passion as his own. Her body arched and twisted against his, any lingering objections lost in the haze of lust and the fire of her desire. The need, honed to a razor-sharp point, ached for satisfaction. Her hands went to his back and her nails raked across his skin.

He groaned, and his mouth left her neck and blazed a trail of hot kisses down to a breast. His mouth clamped down on the rosy tip and he took it between his teeth.

A bolt of electricity went through her when he bit at the rosy nipple, eliciting a gasp. The heat coiled inside. She spread her legs wider, trying to force him to her.

"Damianos!" she cried out as his hand slipped between her thighs and fingers parted the soft folds. He slowly moved a finger up, and then down.

"Yes, my love?" he mumbled as his fingers stopped.

"Don't stop!" she ordered.

He chuckled and his fingers continued exploring the soft, intimate folds. Her body arched, pressing against his fingers. His mouth left her breast, leaving a trail of hot kisses down the plane of her stomach and replaced his fingers in an intimate kiss. He groaned as he tasted her, his tongue probing and caressing the soft folds.

"Damianos—" His name was a plea on her lips.

"Mmm? What do you want, my love?"

"You! Dammit, you!" she gasped.

He lifted his head and dropped a kiss in the dimple of her navel. "You have me," he purred against silky skin.

"I want you!"

"What do you want me to do?" he asked as he dropped a kiss in the valley between her perfect breasts.

She answered by leaning up and wrapping a hand around his erection. She caressed the length of him and he groaned. Her head swam as she guided him to her. He entered her with one deep thrust and she gasped at the sudden fullness.

Her nails raked across his back and urged him on. He thrust into her as deeply as he could go and slowly started to withdraw.

"Damn you!" she growled.

Something bothering you?" he asked as he dropped a kiss on her chin.

Akantha wasn't good at helpless or surrendering, but Damianos would have her just the way he wanted, at just the speed he wanted, and there was nothing she could do about it. "You're the most—"

"Wonderful man alive? Why, yes, I am," he said as he thrust into her. She moaned and he rewarded her with another deep thrust.

"Gods damn you." She arched her hips against him.

He laughed and thrust again. "What do you want?" he asked her and took an earlobe between his teeth.

She hated him so much. "You. Faster. Harder."

He kissed her, swallowing her groans and cries, as he increased his speed.

She moved her hips to meet his thrusts and the pressure twisted inside of her. Each movement was harder than the one before, lifting her to greater heights, taking her closer to the cliff. "Gods," she moaned, half-crazed with anticipation. Dazed, she looked up and met his gaze. His face was a mask of concentration and sweat beaded on his forehead. He groaned her name and kissed her hard. His hands moved to her hips, helping her match his rhythm.

The tightness building inside of her snapped and a wave of ecstasy crashed all around her, pleasure coursing through her with the fury of a storm. She tilted her head back and screamed his name. His mouth came down on hers, swallowing the end of the scream.

He continued to thrust until his body clenched and he poured into her.

Wet with perspiration, sated and exhausted, he remained atop her. Their breathing was ragged and they both remained still, waiting for it to return to normal. He dropped a kiss on her mouth and smiled. His hands released her hips and fingers threaded into dark hair. He kissed a corner of her mouth. "I love you," he murmured against her lips.

She bit back the words lingering on the tip of her tongue and swallowed them. *It was just sex*, she told her treacherous self. Sex didn't mean love and this was a one-time thing, an exchange of need. It was a bandage for her broken heart. Her need for physical comfort, and his need to protect and comfort her. Tomorrow she would erect the walls and go back to hating him.

He rolled to the side and rested his head on her chest. His arms went around her and she snaked her arms around him. Tears formed in the corners of her eyes as emotions coursed uncontrolled and wild inside of her. Her fingers threaded through his thick black hair as she tried to push down the terror of loving him and getting her heart broken. She wanted to love him, but just the thought caused her chest to tighten, and fear wrapped around her heart. She wanted to run away, put as much distance between him and her as she could, and never have to face the fear that now consumed her.

Damianos closed his eyes and focused on the steady beating of her heart. His head rested on the uninjured side of her chest, his arms were around her, and his legs were entwined with hers. Nothing mattered at the moment. Not the war, not the Nazis, and not even the Spear of Destiny. All that mattered was the woman in his arms. He closed his eyes as her fingers moved through his hair. He was home.

"Did I hurt you?" he asked. He turned his head and dropped a kiss on a plump breast.

"No," she replied.

He smiled against her breast. He knew she wasn't telling the truth, but he wasn't going to call her on it. He had tried to be mindful of her injuries, but he had been caught up in the moment.

"Are you sure?"

"Yes."

"Would you tell me if I did?"

"You should know better than to ask that."

Point. Akantha had never been shy about telling him, or anyone else for that matter, if something bothered her. On the other hand, the woman was stubborn as all hell and wouldn't say something if he had hurt her. A wise man wouldn't press the issue and he didn't.

"I love you," he murmured as drowsiness settled upon him. She didn't answer and he didn't expect her to. He expected a denial, but one didn't come. It was progress. Her fingers continued to move through his hair and occasionally they would move to caress his cheek. Occasionally she dropped a kiss on the top of his head. If she truly didn't love him, they would not be lying together enjoying such intimacy.

A yawn escaped her. He lifted his head and looked at her. "What?" she asked.

"Are you okay?" he asked.

"Just tired."

He could tell it was not just a lack of sleep, but a lack of hope and happiness that made her act the way she did toward him. He wanted to take all the hurt away and see her smile. Not smile because of him, just to see her smile at anything. "Get some sleep."

He put his head on her chest and he refocused on her heartbeat. Time ticked by in the darkness. Her breathing turned into a slow rhythm and her heartbeat slowed. Her fingers were still but remained in his hair. He closed his eyes and surrendered, joining her in sleep.

Her body jerked and he opened his eyes. She cried out and he sat up. Her eyes were closed and she slept. She cried out again. "Akantha," he said, gently shaking her.

Her eyes opened and she stared blankly at him. She blinked and he watched the tears well up in her eyes. He slid up and wrapped his arms around her, carefully cradling her against his chest. She didn't resist and buried her face to his chest. He stroked her hair as she cried against his chest.

"Bad dream?"

She nodded against his chest.

"I'm sorry," he whispered before dropping a kiss on the top of her head.

She said something, but the words were mumbled and he couldn't understand them. It didn't matter. All that mattered was that she was hurt and he could offer comfort.

He didn't know how much time passed before her sobs and crying stopped. She went still.

"Thank you," she murmured against his chest.

His arms tightened around her and he pressed a kiss to her forehead. "You're welcome. Would you like to talk about it?" She'd refuse, but he had to ask.

"It was just the usual nightmare," she replied, her voice steadier.

"I'm sorry," he said again.

"It's okay. It's not your fault."

That surprised him. She usually blamed him for everything, even the rain at times, and expected her to blame him for her bad dreams. He did the only thing he could, he held her.

"The camps," she said. It took him a moment to remember what she was referring to. He couldn't imagine such a thing. He had seen camps for prisoners of war before, but there would be no release of these people, and they were innocents, not soldiers.

"What can I do for you?"

"Nothing." A long pause. "Just hold me."

He smiled and kissed the top of her head. "I can do that, my love."

She was quiet for a few moments. "Thank you."

He squeezed her and kissed her head, a long sigh slipping out afterward. His top priority was serving her Matheus's head on a platter. Then as many Nazis as he could kill.

"Try to get some more sleep. Dream of your house in Maine and that walking carpet. Dream of anything except this horrible war." He placed another kiss on her head and gave her a squeeze.

She returned the squeeze and he smiled.

CHAPTER TWENTY-ONE

Akantha woke with the growing light of morning and greeted the day with a small smile on her face. The events of the previous night came rushing back in a flood of memories and the smile on her face faded as quickly as it had appeared. A scowl replaced it. How could she have been so stupid to sleep with Damianos? Now the man would be even more insufferable, if it were possible. Knowing him, he would see this as her having feelings for him and he'd want more than just a night. She'd never admit it, at least out loud.

She pushed herself to a sitting position and swung her legs over the side of the bed. The thin sheet covering her fell off and she shivered at the sudden feel of the cool air. She stood, stretched, and began searching for her discarded clothes. She heard him moving but didn't dare turn around and look at him.

"Morning already?" he mumbled.

"Yes, and we need to get moving."

"Or we could stay in bed for a few more hours. We both rather enjoyed ourselves last night."

"I'm trying to forget most of last night."

Her words cut deeper and caused more hurt than any weapon ever could, but if she were hating him, she didn't have time to be maudlin over Matheus. He'd take a few harsh words if it meant she didn't sink into depression. "Such sweet words of love fall from your lips."

"Get dressed," she ordered. "Or I leave without you." He sighed and she smiled. Okay, it was petty that his frustration brought her some amount of pleasure, but after all he put her through in their long lives, she felt justified.

"I'm getting dressed," he grumbled.

"Matheus probably isn't too far from here," she commented as she pulled on her blouse. "He's had enough time to heal his wounds, enough to be able to function."

"How are you doing?"

"Sore, but able to move," she replied. She grabbed her trousers and pulled them on. They were more comfortable than her usual skirt and allowed her a greater range of movement. She just wished they weren't so baggy on her. "Thank you."

"For what?"

"For last night."

He grinned like a cat at a pigeon on a rooftop. "I aim to please."

"Not for *that*." Of course he would take it that way, but she was grateful he held her after the nightmare.

"You're welcome. With luck and good fortune we should have the spear in our possession soon."

"From your mouth to Tyche's ears," Akantha said as she slipped on the uniform's jacket.

"Gods grant us the good," he said.

She collected the leftover food and packed it in the bag he brought it in. They would need it if they had to run from the Nazis. They may not have time to stop until they were out of Nazi controlled territory. "Ready?" she asked and turned to look at him. He was dressed. Would wonders never cease?

"I'm—" He was cut off by the door bursting open and German

soldiers rushing into the room with weapons drawn and pointing at them.

Akantha jumped and went for a weapon, but she froze when she saw Matheus walk into the room. Damianos had hit him with a head shot, evident by the bandage on his forehead, but he was moving stiffly. Maybe he hadn't healed as much as they had thought.

"My, isn't this a touching scene?" he asked in German. "Am I interrupting? I hope I am."

Akantha glared daggers at her former lover. "How did you find us?" she demanded in French, refusing to speak in German.

"You're in no position to demand answers, but I will indulge you. The soldiers at the checkpoint recognized you from the warrant for your arrest *Reichsführer-SS* Himmler put out. I radioed ahead to all the places you could possibly go and gave instructions that you were not to be arrested, but for them to contact me personally. Once we reached the city, it was just a matter of time until we found the truck you stole. We're creatures of habit and stay at the places we know from the old days, so I checked the oldest inns in the city."

Akantha's jaw dropped. Matheus had laid a trap and she had walked right into it. She had been so focused on getting the spear, she hadn't thought things through and thought about who she was dealing with. "I can't believe you are doing this," Akantha said in French. "How dare you give the spear to the Nazis!"

"Don't question me," Matheus growled and delivered a backhand to the side of her face. Akantha stumbled back a few steps. The sting of the slap made her eyes water and the side of her face felt as if were on fire.

Once the surprise of the slap wore off, Akantha lunged for Matheus, but Damianos caught her and held her tight. "Don't," he whispered in her ear in Greek. "Don't provoke him. Go along and we'll find a way out with the spear." Akantha struggled to break free for a few moments, but eventually stopped. When she relaxed a little, Damianos released his hold on her. Never in a million years had she thought Matheus capable of striking her.

"Tie her up and make sure the restraints are tight," Matheus ordered the soldiers with him. "I can't have you escaping or causing me any problems."

"What are you going to do with us?" Akantha demanded.

"I haven't decided yet," Matheus admitted. "First, I'm going to take *you* to Wewelsburg, because I cannot spare the time to take you anywhere else. There, I will give the spear to Himmler and then I will decide what to do with you. As for your lover, I see no need for him. We both know mortals are disposable, and it's better to not form attachments." Matheus drew his weapon and pointed it at Damianos.

It struck Akantha that Matheus didn't know Damianos was an immortal. The two men had never met, and Akantha had never mentioned the bastard during the times she and Matheus had spent together. She rarely spoke of Damianos, even to the people who had some inkling of the history the two of them shared. Unless it was to unleash a string of curses aimed at him, of course.

"No! Don't hurt him!" she pleaded. She had to make this convincing enough for Matheus to believe she loved Damianos. "Please, Matheus! Please don't hurt him!"

An unholy smile appeared on his face. "I should have known you'd immediately jump into bed with another man." He drew a gun and shot Damianos point blank in the chest. Damianos crumpled to the floor with a heavy thud.

"No!" Akantha screamed and fell to her knees next to him. She leaned over and pretended to sob in anguish. "He doesn't know you're immortal. Follow us to Wewelsburg," she whispered as she leaned in close. She kissed him firmly, selling the act.

Soldiers pulled Akantha off and started dragging her toward the door. "Justice knows every man's number!" she yelled at Matheus. "You'll be food for worms when this is over!"

"Gag her," Matheus instructed. The soldiers shoved a piece of cloth in Akantha's mouth and tied it off. She watched him kick Damianos's inert form, and thank the gods, Damianos didn't react. "Bring her," he ordered and exited the room. Akantha took one last look at Damianos as the soldiers dragged her out of the room.

She fought them every step of the way down to the truck, but their hold on her was too strong for her to break free. They escorted her downstairs, through the main entrance, and outside to a waiting truck. People watched, but no one dared lend a hand. She struggled against her captors and refused to climb into the truck.

Pain spiked on the back of her head and darkness closed in around her.

The door slammed shut and Damianos pulled himself up into a sitting position. Curses, in a few languages, fell from his lips. He looked at the small table, wondering if he could make it there without too much pain or too much blood loss. The small medical kit sat there and in it, morphine. He put a hand on the wound, wincing against the pain. Stopping the blood loss was more important. He climbed to his feet, trying not to pass out. The door opened and he froze, thinking it was the Nazis coming back, but it turned out to be the elderly wife of the proprietor.

"I heard a gunshot," she said in Serbian.

"I got shot," he replied, brushing the dust off his Serbian.

Her eyes went wide when they came to rest on his chest. "Oh my! Sit down and I will go get bandages."

"It's not necessary," he told her.

"Sit," she ordered, and Damianos sat on the edge of the bed. "You stay." He nodded, and she left the room.

Minutes later, the woman returned with her husband carrying a towel and some bandages. She motioned for him to set them on the bed next to Damianos. He did as instructed.

"There's a medical kit on the table," Damianos said as the woman started wiping the blood away from the wound. Her husband walked over to the table and grabbed the medical kit. He brought it over to his wife. She set the towel on the bed and removed the small morphine syrette. She broke the seal and inserted the needle into his skin. The morphine burned as it went in. He wasn't the first wounded she had attended by the way she handled the syrette.

She worked without talking, and her husband handed her a needle and thread without being asked or told. She threaded the needle and started sewing muscle back together. Damianos kept as still as possible, but pain spiked each time the needle went into muscle. She finished with the muscle and started working on the flesh. Her movements were efficient and in hardly no time she had the wound closed.

"Turn," she said and Damianos obeyed without comment or hesitation. He felt the towel wiping away blood and then a moment later the needle went into muscle again. He squeezed his eyes shut against the pain. It took her longer to suture the muscles of his back than it did for his chest. Exit wounds were always larger than entrance wounds. It was the nature of ballistics.

She finished with the muscles and he felt her working on suturing the skin.

"You are lucky to be alive."

He opened his eyes. "I've always been lucky."

"What happened to your wife?"

They had checked in as husband and wife, receiving no judgmental looks from the others. It hadn't been the first time they had posed as a married couple and it probably wouldn't be the last. If he thought she'd agree, he'd ask her to marry him and they wouldn't have to pretend. She'd never go for it, though. When they had Eleni, she had come close, but that was during a time they had gotten along the best since they met. "The Germans took her."

"I'm sorry."

"No need to be sorry. I'm going to get her back."

"You can't take on the Germans," the man said, staying out of the conversation until now.

"I will if I have to," Damianos said, the edge in his voice hard. He'd go through the whole German army if he had to. She was the best thing about him and his only chance at redemption.

Other immortals found something to do with their lives, but not him. Akantha and the other Guardians had their cause of keeping things away from mortals, even Richard's bastard, Philip, gave up fighting in favor of reading books a long time ago, and George traveled the world searching for songs and music. Damianos lived from battle to battle, war to war, and even when he wasn't fighting in a war, he helped police the supernatural world for the organization he helped found over a thousand years ago. Akantha was the one thing in his life that didn't involve blood or wars. She was worth fighting for and worth dying for.

"I am finished," the woman said. Her husband handed her two bandages and adhesive. She applied one to his chest and the other to his back.

Damianos had been so lost in his head he didn't realize she had finished suturing. "Thank you."

"Now you must get some rest."

He shook his head. "No. I must go after her."

The woman's face grew hard. "No. You will rest. Later I will bring you food and change your bandages."

Damianos opened his mouth to argue, but quickly closed it when the look on her face grew harder. He looked at her husband for a little help, but the man looked away. "Fine," he sighed.

The woman smiled. "Now, lie down and rest. I will be back later."

Damianos did as instructed and stretched out on the bed. Just moving a little caused excruciating pain and he knew he wasn't going anywhere soon. As soon as he could move without too much pain he was out of here and going after Akantha.

CHAPTER TWENTY-TWO

Germania Countryside 1941

Akantha woke as she jostled around in the back of the truck. Throbbing pain on the back of her head was added to the list of bodily complaints, but it lessened the pain in her shoulder and side. Her hands were bound in front of her and there were bindings around her ankles. The tight restraints bit into her skin and the gag was still in her mouth.

Akantha looked around and saw two soldiers sitting in the back with her. They were young, but most soldiers were. The young fought the wars of the old, just as it always was and always would be. She remembered seeing fresh-faced men marching off to war many times, only to end up littering the battlefields with their bodies. Akantha studied them and one looked over in her direction. Their eyes met and the soldier looked away first. Even with her mouth gagged, hands and feet tied, Akantha could still intimidate someone.

The truck stopped suddenly and Akantha was thrown forward. She managed to keep herself from falling over and she looked at the back of the truck, waiting. Eventually, Matheus's face appeared. Her eyes narrowed and murderous thoughts raced through her mind.

"Bring her," he ordered.

The two soldiers moved toward her. One unfastened the binding around her ankles, freeing her feet, and they each grabbed an arm and pulled her to her feet. Akantha moved along with them, not resisting. They removed her from the truck and escorted her toward a small farmhouse. She didn't look at Matheus.

They entered the house and shoved her into the dining room. They sat her in a chair, removed the bindings around her wrists, and removed the gag from her mouth. They moved to stand on either side of the doorway. Out of the corner of her eye she saw Matheus come into the room, but she didn't look at him or acknowledge his presence. He sat down at the table across from Akantha. A woman came into the room and placed glasses on the table in front of them. She left the room and returned with a bottle of wine and a pitcher. She set the bottle on the table near Matheus and she filled Akantha's glass with water from the pitcher.

Matheus poured wine into his glass and raised it toward Akantha. "To the Spear of Destiny and a new world order," he toasted. Akantha didn't make a move toward her glass and continued to stare at the table. The woman returned with a plate laden with food and set it down in front of Matheus, then disappeared into the kitchen. Akantha wondered if this was supposed to be some sort of torture. Watching him eat wouldn't affect her like he thought.

The woman came back into the room carrying another plate. She placed it in front of Akantha and disappeared from the room. Akantha glanced down at the plate and saw a chunk of bread and some cheese.

"My dear, you should eat," he said after swallowing a mouthful of food. His plate contained bread, potatoes, beans, and a chicken leg. "You need to keep up your strength."

Akantha glared at him.

"Ever so stubborn," he said. "Did your former lover know how stubborn you are? I suspect not."

Akantha reminded herself that the man sitting across from her was not the man she met in 1307. That man was kind, caring, and loving. She had to remember him as he was then, not who he was now. She remained silent and just looked at him.

"Did he know your secret?" Matheus asked. He stabbed a piece of chicken with his fork. "I would say no. Otherwise you would have made him immortal, no?" He shoved the piece of chicken into his mouth.

Akantha remained silent. She brought up pleasant memories of him from days gone by. She remembered sitting at the table with him as they shared meals. The meals would be simple, like the one now before them, and he would talk about his adventures with the Knights Templar and his visit to Jerusalem. She'd tell him stories of her travels around the world and the people she met in exotic lands. Meals had been long affairs and she always looked forward to them.

"I remember meals with you being a more interactive affair," he commented.

Akantha came out the memories of the past and looked at him. She blinked. He had voiced what she had been thinking about. "I remember you being a kind and caring man," she said.

"She does talk," he said with a half-smile. The smile didn't reach his eyes. Any warmth and compassion he once possessed were gone. All traces of the man she had known and loved were gone.

"I'm surprised by you," she said as she watched him eat. "Since the death of your brothers you have always been a champion of the oppressed and persecuted. Yet, here you are, working with a group that is slaughtering the Jews and others, just like Philip slaughtered your brothers."

He went still for a moment before erupting with fury. "You know nothing!" he bellowed.

"I know you have become just like Philip and Clement! You have become as despicable as them!" He bolted to his feet and crossed the distance between them. His hand grabbed her throat and he yanked her out of the chair. The chair fell backward and crashed on the floor with a loud clatter. Her feet dangled a few inches off of the floor as she hung limply in his grasp. She put her hands on his wrist.

"You know nothing!" he screamed in her face.

"You've become them," she croaked, trying desperately trying to pull air into her lungs.

A growl escaped him and his hand tightened around her throat. Immortal she may be, but she could still pass out due to lack of oxygen. Black spots danced in her vision and her head swam. She kicked at him, her feet meeting his shins. He stared into her eyes, and Akantha saw what could only be called a look of pleasure crossed his face as he watched her suffering.

"Matheus," Akantha rasped.

He softened for a moment, only to harden a moment later. He sneered, and then threw her to the floor. Akantha landed on the hard, wooden floor, and a jolt of pain traveled through her body. She sucked air into her lungs, filling them with much needed oxygen. Breathing was never sweeter.

"Tie her back up," Matheus ordered the two guards in the room. "Then throw her in the truck." The soldiers grabbed Akantha and pulled her to her feet. They quickly tied her hands behind her back, the ropes cutting into her wrists. She winced against the pain."Gag her," Matheus ordered. The soldiers obeyed and shoved a cloth into Akantha's mouth and tied it off. One grabbed her upper arm and pushed her forward. She glanced back at Matheus with a look that promised retribution, before the two soldiers escorted her out the door.

Akantha shivered in the cool late afternoon air. When this war was over, she was going to find a nice tropical beach somewhere and spend a decade or two alone. Completely and utterly alone. No men, or women for that matter, around to cause her grief or annoy her. Munchkin was the only company she needed.

Akantha leaned back against the side and waited. The two soldiers climbed in and took up their positions. Time passed and Akantha grew tired. It didn't look like they were going to be traveling anymore tonight. Knowing Matheus, he wanted to arrive in

Wewelsburg in the morning. He did have a thing for dramatics at times. Akantha closed her eyes and let sleep claim her.

She woke to the sound of the truck engine starting, and the truck lurched into motion. Her two soldiers were still there and they looked as tired as she felt. While she had slept, it was in a very uncomfortable position and she wasn't as young as she used to be. Akantha yelled to get their attention, but it was muffled by the gag. One looked at her and she made noise again.

He shook his head. Akantha made more noise and he shook his head again. Akantha growled through the gag.

"Maybe she's having a hard time breathing," one soldier said to the other.

"It's a trick," the other replied. Akantha shook her head and yelled against the gag.

One soldier eyed her. "You speak German?" he asked.

Akantha nodded.

"Maybe we should remove the gag," the other suggested.

"What if Herr Holtz finds out? We will be disciplined, or worse," he replied.

"What can it hurt to let her speak? It's not like she can escape by talking."

"Fine. Remove her gag, but if Herr Holtz finds out, he'll know it was you who removed it."

The soldier moved to the back of the truck and removed the gag from her mouth. "Thank you," Akantha said. "You're most kind."

"You're welcome," he said. He returned to his position in the back across from his fellow soldier.

"Where are you from?" Akantha asked.

"A small town outside of Munich. Where are you from?" Only the one soldier spoke, the other kept quiet.

"Turkey." It was close enough to the truth. The town she was born in no longer existed, but the ruins lay inside the current country of Turkey. "I haven't been to Munich in quite some time. It has always been a favorite city of mine."

"You have an interesting accent. Where did you learn German?" he asked.

"From a friend." She learned High German back in the tenth century and Standard German in the sixteenth century. Damianos had taught her Standard German during one of the times they had gotten along rather well. "Where are you from?" she asked the second soldier.

"Outside of Salzburg," he reluctantly replied.

"Beautiful city, and the birthplace of Mozart," Akantha said with a fond smile on her face. "The *Festung Hohensalzburg* is incredible and the Golden Hall is magnificent."

"You've been there?" the second soldier asked.

"Yes." The truck hit a bump and knocked Akantha off balance. She fell over and found her face pressed into the floor of the truck. Pain coursed through her shoulder and she grunted.

"Are you okay, Fräulein?" soldier one asked.

Akantha rolled to her side and then sat up. "I'm fine. Mostly embarrassed."

"We all have our moments," he said. "What's your name?"

"Alexis Rowland," she answered. "What are your names?"

"I'm Alfons Boden and he's Gunther Manz."

"Nice to meet you, despite the circumstances. How long have you been with Herr Holtz?"

Alfons smiled. "It's nice to meet you. I've been under his command for the past month. Gunther has been under his command for six months. How long have you known him?"

Akantha nodded. "It seems like a very long time." Six and a half centuries, but she didn't know the man now wearing Matheus's face.

"It cannot be that long. You don't look to be old."

"I am older than I look, but thank you."

An awkward silence settled over them, and Akantha was content to lean against the side of the truck. The small talk was over and there wasn't much more they had to talk about and she didn't want them replacing the gag. The ride was bumpy and she needed the support of the back of the truck. She wasn't about to make herself look like a fool again.

The truck rolled to a stop and Akantha took a deep breath, steeling herself for whatever was to come. Matheus's face materialized at the rear of the truck a few moments later.

"Bring her," he ordered.

The two soldiers jumped to their feet and grabbed her arms, pulling her to her feet. Akantha didn't resist. They helped her out of the truck and she stopped a moment to look around. Wewelsburg castle rose before them. The place was Himmler's pet project, and construction on the castle had progressed since the last time she had been here. Gunther gave her a shove and she moved toward forward.

CHAPTER TWENTY-THREE

They moved her from the truck and escorted her to an underground room. It wasn't exactly first-class accommodations, but she had stayed in worse. She had expected to be put in a dark, damp cell. The walls and floor of the room were stone, and the door was made of thick wood, probably oak. It wasn't damp or wet, and it seemed more like an unused storeroom than a cell. A bare bulb hanging from the ceiling was the only source of light. This was an area Himmler had never visited when she had accompanied him on a visit to the castle. She was surprised Matheus allowed them to keep the gag out of her mouth and untie her.

Matheus didn't let her have something to sleep on except for the bare stone floor. It wouldn't be the first time she slept on hard stone and it probably wouldn't be the last. At this point in her life, Akantha could sleep almost anywhere. She assumed the bucket sitting in the corner was for relieving herself and she was grateful to at least have that.

The door opened and Matheus entered.

She stared at him.

"I'm disappointed we couldn't find you worse accommodations," he said. He wasn't moving as stiffly as before, and Akantha made note of it. "It will be a few days before Himmler arrives," he told her.

"Since I can't have you escaping before he gets here..." Matheus pulled a gun out, took aim, and shot her.

The bullet slammed into her chest, and Akantha stumbled back against the wall. She squeezed her eyes shut against the pain and struggled to breathe. Murderous rage quickly replaced shock. If her chest hadn't been on fire, she'd lunge for him and pound his head into the floor.

Akantha glared at him. "You will pay for all of this," she threatened.

"I beg to differ, my dear."

A cold smile appeared on his face and he left the room. The door slammed shut and Akantha slid down, her back against the wall. The new wound screamed with pain and her head was swimming. Tears formed in her eyes and she refused to cry. She didn't want to move, but she had to try to get the bullet out before she started healing. The trick was doing it without passing out.

She clenched her jaw and started to remove the jacket. Pain shot through her body and the room started to spin. After what seemed like forever, she slipped her arms out of the jacket and let it fall. She paused, putting her head back against the wall and breathing heavily. The simple act of breathing was agony and the spinning increased.

She took a deep breath and shoved her thumb and index finger into the wound. White spots danced in front of her and darkness formed at the edges of her vision. She yelled against the pain and continued to search for the bullet. Her willpower and determination couldn't help her. Darkness closed in and swept her under.

———

Akantha woke to someone moving her to a sitting position. She blinked and the world slowly came back into focus. She stared at the person in front of her.

Alfons leaned in and pressed a metal cup to her mouth. "Drink."

Akantha drank deeply and the cotton feeling in her mouth went away. "Thank you."

"You're welcome," he said.

Her right hand came up and lightly touched her chest, and she looked down when she touched fabric. Her wound had been bandaged and she had been put into a prisoner's uniform. At least she wasn't naked. She was thankful for the small things.

"I removed the bullet and stitched your wound," Alfons told her.

"Thank you. You're very kind." She didn't know if Alfons was going against orders or not, but if he were, it restored a little of her faith. There were still some decent people out there. She promised herself she wouldn't kill him when she escaped.

His eyes met hers and he smiled. "You don't need to thank me for doing the right thing."

Akantha smiled in return. She knew that every solider wasn't in the army because they followed the Reich's dogma. For some it wasn't a choice. For them it was either join or be punished, possibly killed.

"It's a miracle you're still alive. I will bring more water and possibly some food."

It was a curse she was still alive, not a miracle. "Thank you."

"You're welcome," he said and rose. He started for the door.

"Wait. How long was I unconscious?"

He stopped and turned around. "A few hours."

"Thank you."

He smiled and left the room.

Akantha sighed heavily. She learned a long time ago to never trust Damianos, but Matheus—he had been the one man she could trust. He had been a shining light in a dark world. Akantha sighed heavily and mourned the lost trust. It was one thing she had counted on and she got burned. Never again.

Akantha didn't know how much time passed. It could have been days, or mere hours. The only way she could measure the passage of time was Alfons coming in to change her bandage and bring her some water and bread. She didn't know if he did it on a regular schedule or when time permitted. She spent most of the time sleeping and remaining still so she could heal.

The door opening drew her attention.

She didn't bother to stand when she saw Matheus, with spear in hand. She was in too much pain and she no longer respected him. He tilted the tip of the spear toward her, almost as if in a salute. The plaster coating had been removed and the wooden shaft was polished. The tip reflected the light from the bare bulb overhead. "Come to see if you've broken me?" she asked with a raised brow.

"No. I know it takes a lot more to break you," he said. "I just came down here—"

"To gloat," she finished for him.

"No. To check on you."

"Your concern is touching."

"Believe what you want, but I did come to check on you. I could bring something for the pain if you want.""

"I bet you sleep with that thing," she said, nodding to the spear. She ignored his offer. He wouldn't bring her anything for the pain and she wouldn't take the bait. He scowled and on some level it amused her. Her chances of escape were slim, but she couldn't let it stop her. It was escape or death. She wasn't ready to die.

"Himmler is on his way," Matheus said. "I'm sure he'd be interested in seeing the spy who had managed to find her way to his bed."

The inflection on the word bed made her raise her brow in inquiry. "Are you jealous?"

"Of course not," he replied. "I'm sure in the years since we've been together, you've been in the beds of hundreds of men."

"You give me too much credit," she countered. "The number is way less than you would think."

"You were always an excellent liar, my dear." He squatted down in front of her and was now eye level with her. "It only took you a few hours to crawl into the bed of another man."

"Believe what you want, Matheus."

"I know you, Akantha. Better than you know yourself."

She remained silent. Let him think he knew her. She could use it to her advantage later. "What's going to happen to me?"

"I haven't decided yet," he admitted.

Akantha didn't believe him. In his current mental state, he would probably enjoy seeing what the Nazis would do to her. The Nazis learning there were immortals in the world would be a very bad thing, almost as bad as their getting their hands on the spear. They would want the secret, and the thought of immortal Nazis made her blood run cold. "So, I'm at your mercy then?"

"It would seem that way."

Akantha bit back a response and kept quiet.

"Nothing to say?" he asked.

"Why are you giving the spear to the Nazis? You know the rumors surrounding it and you know what will happen if they have it."

"I do and I'm counting on it," he said.

"Why?"

"You know why," he said.

"No. All that you've said is something about restoring order and writing wrongs. What order? What wrongs? "

"They slaughtered my brothers!"

"That was Philip and Clement! They've been dead for almost seven hundred years! The Nazis are slaughtering the Jews, Romany, and others. They're no better than Philip and Clement."

He shook his head. "No. They're different. The Germans will bring order to this insane world. Then, I'll rip the spear from their grasp."

"And then do what?"

He smiled again and like the first, there wasn't any warmth behind it. He leaned closer, his face inches in front of her face.

"Hitler, Himmler, and all of the others won't live forever. I, on the other hand, will."

"This doesn't make sense. You're not like this. What happened to showing pity for the weak, and steadfastness in their defense?" she challenged. "He must at all times champion the good against the forces of evil?" She wielded the tenets of his former order against him like a weapon.

"It's a different world and it has lost its way. I will show the people of the world the true path. There is no future without order."

Her temper reached a breaking point. "You're deranged," Akantha spat.

The backside of his hand caught her across the face. Pain spiked and she winced. He grabbed her chin and turned her face to his. Defiance burned in her soul and eyes. "You may think that," he said. "But know in the end this is all because of you. You made me who I am."

Akantha willed herself not to physically react. The slap across her face hurt less than his words. Her face remained a mask of indifference, but inside her heart was in a million pieces. Guilt welled up and consumed her. She was responsible for Matheus, and his immortality, and the burden of stopping him was hers.

"I'm sure Himmler will want to execute you for being a spy," he told her, not releasing his hold on her chin. His grip was painful, but she kept her face passive. "I could save him the trouble and see if the spear is powerful enough to kill an immortal right now." He put the point of the spear against her chest, right on the bullet wound. She wanted to scream from the pain, but doing so would give him pleasure. Instead, she clenched her jaw.

Akantha didn't blink or look away. She did not allow herself to show any weakness. She stared into his eyes, almost daring him to do it. Anger kept her focused on him and not on the white-hot pain in her chest.

"You always did possess an indomitable spirit," he said. "It's one of the things I loved about you, but it will not help you now."

She responded with an icy glare.

He looked at her for a long moment and his hand released her chin. He rose, looked at her and then left the cell. The breath she had been holding escaped with explosive force and Akantha slumped with relief. A moment later the light went out, casting the room into darkness.

Akantha embraced the darkness. She slowed her breathing, inhaling through her nose, and exhaling through her mouth. Her mind emptied with each breath and her thoughts became still, even the pain in her chest dulled.

Time passed, but how much she didn't know, and the bulb flared to life once more. She squinted against the sudden brightness. Matheus, minus the spear, filled the doorway, and Himmler's face appeared over his right shoulder. The two men entered the room and Akantha didn't move.

"Stand up," Matheus ordered.

Akantha refused.

"Stand up!" Matheus bellowed.

She glared up at him but didn't move. He moved to her side and put a hand on her upper arm. His grip was a vice and he pulled, and Akantha didn't resist. She went limp and became dead weight. Matheus jerked her arm, but it did not bring her to her feet.

"Enough," Himmler said. He moved to stand directly in front of her.

Akantha didn't look up at him, instead she entertained murderous thoughts as she stared at a point past his legs.

"You will be executed for being an enemy agent, after you give us the names of other agents in Berlin."

She didn't respond.

"It would be in your best interest to tell me the names of your contacts in Berlin now. We will get the information and will use whatever method at our disposal. I can guarantee they will be most unpleasant."

Akantha remained quiet.

"Nothing to say? Very well then. In the morning we shall talk."

I will be gone from here by then, she thought, keeping her eyes fixed straight ahead. He turned on a heel and headed for the door.

"Wait," she said.

Himmler turned around and walked toward her. He leaned in. "Yes? Do you have something you want to tell me?"

Akantha's mouth twisted up into a smirk. "You're lousy in bed. I faked it. Every single time."

His faced turned red and a hand struck her face.

Her head whipped to the side and fire exploded on her cheek. She didn't cry out or react. Compared to the pain of the bullet wounds, a slap across her face was a bee sting.

"That may be, but tomorrow your screams will not be fake." Himmler left the room.

Matheus lingered.

Akantha glanced up at him, searching for the man she once knew.

"Himmler is expecting to torture you in the morning and will eventually kill you. Well, he'll give it his best try. I can prevent him from finding out about your immortality. Say the word and I'll use the spear, making it a quick death."

"Burn in Tartarus," she spat.

"Have it your way. When you don't die, the Nazis will experiment on you and do unimaginable things to you to find the source or your immortality. I will show you some kindness and give you a few hours to make your decision. For your sake, I hope you make the right one."

The murderous glare she gave him would have made lesser men crumble.

"Until later." He gave her a smile that was all malice and left.

She sagged against the wall, using it to keep her sitting up right. Tension drained out of the room and leeched out of her muscles and bones. The light snapped off and darkness rushed into the cell.

CHAPTER TWENTY-FOUR

BELGRADE, YUGOSLAVIA 1941

The bullet wound was sore and ached, but it wasn't the worst wound he ever received and wouldn't be the last. Damianos just wished he had more time to let it heal, but the Reich currently held Akantha and they had the spear. Both situations were unacceptable and he was going to correct them. *Damned woman,* he thought. She always caused him grief, but he still loved her. Two millennia hadn't diminished his love for her.

The streets of Belgrade were mostly empty, but a few pedestrians kept it from complete desolation. As he walked, he devised a plan to get him to the next step in retrieving the weapon and Akantha. His experiences in war zones came in handy at such times. The years passed, the weapons changed, but men did not. It wasn't long until he found what he wanted.

The small pub sat on a side street, filled with German soldiers. Music and laughter flowed out of the opened doors and windows even at this relatively early hour. The scowl on his face smoothed into a friendly expression. He hated the Nazis—they were a scourge worse than he had ever encountered during the centuries, and if they had left Akantha alone, more of them might have survived this war. He would make it his mission to kill as many as he could after he retrieved her and the spear.

No one noticed the stranger as he slipped between two soldiers and kept his eyes averted. He wore a German uniform, but he didn't want to interact. In the past, he might have courted attention for the entertainment of the ensuing fight, but not now. The uniform he wore was serviceable, but he needed an officer's uniform for the next part of his plan. An officer's uniform wouldn't be questioned or stopped, and he had to move freely in occupied territory.

He asked for a beer and made his way to a table in the corner. The drunken soldiers ignored him as he sat back into the shadows to watch.

It didn't take long. There was a *SS-Standartenführer* enjoying himself with free-flowing beer and a barmaid on his knee.

The Germans could certainly drink beer, even wartime beer. The whole world had been at war so long they'd forgotten what real beer tasted like. Good beer took time to make. Great beer couldn't be rushed. This war, like most wars, was all about rushing to the next battle. The loss of life, of dreams, and good beer. And coffee, another casualty. He remembered a time when Germanic armies were more disciplined. There were a few times he had led German troops into battle and they had been better than this.

He watched his target down beer after beer and fondle the poor girl. The man had to relieve himself some time. The longer Damianos watched, the more he became certain that the officer had hollow legs. The beer went in, but it wasn't coming out.

Just when he thought he'd have to move and find another target, his prey pushed the girl off his lap and staggered to his feet amid jeers and laughter. He weaved his way to the door and disappeared, practically falling out onto the sidewalk.

Damianos waited a few moments to be sure no one followed the officer, stood, and crossed the pub. A drunk soldier bumped into him and he gently pushed him away. The soldier glared at him for a long moment and he waited for the punch, hoping the man regained his senses. The last thing he needed was to get caught up in a bar fight. Damianos scowled and gave the soldier his best glare. The man's brain was slow to react, but the rest of him recognized the threat and backed off. Damianos continued to the front door, unnoticed by anyone in the bar.

He stepped out of the pub and looked for his target. He spotted him walking down the street in an unsteady gait and there wasn't going to be a better chance.

Damianos stepped out and followed. With the man's drunkenness and his own steady head, he quickly caught up to him. "Excuse me, sir," he said.

It was the "sir" that got the officer's attention and he swung around on unsteady legs. "What is it?" he sneered.

Damianos ignored the disdain the officer held for those of lower rank. "There is something you should see, sir. It could be important. An officer should report it."

The deferential tone of voice and appeal to his rank pleased the *Standartenführer.* He stood wavering long enough that Damianos feared he'd have to take the man here in the open and risk discovery.

"Very well. Take me there."

Damianos forced himself not to smile. Nazi officers were never short of ego. He gestured for him to follow and led the man to the closest alley.

The officer stopped at the entrance and peered into the darkness. "What's in there?"

"I found a body of an officer in there. It's just behind the trash bin."

The officer nodded and walked into the alley. Damianos followed.

He stopped near a collection of trash piled against a wall. He wrinkled his nose at the smell. "Where?"

"It's right here," Damianos said and brought the grip of his pistol down on the point where the man's head and neck met. The officer crumpled to the ground.

Damianos waited for a moment to be sure he was still alone. It wouldn't be long before other soldiers left the pub and wandered this way.

Once he assured himself that he hadn't been seen, he dragged the man behind the trash bin. A few minutes later, he emerged from the alley wearing the officer's uniform. It would be at least a day before the body was discovered, maybe two, if he were lucky. He settled the hat on his head and whistled as he walked away.

He walked the distance to the makeshift headquarters in Belgrade. It was one of the better residences in the city, forcefully volunteered by a wealthy family with many children. It wouldn't be worth much once the army was finished with it. The family, if they survived, would profit more from burning it down and rebuilding. When he arrived, he motioned to the nearest grunt. "Bring me a car," he ordered.

The grunt saluted and disappeared.

The car arrived and the driver ran around to open the rear door for him with a salute.

"I'll drive myself," Damianos said dismissively.

The soldier was surprised and it showed on his face. Damianos's scowl deepened. The man backed away and saluted again.

Damianos climbed into the car. He cursed under his breath as he pulled away, heading to Wewelsburg.

After a few hours, he watched as the sun rose over the green hills, but he was in no mood to enjoy the rolling farmland of Yugoslavia and Germany. Thoughts of dark hair and gray eyes, and what the Nazis could be doing to her now, chased around in his mind and squeezed his heart.

He knew she could handle anything, *had* handled situations that would have defeated lesser men, but she didn't deserve it. Immortality was a special hell for women as long as men treated them like property. However, it wasn't his greatest fear for her. If Mathias took it in his head to see what the Spear of Destiny could do to an immortal, he had a prisoner close at hand to test his theories. It might end her life, and his, in one lethal strike. There was no denying he loved her, he never stopped, but there were times when she tested his love. He had endured countless years of animosity and physical wounds from her. Hell, he had given her a few wounds. She had him arrested a few times and left him to rot in prisons.

Thoughts of walking away and never seeing her again crossed his mind on occasion, but the thoughts were fleeting. There were a few centuries where he didn't see her and they were the longest centuries of his life. No matter his location, every evening he looked up at the stars and the moon, wondering where she was and what she was doing, and he even went so far to think she thought about him. His thoughts always returned to her, even when he had another woman in his bed. The other women all shared the same problem: they weren't her. He'd never stop loving her and would storm the gates of the underworld to save her. He only felt alive when he was with her, ironic given all the times she had threatened to kill him.

There had been times when he came close to telling her the truth about what happened so many centuries ago. Early in their first millennium, he refused to tell her out of spite for her lack of faith. Later, he lacked the courage. He charged head first into battle without hesitation too many times to count and faced dangers that would have made lesser men run, but he couldn't utter the words, telling her the truth.

CHAPTER TWENTY-FIVE

Six months of non-stop work left Damianos exhausted, but he was home and looked forward to being in Akantha's loving arms. He took every job he could, stepping off one fishing boat to immediately step onto another one. Six months at sea earned him enough money to allow him to provide better living quarters for the two of them and, the gods willing, have daughters with their mother's gray eyes and strong sons to help him on his own boat someday.

The thought of a family made him smile and carried him through the crowded city streets. People passed him and the wary looks they gave him didn't go unnoticed. He was a fool in love with a beautiful woman and he now had the means to give her everything he promised.

Thoughts of Akantha fueled his steps and quickly brought him to the door of the building where they rented a room. In a few days, they would have a place two or three times the size of what they shared now. He entered the building and climbed the flight of stairs to their door. He opened it. An empty room greeted him, and for a brief moment he thought she was out running an errand or perhaps still working at her laundress job. Then he noticed what few possessions she had were gone. The comb he bought her when they first came to Athens was not on the small stool next to the bed and the few pieces of jewelry he bought her were gone. She only wore them for him. It was as if she had never lived here.

She couldn't be gone. He loved her and she loved him. She would never leave him after everything they had been through and the promises they made to each other. There had to be an explanation as to why her possessions weren't here and why she wasn't home. He refused to think she had left him, and he refused to believe something happened to her.

Closing the door behind him, he headed out into the street. He looked left and then right. The street was filled with people, but none of them were her. Where could she have gone? Neither direction provided an answer, but he spotted an old woman across the street. He knew her. She loitered near the door to her building every day and saw everything that happened in the area. Damianos crossed the street and approached her.

"Gods be with you, Agathe." He smiled in greeting.

"Damianos. Six months have passed since I last saw you." She smiled a toothless smile up at him. Her gray hair was pulled back and gathered at the base of her neck, and wrinkles lined the tanned skin.

"I have been out on the boats earning enough money to give Akantha a house and a family," he said. "Have you seen Akantha today?"

She shook her head. "No. She has not been this way for almost as long as you have been gone."

His chest tightened at the implications of her words. He refused to believe Akantha left. "Akantha hasn't been home for almost six months?"

The old woman nodded. "She came by one day about three weeks after you left. A young man was with her and she left with him."

"Who? Who was with her?" he demanded as his stomach twisted into a knot.

"That young fellow you brought home a few times."

"Androkles?"

"Yes, him. They came here and then left after a short time. I have not seen them since."

Damianos smiled and relief flooded through him. Akantha didn't leave him. She probably thought him dead. Now he could go find her and show her he was still alive and how much he loved her. Then, they could start their family. "You have helped a great deal. Thank you, Agathe."

She smiled up at him. "You're welcome. Go find your love."

He nodded and then left the old woman where she stood. He cut through alleys to avoid the busy streets and crowds. Even the alleys saw heavy foot traffic and he had to dodge and weave in and out around people. The afternoon sun was bright and the air was warm enough for him to work up a sweat in the shaded alleys.

It didn't take long to reach the entrance to the building where Androkles lived. It was similar to the one he and Akantha currently lived in. Akantha's laughter cut through the surrounding noise as he stood there staring at the door. He turned to see her walking toward him, Androkles by her side. She hadn't seen him yet. Androkles' hand reached over and took hers, bringing it up to drop a kiss on her knuckles. She laughed and smiled brightly. Androkles stole a kiss from her, and Damianos's stomach fell to the ground.

A hollow feeling developed in his chest and it became difficult to breathe. The world spun and came crashing down around him. Akantha had left him for his best friend after vowing to always be with him. His best friend had stolen away the woman he loved more than life. The sharp knife of betrayal stabbed his chest and ripped his heart out.

The pair drew closer and he knew he couldn't face them. He wanted to give into the rage building inside of him, but he couldn't speak or think. He only knew he had to get away from them. He couldn't stomach the sight of the two of them together, or see how happy they appeared to be.

His feet were as heavy as lead, but he managed to move them. He stumbled into an alley and turned the corner, putting his back against the wall for support. Blood pounded in his ears and the emptiness inside of his chest grew. Love was as fickle as the gods. He squeezed his eyes shut against the pain, and his hands went to his knees to help steady himself.

Through the din he heard her laughter again, taunting him and twisting the knife, and then the closing of a door followed. The sound seemed so final to his ears. He pushed away from the wall and stumbled into the street. For a long moment he stared at the door and then willed his feet to move. Every step was filled with agony, but they carried him away from the building and away from her.

CHAPTER TWENTY-SIX

Damianos caught up to her fifty years later and she had been full of vitriol and accusations. He had tried to apologize and explain he hadn't left her, but she would hear none of it. She threw her happiness with Androkles in his face, driving a knife deeper into his heart and soul. Nothing in the two thousand years since hurt him as she had hurt him that day.

There were many times over the long centuries he wanted to tell her the truth about Androkles' betrayal, but the words never came. He couldn't even tell her in the brief moments when she set her anger aside and the two of them enjoyed a temporary truce. So much time had passed she wouldn't believe him, and he didn't want her to believe now. If she believed, she would blame herself, and he didn't want that. The only thing he could hope for was her forgiveness.

He sighed heavily. *Damned woman.* He wouldn't be driving into the lion's den if it weren't for her. He could be anywhere else getting friendly with a woman. Maybe a blond, though he always preferred brunettes. He banged a fist against the steering wheel and stomped on the accelerator. The car lurched forward in a burst of speed.

Many hours later he pulled into the town of Wewelsburg. His chest hurt and exhaustion settled in his bones. Those were just two of the bodily complaints, but as much as he wanted to find what passed for a soft bed and sleep, he had to find Akantha. He promised himself a week in bed when this was over, preferably with Akantha naked and stretched out beside him.

He climbed out of the car and stretched his legs. At least this time he had an easier way in. He wouldn't be leading a frontal assault with an army behind him, and no one would be firing arrows or dumping burning pitch over the battlements. He didn't miss the old days. There was something to be said about subtlety.

He looked up at the castle looming over the village. In the growing light, it was almost gargoyle-like, large and imposing. He had gotten into more secure places, but he had time to prepare and plan. He was making this up as he went. "I'm coming for you, Akantha. Hold on a little while longer. I promise you can slaughter all the Nazis you want."

Damianos climbed back in the car. He put it into gear and pulled out. The trip through the town didn't take long and he pulled up to a stop before a narrow bridge on the eastern wing. No one came out to meet him and he waited a moment before shutting the engine off and exiting the car. There were guards outside the heavy gates, watching, and this was where his charade began. He wore arrogance like a cloak, daring anyone to question him. The guards standing watch at the entrance saluted him, and he returned it.

He crossed the bridge, passed under the arch, and entered the inner courtyard. Akantha would be held somewhere within the walls, and his money was on some place underground. He had to narrow it down and get a better idea of her location. The last thing he wanted was to be wandering around the castle trying to find her. Matheus and the soldiers that had been with him knew his face, and it would only be a matter of time until one of them spotted him.

His tactical mind worked as he scanned the courtyard. He made note of certain features and potential problems if they had to make a quick exit. He also noted where soldiers were stationed. Damianos counted each one, keeping a running total in his head as he walked. The smallest detail could mean the difference between success and failure.

He crossed the courtyard and nodded to the soldier standing at the door. The soldier opened the heavy wooden door and held it. Damianos entered and the door closed behind him. He started down the hallway to his right. The castle was triangular in shape, and there was little chance of getting lost in unexpected twists and turns.

It didn't take long to spot a stairwell going down and he quickened his pace. He was about to turn the corner and head down the stairs, when the sound of footsteps coming up the stairs reached him. He stopped and took a step backward into an alcove. He bumped into a pedestal and turned to make sure the marble bust hadn't moved. He slid deeper into the alcove and watched to see who appeared in the stairwell.

The person's back was to him, but he would know that ass anywhere. He had spent a lot of time admiring that ass through the centuries. He moved out from behind the pedestal and slid up behind her. He reached out, putting one hand over her mouth and another on her shoulder to spin her around.

The lone bare bulb flared to life. Akantha opened her eyes and blinked against the brightness. Once her eyes adjusted, she saw Alfons coming in through the doorway holding a metal cup and a small bowl.

Akantha stood. Her shoulder with the bullet wound hurt and her chest was on fire, but she could move without debilitating pain. Time was slipping by and Matheus would be returning any moment. She walked toward Alfons and offered him a smile. "Thank you," she said as she accepted the cup. Akantha gulped down the water and held out the metal cup to Alfons. She took a deep breath and steeled her will. This was going to be hard with her injuries, but she had to get out of here now. She had no doubt Himmler would have her executed and she didn't want him learning her secret.

Alfons returned the smile. "You're welcome."

A calmness enveloped her and she slowly exhaled. Her movements were quick and efficient, her legs and feet a blur. She brought a knee up to connect with his groin. The cup and bowl hit the floor with a clatter and he doubled over in pain and she brought a roundhouse kick around. Her foot connected with the side of his head and he dropped to the floor. Akantha went down to her knees and removed the knife and pistol he carried. She tied his hands and gagged him. She knew she should kill him, but he had shown her kindness and she could return it. Not all Nazis were the embodiment of evil.

Akantha took a deep breath and stood up, trying to ignore the pain of her wounds. She could relax and finish healing later. She paused by the door for a moment before pulling it open. The other guard outside didn't react. He had been expecting Alfons and Akantha used it to her advantage. She used the butt of the weapon and brought it down on the back of the soldier's neck. He crumpled to the floor. Akantha put her hands on each side of his head and gave it a sharp twist. A loud crack echoed in the hallway. This soldier hadn't shown her any kindness and she wasn't under any obligation to show him any. Akantha pulled the dead soldier inside. A few moments later she emerged wearing his uniform, boots, and hat. She wished the boots weren't two sizes too big. Matheus would keep the spear close to him, even if Himmler were here. She just had to find Matheus, get the spear, and get out of here. Killing Himmler would be an added benefit. Stopping the tides or stopping the sun from coming up may prove to be easier tasks.

She started down the hallway. Thankfully, there weren't any other guards in the hallway. It tickled her a little that Matheus had thought she needed guards on her cell. She walked stiffly, which wasn't all an act. Wounds and days of sleeping on a stone floor made her sore, stiff, and feeling her age.

She wrapped arrogance around her and strode down the hall with purpose. Sometimes, confidence could get you a lot further than a simple disguise. People who moved with an air of authority usually weren't stopped or questioned, not to mention the lower ranks made it a point to avoid authority figures.

She reached a set of circular stairs leading up clockwise and stopped at the base. She listened for anyone moving above. Silence echoed down and she started her ascent. She took each step with caution since she knew old castles had uneven steps, but it wasn't due to the masons not being able to measure. They were uneven to slow down attackers trying to reach the top.

She stopped at the top and peeked around a corner. Luck smiled on her as the hallway was empty. Judging by her location, she guessed she wasn't too far from the North tower.

Akantha took a step forward and immediately took one backward. Carefully she put her head around the corner. Two soldiers appeared at the end of the hallway and were coming down the hall. She tensed up and she waited. The dark uniform she wore helped conceal her in the shadows, but movement would give her away. The two soldiers stopped half way down the hall and opened a door before entering. The sound of the door closing echoed in the hall and the breath she held escaped with explosive force.

She didn't immediately move. Even though the hallway was clear, she didn't want to take the chance of the soldiers coming out of the room, or more appearing. A hand clamped over her mouth from behind and another went to her uninjured shoulder. The hand pushed her shoulder and she spun around. Akantha brought a knee up and the attacker doubled over in pain. A whoosh of air escaped the man and he groaned. She cursed herself for not hearing someone sneaking up behind her.

"Akantha," he hissed.

"Damianos!" she gasped. A pained expression adorned his face and small amount of guilt welled up inside of her. He had come to rescue her, even though she didn't need rescuing, and she hit him where it counted.

"Not the greeting I wanted, but the one I should have expected."

Akantha grabbed the front of the officer's uniform he now wore and planted a kiss on his mouth.

When the kiss ended he smiled. "Now that's a greeting I like."

Akantha ignored the comment and regained her composure from the momentary lapse in judgment. "Matheus is somewhere in here. Himmler is here, so we need to act quickly."

"Once we're out of here we're going to discuss that kiss."

"It meant nothing," Akantha argued. The momentary feeling of guilt was gone. "I was just glad to see you for once."

"Of course," he said with a smirk on his face. "What's the plan?"

She eyed him for a long moment and knew he was seeing more to the kiss than was actually there. He would keep bringing it up for the foreseeable future. "Find Matheus, get the spear, and get out of here without any more bullet wounds."

"You're wounded? Where?"

"Matheus was nice enough to give me a bullet to the chest."

"Are you okay enough to go through with this? Maybe you should head out to the car I have waiting and let me take care of your insane ex-lover."

"No. I'm seeing this through to the end."

"Any idea where he may be?" Damianos asked.

"I have an idea, but we'll confirm it. I don't want to spend too much time looking for him. It won't be too long before someone discovers I'm not in my cell."

"After you," he said with a sweeping motion of his hand.

She shook her head and checked the hallway. It was still clear.

"See anything?"

"No."

"You should go first and I'll follow at a distance," he whispered. "If someone notices, we both won't be caught."

Akantha nodded. There was wisdom and sense in his words.

"Fortune favor you," he said and added, "I love you."

"Fortune favor you," she echoed. No matter how many times he told her he loved her, she would never say it back. Even if it was the smallest bit true.

Akantha stepped into the hall and didn't look back to see if Damianos followed. He always had her back, no matter what. It was the one thing about him she could count on. She pushed back thoughts of the other man she had trusted.

She assumed an air of authority and walked confidently down the hall. The stone walls met overhead in a graceful arch and the morning light poured in the windows. She couldn't duck or hide in shadows if someone came into the hall. A soldier came from the opposite direction, but he didn't seem to take any special notice of Akantha.

"Where is Herr Holtz?" she asked, deepening her voice.

"In the *Obergruppenführersaal* in the North Tower."

Akantha nodded and walked past him. Himmler's ego practically demanded he have a hall for the upper echelon of the SS. She quickened her pace and put what she hoped was a more determined look on her face.

It worked. She passed a few more soldiers on her way to the North tower and not one stopped her or gave her a second look. She approached the door and her heart sank when she saw two guards at the entrance. She focused on the door as she approached. One of the guards moved into her path and she stopped. Dealing with them wasn't an option, as she had nowhere to stuff the bodies, and bodies lying on floors garnered attention quickly.

"I have an important message for Her Holtz," she told the guard in front of her.

The guard eyed her for a long moment. "He left instructions not to be disturbed."

"It's very important that I deliver this message to him," she said.

The guard looked over at the other guard. The second guard nodded and the first guard stepped out of the way.

"Thank you." She paused for a moment before opening the door.

Akantha read the inscription above the door. *Domus mea domus orationis vocabitur.* "My house shall be called a house of prayer." It seemed out of place, but she assumed the place was once a chapel. Akantha took a deep breath and then opened the heavy wooden door.

CHAPTER TWENTY-SEVEN

Matheus stood in the middle of the circular room, illuminated by the morning sun streaming in through the windows, and an unholy smile crossed his face when he saw her. He held the spear tightly in his right hand, knuckles white from the effort. Akantha swore under her breath, but thankfully Himmler was nowhere to be seen.

"Come in, my dear," he said. "I've been expecting you. I knew you would find a way out of that cell and come looking for the spear. Even with your injury."

Akantha took a deep breath and walked into the room, the door closing behind her. Twelve pillars rose from the floor around the circular room and were connected in a groined vault, if Akantha recognized it correctly. A dark green sun wheel with a gold center was embedded into the center of the floor and the room was illuminated by twelve windows in their own niches. Construction was still going on, along with the rest of the castle, and Akantha wondered how much Himmler was spending for this ego trip.

"I would hate to disappoint," she said as she reached the center and stood on the gold plate.

"You never do," Matheus said. "Is this what you are after?" He tilted the tip of the spear toward her, almost as if in a salute.

"I can't let the Nazis get their hands on it."

"You seem confident this is the real spear," Matheus observed.

"It could be. This is just one of a number people think is the true spear," Akantha replied. "I'm just covering all of the bases."

"You didn't go after any of the others," he pointed out.

"You seem confident I'm acting alone."

"Yes, your little secret group."

Akantha didn't respond.

"Are you ready to test the spear?" he asked. "Himmler is expecting to question you in an hour or two. We can save him the trouble and spare you the rigors you will endure at his hands."

"Hand over the spear and I'll test it on you," she replied. The gun she liberated with the uniform remained in the holster at her waist; it wouldn't do anything more than slow him down.

Matheus smiled, but it didn't reach his eyes. "To think people have accused you of not possessing a sense of humor."

"I do have one," she defended and started walking to her right to circle him. She knew Damianos was somewhere outside of the room and to have a chance of succeeding, she needed Matheus's back to the door. "I just don't find humor in things most people find funny."

"You never did," he said and his gaze followed her.

Akantha shrugged and moved behind him. She knew he would turn, he had to. He was a trained knight and he couldn't ignore a threat. He turned as predicted and Akantha smiled on the inside, her face remaining passive.

"Don't force me to use the spear on you," Matheus told her.

"Force you? If you use it on me it will be because you chose to do it, not because I forced you," she countered. "I'm not forcing you to do anything. You brought everything upon yourself. Matheus, it doesn't have to end like this. Give me the spear. Let me take it out of the reach of mortals." She now stood opposite the door and his back was to it, exactly where she wanted him.

"We both know how this is going to end," he told her.

"Please, Matheus," she begged. She needed him to believe that she wouldn't do whatever it took to get the spear. "We loved each other once. Don't let something like this happen."

"If you think any feelings for you will sway my decisions or actions, you're mistaken." He sneered.

His words spoke volumes. Akantha knew he wouldn't hesitate to use the spear on her. For the first time since she was mortal, she feared for her life. "Matheus, please. Let's leave all of this behind us and go somewhere and be alone together. Remember how wonderful life was when we were together? Over two hundred years of happiness. We could have it again."

He paused and seemed to be considering the proposal. Behind him the door started to open and Akantha kept her eyes focused on Matheus. Just looking at the door could alert Matheus to Damianos's presence and they would lose the element of surprise. She sent a silent prayer the door wouldn't make a noise.

"Please Matheus," she continued. "Let's go. We can get lost in central Asia or the heart of Africa. We can spend time getting lost in the grasslands of the Serengeti."

Matheus was a statue, and the door behind him opened ever so slowly. Akantha took a step toward Matheus.

"Please," she whispered. "Please come with me."

Matheus wavered and the tip of the spear dipped a little. Akantha stepped closer to him. "Please. Come with me," she repeated. She closed the short distance between them, stopping a few inches in front of him. Her stomach twisted up and she swore she could feel her heart pounding in her chest. He could easily run her through with the spear if he chose to. "Matheus." His name was barely more than a whisper.

"Akantha," he muttered.

Akantha took a deep breath and leaned in to kiss him.

"Did you honestly think I would fall for this?" he said his mouth an inch away from hers. He put out his left hand and pushed her back. He jabbed the shaft backward. It connected with Damianos's gut and he grunted.

Matheus spun and stabbed at Damianos with the point of the spear. Damianos had recovered enough to avoid the thrust. "You're supposed to be dead," Matheus growled.

Damianos grabbed the shaft of the spear and tried to yank it out of Matheus's hands. Matheus pulled on the spear and then suddenly pushed, sending the shaft toward Damianos's face. It connected across the man's nose with a loud crack. Blood gushed out, but he didn't seem to notice.

"I should have suspected she made you immortal."

"She didn't," Damianos replied as he tried to wrestle the spear away from Matheus, but Matheus's grip on the spear was strong enough to keep it from happening. He took one hand off the spear and used it to deliver a punch to the gut. Matheus grunted from the pain, but his grip on the spear didn't lessen. "We became immortal together."

With the men grappling for the spear, Akantha kicked the back of Matheus's knee. The leg buckled and he yanked on the spear as he fell backward. Damianos's hands slipped from the spear, and Matheus regained his footing. He lashed out with the spear, swiping at Damianos. The edge sliced across Damianos's chest, going through uniform and skin.

Fire laced across his chest and he yelled in agony. Countless battles and wars brought wounds and scars, but this was worse than all the wounds he had suffered in the past two thousand years combined. Damianos staggered as the world tilted for a moment. His chest tightened and he couldn't breathe. Pain consumed him. He used every ounce of strength and willpower he possessed to remain standing.

He looked at Akantha. Their eyes met and worry dominated the gray depths. He didn't have time to ponder it more as Matheus recovered and tried to run him through with the spear. He sidestepped the thrust and grabbed the shaft of the spear, keeping Matheus's attention. If one of them had to die, he'd prefer it be himself. No matter what happened, Akantha had to live.

Matheus tried to jerk it out of his hands, but Damianos's grip held. He couldn't let the man have the chance to use the spear on Akantha. His chest burned and protested each moment with pain, but he held on. Matheus pulled and Damianos's hands slipped a little. Sweat made his grip precarious. Movement caught his eye and he saw Akantha draw a gun and take aim.

Damianos nodded as he tried to yank the spear from Matheus's grip. Sound filled the chamber, the shot seeming louder than normal. The bullet slammed into one of Matheus's legs and it buckled under him, but the man didn't release the spear. Matheus yanked the spear and Damianos's hands slipped free. He turned it around and Damianos stared at the point aimed right at him.

Matheus thrust it forward and Damianos jumped backward. Pain spiked with each move, but he couldn't afford to remain still. Akantha fired again and the bullet slammed into Matheus's back. He stumbled forward and Damianos lunged for the spear, his chest protesting with pain. He grabbed the shaft and yanked, but Matheus was stronger than he looked.

Matheus slumped and Akantha charged forward, grabbing the shaft. She yanked with all of her might and the spear came free from Matheus's hands. She spun it around and put two hands on the shaft and maybe it was her imagination, but she swore she could feel power radiating from the weapon. Matheus spun around to face her. The point went to Matheus's throat and their eyes locked. Time seemed to stop, seconds dragging out to an eternity. Blood thundered in her ears and her heart pounded in her chest. Her mouth went dry, sweat formed on her palms, and her stomach twisted up into a knot.

She glanced over at Damianos and looking at him made her wonder how it came to this. The man who broke her heart, and had given her nothing but grief for over twenty-four hundred years, was helping her, and the man she still loved would kill untold numbers for a misguided sense of protecting the innocent. The gods and the Fates were playing some cruel joke on her. Akantha knew she didn't have a choice. Either she had to do it or Damianos would. "Gods be merciful," she said under her breath and brought the spear back for a thrust.

Matheus lunged at her. Akantha reacted without thought. The spear thrust forward and buried into Matheus's chest. His eyes went wide and he looked at the shaft of the spear sticking out of his chest. His eyes locked with Akantha's and then he fell backward. The gun in his hand went off.

Akantha froze at the sudden realization of what she had done and time seemed to stop. Her hands shook as she watched the color drain out of Matheus's face. The sound of a weapon firing made her jump and bring her back to the moment. The world jerked and time started moving again. Matheus collapsed on the floor. Akantha fell to her knees at Matheus's side and pulled him into her lap.

"Eleanor," he said using the name he had first known her by.

Tears gathered and his face blurred. "Matheus," she choked out as the tears spilled from her eyes and ran down her cheeks. Her stomach twisted and she tasted bile in her mouth.

"Not your fault," he gasped in the struggle to draw another breath.

She bit back a sob and nodded. Pain and grief flooded her, threatening to consume her. "I'm sorry," she said, forcing the words past the lump in her throat.

He managed a weak smile. It was the first one to touch his eyes since the night they spent together. "Forgive me."

"I do," she said with a sob. She placed a hand on his cheek. "I forgive you."

He smiled again. "I go to join my brothers," he said, his voice thin and thready.

The tears continued to fall from her eyes and they blurred his face. She was no stranger to death. She had felt its presence so many times, coming to take the people she cared about and loved with its icy hands. Now death was reaching to claim Matheus. "I love you, Matheus. Godspeed."

Life slipped from his body. His final breath escaped and his empty eyes stared into space. Akantha gently closed his eyes and laid his head on the floor.

"Akantha, we must go," Damianos said. His deep voice was soft and seemed to reverberate in the room.

Akantha looked up to see Damianos standing over the inert bodies of two soldiers. They were the guards from outside the door. She had been so distracted by Matheus, she hadn't heard them enter or notice Damianos had fought them. She looked up at him and nodded.

Akantha leaned over and brushed her lips across Matheus's. She pulled back, hastily wiping tears from her cheeks and climbed to her feet. Her hands wrapped around the shaft of the spear and she pulled it free. It came free with a sucking sound that turned her stomach. The metal was slick with crimson blood, dripping to the floor, red contrasting against gray stone.

"Akantha," Damianos said again.

Akantha looked at him. He grabbed the guns from the downed soldiers and tossed one to Akantha. She caught the weapon and put it in her right hand. The spear, useless against soldiers with guns, she put in her left hand.

"We should take him with us," she told him.

Damianos shook his head. "We can't."

"He deserves a burial befitting a Templar."

"I know and I agree, but it's not possible. It's going to be difficult enough getting out of here without carrying a body."

"Damianos." She knew she'd win this battle of wills, and she owed Matheus a proper burial.

"This is a mistake," he cautioned as he picked up Matheus's body. "You were always so stubborn." He hefted the body over a shoulder with a loud grunt.

"I know. I can't leave him here." She went to the door. "Ready?"

He nodded and followed her out of the door.

The gunshots had alerted the rest of the castle to their presence and soldiers poured into the hallway. Akantha walked with confidence and an air of authority.

"Find the person who shot Herr Holtz!" Damianos ordered in a loud voice. "Now!" Soldiers stopped for a moment and then resumed with more energy than before. The hallway emptied a little. They had to hurry. The charade wouldn't last.

Akantha continued down the hall, Damianos on her heels. So far no one questioned them, but Akantha knew their luck wouldn't hold.

"Halt!" a soldier yelled from behind them when they were near the main entrance.

Akantha stopped and swore under her breath. Damianos cursed behind her.

"Identify yourselves!"

Akantha turned around to face the soldier. The soldier paused as if trying to decide what he was going to do. Akantha fired and the bullet slammed into the soldier. He crumpled to the ground. The noise got the attention of another soldier at the far end of the hall. Akantha shot at him. Her first shot missed, but her second slammed into a leg. He fired and the bullet ricocheted off the wall next to Akantha. She fired again and shot the soldier's other leg, and he fell to the floor, screaming in pain.

"Come on," Akantha urged Damianos. "We're going to have more company soon."

"You don't need to tell me twice," he said. He readjusted Matheus's body on his shoulder and followed Akantha.

They reached an exterior door when there was another shout from behind them.

"By Zeus's beard! Go," she ordered. "I'll be behind you." She stopped and turned to see three more soldiers at the far end of the hall running toward them. Damianos brushed past her and went through the door.

Akantha took aim and started firing. Gunshots rang out in the stone hallway. The soldiers stopped and returned fire and she was glad they weren't good marksmen. Bullets flew by her and Akantha had to do something. She turned around and ran out the main door as bullets whizzed by her. She slammed the door shut and moved to the side away from the door.

As soon as the door opened, she fired two successive shots and took down the two soldiers. It was easier when they were closer. She glanced over her shoulder to see Damianos going through an archway. Two soldiers stepped into the middle after he passed through. They brought their weapons up and aimed at Damianos's back.

Akantha charged across the courtyard and fired. One took a bullet in the back of the head and the other took a bullet in the back. She looked up and saw Himmler standing on one of the parapets and shouting orders to anyone in the general area. Akantha couldn't resist and fired off a few shots. Himmler ran and disappeared. Akantha swore and turned her attention back to Damianos.

Damianos dropped Matheus's body in the backseat of a car and ran to the driver's side. He climbed in and Akantha ran to the passenger side. The car was in motion as she yanked open the door. She jumped and landed in the seat, yanking the door shut as they sped down toward the town.

CHAPTER TWENTY-EIGHT

The car sped through the streets of Wewelsburg, and Akantha kept an eye on the side mirror for any signs of pursuit. Damianos weaved in and out of traffic, avoiding the other vehicles and other things. He slammed his hand on the horn as people moved to get out of the way. People on the sidewalks stared at their passage.

"Did you get hit?" he asked, glancing over at her. There was no response. "Akantha!"

"What?" she snapped and looked over at him.

"Did you get hit?"

She shook her head. "No. You?" No new injuries to add to the existing ones.

He shook his head. "Not by bullets."

Akantha glanced over and saw the line of red across his chest. She had thought Matheus had missed him with the spear, but his chest proved otherwise. Blood seeped out of the wound, soaking up into the uniform. Injured, he still managed to carry Matheus out. "Are you going to be okay?'

"Hurts like nothing else," he said, "but I'll be fine."

Akantha turned her attention back to the mirror and saw a truck closing in on them. "Hurry!" she yelled at Damianos.

"I am!" he yelled back.

"It sure doesn't look like it," Akantha growled.

"Would you rather drive?"

"Yes. I'm a better driver than you are," she countered. "Always have been."

He snorted and jerked the wheel to avoid a dog in the street. Akantha clutched the handle above the door to help keep her balance as the car sped up.

"Where are we heading?" he asked as he checked the mirrors. The truck behind them was closing in, but he didn't want to do anything about it here in the town. He pushed the accelerator pedal down as far as it would go. The car shuddered and then sped ahead.

"My estate in France," she replied. "Near Paris."

"Why are we going there? Shouldn't we make our way to England, or even Switzerland?"

She shook her head. "No. We're going there so I can bury Matheus."

"Akantha—"

"We're going there," she said in a voice that didn't encourage any further discussion.

"Fine." She rolled down her window and he glanced over. "What are you doing?"

"I'm going to see if I can do something about the truck behind us," she answered as she climbed up and sat on the edge. She held on with her free hand and took aim, firing at the truck. One bullet hit the windshield and another hit the front grill, but the others went wide. The car swerved and Akantha was almost jarred from her precarious perch.

The truck behind them sped up and collided with the rear of their vehicle. Her grip slipped and she fell backward.

"No you don't," Damianos said as he reached over and grabbed the front of her blouse. For a few seconds she teetered on the edge of falling out of the car. Damianos yanked and she righted herself back into a sitting position.

"You owe me!" he called out to her.

She hated to think what she owed him. The other truck pulled up alongside, and Akantha fired over the roof of the car. The bullets harmlessly hit the side of the truck and it swerved once more into theirs. Damianos jerked the wheel to the left and plowed into the other truck. It went veering off to the left and gave Akantha a better angle on the driver. She fired another shot and this one went into the windshield but missed the driver.

The truck slammed into them again and Damianos fought to keep the car on the road. Akantha clutched the door frame, trying to keep her seat. She saw a soldier in the other truck turn toward the window and aim a weapon. She ducked a second before a shot rang out. Akantha sat up and took aim. She squeezed the trigger and the shot went into the soldier in the passenger seat. He doubled over and his head collided with the dashboard.

Akantha watched the driver of the other truck pull a weapon and fire at them. Akantha fired her last two shots and the second one hit the driver. The truck swerved and slowed. Akantha slid back into her seat and she glanced over and saw the pained look on Damianos's face.

"What's wrong?" she asked.

"Chest's hurting."

Akantha swore.

"You could make a sailor blush and walk out of a room."

"Pull over so I can stitch you up," she told him.

He shook his head. "No time. You can do it as soon as we're outside the town."

"Damianos—"

"It's nice to know you care."

"Don't pass out," she commanded. He wouldn't die—he couldn't —but passing out was a real possibility and it was the last thing they needed while he was driving.

"I won't pass out," he assured her.

"You always say that and you end up passing out from blood loss."

"I do not," he countered.

Akantha harrumphed and turned away from him.

Silence hung between them for the rest of the trip out of Wewelsburg. Akantha occupied herself by looking out the windows. She didn't want to look at him or talk to him. She just wanted a few moments of peace and quiet.

The car slowed and he pulled off to the side of the road. He left the engine running and climbed out. He walked around to the passenger side and opened the door.

"What are you doing?"

"You're driving," he said. "I'm starting to get dizzy."

She smirked. "I knew it." Akantha grabbed the small medkit and climbed out. "Do you want me to sew you up?"

"No. We're still too close. I'll be fine for a few hours."

"Are you sure?"

"I'm sure. We can't spare the time."

Akantha put the medkit on the hood and opened it. She pulled out a roll of bandages and motioned to him.

"We don't have the time," he insisted.

"Let me put a damned bandage on and we can go."

He walked over to her and she grabbed his arm when he was close enough. "Ow!"

"Oh shut up and don't be such a baby," she said. "You used to be a lot tougher. Remove your jacket and shirt."

"You used to be a lot nicer," he said. He slowly removed his jacket and shirt. Akantha bit back a gasp when she saw the wound. It ran straight across his chest, from arm pit to arm pit, angry and red. Blood flowed from the wound and without shirt and jacket to absorb it, it started to run down his chest. The edges of the wound were smooth, attesting to the sharpness of the spear.

She didn't respond to the bait and grabbed the roll of bandages. She rolled the bandage over the wound and put her arms around him, passing the roll from one hand to another. She looked up at him and the breath stayed in her chest. He looked down at her, dark eyes looking down into her soul. He radiated heat and she wanted to get closer and soak up the warmth. The world spun a little and she let out the breath she held. She wrapped the roll around him again. She ripped the bandage from the roll and tied it off. He groaned loudly. "There."

"Thank you," he said and dropped a kiss on her forehead.

"You're welcome," she said and placed a kiss on the tip of his chin. Then kicked herself for doing it.

When he pulled away she walked over to the driver's side and climbed in. She put the car into gear. It started moving and Damianos scrambled to climb in before she pulled away. He didn't say anything. He settled in the seat and leaned against the door. Akantha glanced over after he didn't say anything after a while and saw his eyes were closed. At least part of the drive would be quiet.

CHAPTER TWENTY-NINE

Akantha pulled up outside a modest manor house about ninety miles northeast of Paris. She glanced over and looked at Damianos. The man was still passed out and the drive had been done in blissful silence. It had allowed Akantha to think and deal with the turbulent emotions swirling inside of her. She had always led a complicated life, but recent events had seemed more complicated than usual. She blamed the man passed out on the passenger side and rightfully so. Her life always grew more complicated when he showed up.

She climbed out of the car and walked around to the passenger side. She opened the door and put a hand on his shoulder, shaking him. No response. She shook him harder.

Her stomach twisted. "Damianos!" she yelled, panic seeping into her soul. She put two fingers on the side of his neck. The steady pulse calmed some of the rising panic and worry. She caught a glimpse of the bandage beneath his shirt and saw it was almost completely blood-stained. The edges of the bandage were almost brown while the center, right over the wound, was a bright red.

Blood was still coming out of the wound. He should have stopped bleeding by now.

She placed a hand on a pale cheek and she frowned. His skin was hot to the touch. He shouldn't have a fever. Worry settled in. "You'll be all right," she said, trying to convince herself he was going to be okay.

"Akantha?"

The sudden voice behind her caused her to jump. She spun around, ready to attack if necessary. A warm smile greeted her and she relaxed. "Zenon." His head was still shaved like it had been when she first met him over two thousand years ago. The hair on his upper lip and chin was neatly trimmed as always. His dark eyes were full of concern. He leaned in and placed a kiss on her cheek. The immortal had been a father figure to her for over two thousand years and helped her adjust to life as an immortal. He brought her under his wing and had made her a Guardian.

"What happened?" he asked, looking around Akantha at Damianos. Then he noticed and looked at the body in the rear seat.

"Nazis," she grumbled. "Can we stay until he's healed enough to travel?"

"Of course. I thought I would never see Damianos so incapacitated. What about the man in the rear seat?" He leaned in and pulled Damianos out.

"Dead," Akantha said as she put a shoulder under Damianos's arm. Zenon was on the other side. Slowly they started toward the house. "It's Matheus."

Zenon stopped for a brief moment. "I am sorry, Akantha."

"Thank you," she said. She wanted to say she didn't want his sympathies after what Matheus had done to her and in general, but she had loved Matheus. The man she knew was the gentle knight fleeing Philip's men, not the man who had stood with the Nazis.

"How did he die?" Zenon asked as they continued toward the house.

"The Spear of Destiny."

That got another pause. "You found it?"

"Yes," she answered and they started walking again. "We found it and Matheus ripped it from my hands, intending to hand it to the Nazis. Damianos helped me get it away from them."

"Did the spear injure him?" Zenon asked, nodding at the man suspended between them.

"Yes."

His brows came together and Akantha's stomach turned over. Did he know something about the spear she didn't? "Let's get him inside and take a look at his wound."

"Is there something we should be concerned about?" Damianos dying bothered her on a level she couldn't put into words. With the look on Zenon's face, and the feel of Damianos's fever-hot skin, a pit formed in her chest. Drawing in breath grew difficult.

"I don't know. We'll learn more when we get him inside."

It didn't take long to get Damianos into the house and into a bed in a room on the first floor, but to Akantha it seemed longer than her life. Once he was laid out on the bed, she removed his shirt and then noticed Zenon had disappeared. He reappeared moments later and handed Akantha a pair of scissors.

"Thank you," she said, accepting the scissors. She cut through the bandage on both sides of his body. She dropped the scissors on the bed and peeled away the bandage. Blood dripped from the bandage as she removed it and her chest tightened. Zenon held out a porcelain bowl and Akantha dropped the soaked bandage in it. He set the bowl on a nightstand and handed her a clean towel.

"Thank you." She wiped the blood from his chest as gently as she could. Normally he'd be complaining and demanding she be gentle, but silence dominated the room. She glanced up at his face and willed his eyes to open. The times she had wanted him to shut up had been too many to count, now she just wanted nothing more than to have him say anything. Even something that would make her mad or annoy her.

"I'm curious," Zenon said as he accepted the bloodied towel from Akantha, "why you're trying to save his life. I cannot count the number of times I've heard you swear to the gods you'd kill this man given the chance." He handed her a sterilized needle along with thread. "Your life would be less complicated if you left him to die, yet here you are trying to save his life."

"I have my reasons," she replied shortly, biting back a truthful reply.

"I would guess one of those reasons is you still love him."

Akantha didn't reply. She might say yes if she spoke. Instead, she started suturing the wound close. Her brows came together in concern at how hot his flesh was under her hands. "He needs something to break the fever."

"I will go make some tea. I believe I have yarrow on hand."

"Add lemon balm if you have it," she said as needle went into flesh. "It will help him sleep. And echinacea as well." Her voice wavered as she tried to hold the panic at bay. The fever bothered her on a level she couldn't put into words. She couldn't recall a time when either of them had run a fever.

"Excellent idea," Zenon agreed. "And for you?"

"Black tea, please."

"Of course. I will send someone with some wet cloths for him and I will return shortly."

She glanced up and saw him cross the room, heading for the door. "Zenon?"

He stopped and turned around. "Yes?"

"Could you please see to Matheus?"

"Yes," he said. "He will be given a burial fitting a Knight Templar."

"Thank you, my friend."

Zenon left the room and Akantha turned her attention back to suturing the wound. She was three quarters of the way done when the door opened and she paused to see who had entered. A servant carrying a porcelain bowl entered the room, and Akantha wasn't surprised Zenon still used servants. Most of the Guardians did, but not Akantha. Without needing direction, she crossed the room and set the white bowl on a nightstand. She removed a cloth and wrung out excess water. She looked at Akantha who nodded. The servant placed the cloth on Damianos's forehead.

"Is there anything else I can do, milady?"

"No thank you," she said and resumed suturing. She heard the servant leave and a long yawn escaped her. Exhaustion, injuries, and worry were taking their toll on her. She needed sleep as much as Damianos, but she knew she wouldn't get any. Not while he had a fever. She'd rest once his fever broke. She tied off the last suture and sighed deeply. Damn this man and damn her feelings for him.

She slipped his hand in hers and brought it up to her mouth. The kiss to his knuckles was light, tender. "I love you," she murmured against his knuckles. She released his hand and stood. She moved around the bed and removed the cloth from his forehead. She dipped it into the water and wrung it out, returning it to his forehead.

She pulled a nearby chair closer to the bed, sat, and then took his hand. Leaning back in the chair, she allowed herself a moment to relax and close her eyes. A deep sigh escaped her and she drifted off. Her hand didn't release his.

A hand on her shoulder woke her and she jumped. She looked up to see Zenon looking down at her. In his other hand he held a tray with two steaming teacups.

"I am sorry I startled you," he said.

"Do not worry about it. I shouldn't have fallen asleep."

"Perhaps Damianos isn't the only one who needs to rest," he said with a fond smile.

"I'm fine for now. I will rest later when his fever has broken."

"Stubborn, thy name is Akantha," he muttered as he set the tray down on the end table.

"I learned it from you," she countered. She released Damianos's hand and stood. "If you want to get him into somewhat of a sitting position, I can get the tea in him."

Zenon nodded. "Of course." He walked around to the other side of the bed and put his hands on Damianos's arm and gently pulled him up. Zenon put a hand on Damianos's shoulder to hold him in that position while he maneuvered behind Damianos and sat on the bed. He nodded to Akantha.

Akantha picked up the teacup with the lighter colored tea and brought it up to her nose for a sniff. The familiar smell of yarrow drifted up and she knew she had the correct cup. She dipped a fingertip in it to test the temperature. Satisfied it wasn't too hot, she brought the cup up to Damianos's mouth. Zenon tilted his head back a little and Akantha carefully poured some of the tea into his mouth. Some dribbled down his chin, but most made it into his mouth.

Little by little, the tea went into him, and when the cup was empty Zenon slipped out from behind him and gently laid him down on the pillows.

"Thank you," she said as she sat the empty teacup down on the tray. She'd make more yarrow-based tea later if the fever didn't break.

"You're welcome. With luck, his fever will break. You should get some rest."

Akantha sighed, wishing he would let the subject drop. Although she could imagine how she looked to Zenon. She had to have dark smudges under her eyes, disheveled hair, and her complexion was probably as pale as the sheets on the bed. She was exhausted and would love to sleep, but she had to make sure Damianos would be okay before she could rest. "When the fever breaks."

"Very well. Have you made a decision about what you are going to do with the spear?"

She tore her eyes away from Damianos and looked at him. "What do you mean did I make a decision about the spear? It will remain here with you."

Zenon shook his head. "No. The spear is your responsibility now. You must decide its fate."

"Zenon!" she protested.

"Yes, Akantha?"

"You are the keeper of the spear. It should remain with you."

"My dear, you are now the keeper. It is for you to decide."

"I don't want that responsibility."

"Want it or not, it is now your burden."

"But—" The look he shot her stopped her. Stubbornness was a common trait among immortals. "Fine. I haven't made a decision yet. What to do with it has been driving me crazy since we left Wewelsburg."

"I hold no doubts you will make the right decision."

That didn't help much, but then again, she didn't expect him to help. "What would you do with it if you had it?"

"Hide it away somewhere safe," he said. "Do it better than the last time I had it."

Akantha smiled. "You did a good job at hiding it."

"I could have done better."

Silence settled over the room. Akantha wasn't going to agree. The Guardians did their best to hide items, but sometimes they didn't do as a good a job as they needed to. Hiding in plain sight was a common thing, but sometimes not the best.

"You were right," she said quietly.

"About?"

"Damianos. I love him."

Zenon smiled a fatherly smile. She had missed it. "Of course you do. You have always loved him. Never stopped."

Akantha looked away. "Yes," she admitted.

Zenon walked around the bed to stand next to her. He placed a hand on her shoulder. "You've taken the first step. You've accepted the truth. Now you must tell him when he wakes. "

Easier said than done. She didn't know if she was ready to tell Damianos the truth about her feelings. "I will."

Zenon smiled. "Good. Try to rest. I will let you know when the service for Matheus is set."

Akantha nodded. "I will try. Thank you."

Zenon squeezed her shoulder and then left the room. Akantha returned to the chair and picked up the filled tea cup. She took a sip and the world slightly shifted back to normal.

Damianos walked in the door and was greeted with a smile like sunshine. Akantha was always more beautiful when she smiled and he would never tire of seeing her smile. Dark smudges shadowed her eyes and a general tiredness dominated her face, but she never looked more beautiful. Her gray eyes, even as tired as she was, sparkled. His eyes moved from her face to the small bundle in her arms.

"Come meet your daughter," she said, her voice low.

His chest tightened and his heart swelled. A daughter. Gods help him if she turned out to be anything like her mother. He crossed the room and took a seat on the bed next to her. He looked over at his daughter.

She was a tiny pink thing in her mother's arms. Her eyes were closed and he wondered if they would be gray like her mother's. Wisps of dark hair covered the top of her head. He reached out and touched a little hand with a fingertip. Ten perfect fingers and if he were to look, she'd have ten perfect toes. His eyes met Akantha's and she smiled.

"She's beautiful. Just like her mother. Did you decide on a name?" he asked.

"Eleni," Akantha replied.

He smiled. She always took Greek sounding names for herself and her children. "I like it." He leaned over, careful not to squash the baby between them, and placed a kiss on her forehead. Then he placed a light kiss on Eleni's forehead.

The world blurred and shifted, bringing him to another bedroom. The familiarity of the scene settled over him. His chest tightened and his stomach twisted. The bed linens were soaked in blood and a baby wailed. Akantha held the infant while the baby's mother lay in the bed. Akantha looked at him, her eyes red and swollen from crying. Tears ran down her cheeks. His vision blurred as tears filled his eyes and his heart shattered into pieces.

"Is she?" He couldn't say another word. He just looked at Eleni lying there.

Akantha's lips moved, but no sound came out. She nodded.

His world crashed down around him and grief flooded through him. Eleni was the joy of his life and she was dead.

The scene shifted again. He was back in Wewelsburg trying to wrestle the spear from Matheus's grasp. His hands slipped from the shaft as he watched Akantha rip it from Matheus's hands. She turned the spear in her hands and instead of driving it through Matheus's chest, the point plunged into his own chest. His chest exploded with pain and it spread to other parts of his body. He looked at Akantha, not believing what she had just done. He screamed, but no sound came out.

Damianos sucked in a deep breath and opened his eyes. He moved to sit, but pain in his chest stopped him. He looked down at his chest and touched the white bandage running across his chest with a finger. Then he noticed someone squeezed his other hand. He looked at his right hand and saw a woman's hand. His eyes traveled up the length of her arm and then to her face. Gray eyes looked back at him and he smiled.

"What happened?" he asked.

"You passed out from your injuries. You've been unconscious for two days."

"Two days?" He looked around at the unfamiliar room. "Where are we?"

"Zenon's," she answered. "This was the closest place." He moved to sit and she put a hand on his shoulder in an effort to keep him still. "Don't move. You'll pull your stitches." She released his hand and placed her hand on his forehead. "You're still a little feverish."

"What? We don't—" He settled down into the bed.

"You were running a fever. Zenon and I think it was because you were injured by the spear." Her hand took his and held it.

Realization settled over him. Just a scratch from the spear had caused him more serious injury than any he had received in the past twenty-four hundred years. All the wounds from all the battles he had fought in his life, he had never been unconscious for two days or had run a fever. He looked at her. He didn't ask, but he knew she had been by his side the whole time. If she hated him as much as she claimed, she would have left after dropping him on Zenon's doorstep. He squeezed her hand and she smiled.

"Are you hungry? I'm going to go make you some more yarrow tea."

"A little," he admitted. "What I could use is a shot of whiskey." She started to stand and he pulled her down. "Stay."

"I'm coming back," she assured him. She squeezed his hand. "You can have all the whiskey you want after you've healed."

"You better come back," he said as he released her hand. "And I'll hold you to that."

She leaned over and placed a kiss on his forehead. "Of course you will."

He smiled and watched her leave the room.

CHAPTER THIRTY

FRANCE 1941

The simple wooden cross marked the grave of the last Knight Templar, buried six hundred years after the death of his brothers. The priest who had conducted the simple service walked away from the fresh grave, but Akantha hardly noticed. A part of her heart and a piece of her soul were buried in the cold ground with Matheus. It would take years, maybe a few decades, to get past his death. He would always be the knight she met in the early 1300s, not the man he had been recently.

She held the spear in her right hand, never letting it out of her sight for more than a few moments at a time. Even here, which she considered a safe place, she kept the spear close.

The question of what to do with the spear lingered in her mind. She wanted to return it to Zenon and make him responsible for it, but it was a losing battle. He'd refuse again and at times he could prove to be more stubborn than she. She'd have to mull over the options open to her and choose one of them. When her heart and mind weren't enmeshed in grief, she would figure it out.

She jumped when a hand was placed on her shoulder. She looked at it and then up at Damianos. Her heart ached too much to say anything. Death ended a life, not a relationship. A part of her would always love Matheus, and that part was in agony. The hand moved from her shoulder and the arm went around her waist. She leaned into him and then silently scolded herself for doing it, but she didn't move away. He provided strength and she desperately needed a little right now.

"We can't linger here," he said quietly. "The Germans will find us."

"I know," she said. Yet, her feet wouldn't move. It wasn't too far from here where she first met Matheus and had saved him from the king's soldiers. She didn't want to leave with a part of her heart buried in the ground. She knew German and Vichy French forces were in the area and they would arrest the both of them on sight. A deep sigh, laced with regret and guilt, escaped her. The sun was bright and Akantha was angry it had the audacity to shine. The sky should be full of dark clouds and raining, as if it mourned with her.

Damianos heard the sigh and gave her a gentle squeeze. He'd take all of her pain away if he could. He carried the guilt of hurting her for so long, it seemed like an old friend or a well-worn pair of boots. Matheus was the lucky one; the dead carried no guilt and held no responsibilities. Matheus was in the cold ground and wasn't alive to see the pain etched in her gray eyes. Damianos wanted to resurrect the man only to kill him all over.

He knew she would move on and time would heal the wounds she suffered. She was a fighter and always found a way to survive in the end. Each battle made her stronger and brought her closer to peace. It may be storming in her life right now, but storms didn't last forever.

Akantha glanced over at him and met his eyes.

Sadness dominated her face and he wanted nothing more than to make her happy again. Only he knew he couldn't. "You had no other choice," he said softly. "The Nazis couldn't get their hands on the spear."

"I know. It's just—"

"You loved him," Damianos finished for her.

"I did," she admitted. "And I killed him." She looked at the fresh grave and tears welled up in her eyes. They spilled out and ran down her cheeks. He wiped them away with a thumb. He placed a soft kiss on her temple and she closed her eyes as he did.

"You had to. There was no other choice," he told her. "I should have been the one to do it, then you wouldn't have to carry the burden of taking his life. I would go out and conquer the world and demand peace on Earth if it took this pain away from you."

"He was one of the best." Akantha sighed and dropped the rose in her hand on the grave. "May your god shelter and protect your soul," she whispered.

"Ready?"

"No, but we need to go," she said.

"We do," he agreed. "Is there anything you need from the house?"

She shook her head. "There's nothing I need in there, but we should say goodbye to Zenon. Have you ever thought about it?" she asked, looking at the grave one last time.

"About what?" he asked, not sure what exactly she was asking. The woman could be mercurial and he couldn't keep up with her mind at times.

"Ending it. We now know the spear can kill an immortal."

He shook his head. "No. Not once."

A dark brow rose and she gave him A Look. "Really?"

"Okay, I admit I did think about it in the beginning, but as I got older I realized that living was more important and more of a challenge. Have you?"

Akantha shrugged. "A few times I got tired of living. I remember going back to the temple to end this curse and despairing when I saw the ruins. I wanted to die right there and then. The other time—now I never think about it."

"The other time?" he prompted.

She squeezed her eyes shut. "Eleni."

He sighed deeply and he squeezed her against him. The death of their daughter in 1766 had been a crushing blow to each of them. Eleni had been young, full of life, and had died giving birth to their grandchild. They buried their daughter and raised their granddaughter. One hundred and seventy-five years later they still hesitated to mention her name. Eleni's life was the longest stretch of time the two of them had been together and they had been happy.

He gently turned her in the direction of the house. If they didn't move now, they never would and the Germans would find them. A shroud of silence settled over them as they walked. He was thankful she never decided to end her existence. His fate was tied to hers and he would die a second after her. She wasn't the only one the priestess cursed that night.

They reached the house and Zenon greeted them at the door. He held a covered basket in his hands and offered it to Damianos.

"Food and weapons."

Damianos nodded and accepted the basket. "Thank you."

"What are your plans?"

"We're going to head to Calais and slip across the channel to England," Akantha answered.

"That's a good plan. And the spear?"

Akantha shrugged. "I don't know yet."

Zenon smiled and put a hand on her shoulder. "I know you'll make the right choice."

"Thank you." Akantha slipped from Damianos's arms and hugged Zenon. He returned the hug. He held out a hand to Damianos after releasing Akantha.

Damianos took the offered hand and shook it. "Thank you."

"You're welcome. Gods be with you."

"Gods be with you," he said and slipped an arm around Akantha's waist. He turned her toward the waiting car.

They reached the car and he opened the door for her. She muttered her thanks as she climbed in. He walked around the front and climbed in the driver's side. He started the engine and looked over at her. "Are you okay?"

His voice brought her out of her reverie. "I will be," she answered.

"Maybe we can steal a plane somewhere," he said as he put the car into gear.

"No plane."

He sighed. The woman and her irrational fear of flying. "Fine. We'll see if we can steal a boat."

Damianos felt the weight of her eyes and glanced over. Her eyes were rimmed with red from crying and she had a lost, pathetic look about her. He stretched out his arm toward her and she slid across the seat and settled in next to him. His arm settled across her shoulders and his hand came to rest on her far shoulder, holding her close. He felt her sigh deeply and he kissed the top of her head. She was a woman who didn't need to be saved; she needed to be loved. He would love her if she would give him a chance.

CHAPTER THIRTY-ONE

London, England 1941

"Are you okay?" Damianos asked, coming up behind Akantha and placing a hand on a bare shoulder. She stood by the window wrapped in a sheet, watching the street below. She turned to look at the hand on her shoulder, but she didn't protest his touch or try to pull away.

He affectionately nuzzled her neck and a shiver raced down her spine. "I'm fine," she answered without thought. Was she fine? She didn't know the answer to the question. Her mind was still processing the events of the past week and her heart ached over the loss of Matheus. She had lost people she loved in the past, but none had been by her own hand.

Matheus was another ghost added to a world full of ghosts. The longer she lived, the more haunted she became. Names and faces faded with memories, but they all served to remind her that her heart still beat and her lungs drew breath.

"You don't sound fine," he muttered as he dropped kisses along the smooth skin of her neck.

A truck rumbled on the street below, and Akantha watched it roll past the hotel. The streets of London were quiet at this late hour, save for the occasional vehicle. They had come here from Calais. They were able to find a small boat to take them across the English Channel to Dover. Then, it was a short trip by auto to London.

She sighed contently and her eyes closed at the feel of his mouth on her neck. Yet at the same time she was mentally chiding herself for enjoying it. They played the same game over and over through the long years and no matter the winner, they never changed. They ran circles around each other. She was tiring of the running. "Just processing everything," she admitted. She leaned back into him, soaking up warmth and strength. He gently turned her around and put a hand under her chin to lift it so he could see her face. His face blurred as tears formed in her eyes. He dropped a light kiss on her lush lips. "Mourn him, but eventually let it go. You'll drive yourself crazy if you dwell on it."

Akantha looked into his dark eyes and didn't answer. She knew he was right and hated it. She would mourn Matheus, but she knew life moved on. It always did no matter how much she wanted it to stop or even slow down. "I know," she told him.

"I'm here for you," he said. "Anything you need, just say the word. I'd give you the world if you wanted it."

She felt herself falling under the spell of his gaze and could get lost in the brown depths if she weren't careful. Despite being an ass most of the time, she couldn't deny that he cared. No matter what happened between them, and no matter what nasty things she said to him, he was always there for her. She nodded but couldn't find the words to thank him. She feared she'd start crying if she spoke.

He wrapped his arms around her and held her against his chest. The sound of his steady heart beat spoke to her on a level she couldn't put into words and time slowed around them. She closed her eyes and listened; the world slowly righting itself in the steady rhythm. Her heart still ached, and would for a long time, but in the warmth of his arms things seemed better. The world would move on with or without her and she couldn't wallow in grief. He wouldn't let her, and she was thankful, but she couldn't voice it.

"Have you decided what you're going to do with the spear?" he asked.

She shook her head. "Not yet." The distraction he provided hadn't given her much time to think past the current moment. She knew she had to make a decision soon. There were two choices open to her: she could give the spear to Churchill and the Allies, or hide it away in a vault far from the reach of mortals.

"Giving it to the Allies could turn the tide of the war and save a lot of lives in the end," he pointed out.

"I know," she said. "But there's no guarantee that they'll stop once they defeated the Axis powers, or give it back."

"There's always a risk," he said. "But if the Allies don't succeed, I'd hate to see how many people vanish from the face of the Earth and what atrocities the Nazis would commit."

The Allies winning was the only way the Nazis would stop slaughtering millions of innocent people. Images from the camps appeared in her mind and she shuddered. The spear in Allied hands could prevent similar horrors. "What would you do with it?" she asked.

"It's not my choice," he said. "You're a Guardian and the current keeper of the spear. It's for you alone to decide."

"Hypothetically, if it were your choice, what would you do with it?"

"I'd give it to the Allies so they could win the war and save countless lives," he answered. "Of course, I'd only give it to someone I'd trust to give it back."

It seemed simple enough, but it really wasn't that simple. There weren't many people she trusted and even fewer she'd trust with something as powerful as the Spear of Destiny. Not only would she be giving someone the ability to kill the handful of immortals in the world, but it was also said that whoever possessed the spear would have the power to shape the destiny of the world. Could she risk giving someone that kind of power? Power attracted the worst and corrupted the best.

"I'll have to think about it," she finally said.

He nodded and looked into her eyes. "Gods above, you're beautiful," he said before dropping a kiss on her mouth. "If I had a flower for every time I thought of you, I could walk through my garden forever."

The tender kiss and the Tennyson quote made her go weak in the knees and made her briefly turn into that foolish seventeen-year-old girl who had fallen in love with him. She shook her head and tried to banish such feelings. She couldn't let herself be ensnared by him again, not now when her heart was broken and she was emotionally raw and vulnerable. She pulled back and took a few steps away from him.

"What's wrong?" he asked.

"Nothing," she automatically replied.

"Akantha," he said and took a step toward her.

She moved without thought, taking her beyond his reach. "Damianos. Please."

He sighed heavily. "Akantha," he repeated and closed the distance between them. He wasn't going to let her put distance and rebuild the walls between them. His arms wrapped around her and she stood stiffly in his arms.

Akantha put her hands to his chest, the hard muscles making her feel a bit lightheaded, and tried to push him away. She may have well been trying to push a wall for what good it did. The warmth of his very naked body melted away any resistance she had.

He lowered his head and his mouth claimed hers in a forceful kiss.

Akantha was breathless when the kiss ended. She tried to pull away from him, but the strong arms around her didn't let her move. "Damianos!" she protested.

"Yes, my love?"

"Don't call me that."

"Why not? I love you. I have always loved you and I will always love you."

Akantha harrumphed.

"I'm serious. Why can't you forgive the actions of a foolish young boy? I've spent over two thousand years trying to get you to forgive me."

"It's not that simple," she told him.

"You forgave Matheus," he pointed out. "For worse than I ever did, yet you cannot forgive me. Why?"

"You broke my heart," she snapped. She tried to pull away, but his arms were steel bands around her. Forgiving him would mean removing the knife from her heart and not using it hurt him in return. A part of her wanted to inflict pain upon him for all of the wounds he had delivered upon her heart and soul.

"There's not a day that goes by where I don't regret what I did." He tenderly tucked a lock of hair behind her ear. "I would give anything to be able to go back and fix my mistake. I would do anything to make it up to you and earn your forgiveness."

Akantha looked away. She couldn't stand looking into his eyes and seeing the guilt and remorse in the brown depths. By the gods below, she still loved him and wanted to forgive him, but each time she looked at him she swore her heart broke all over again. She had found it in her heart to forgive Matheus, yet she had a hard time forgiving Damianos. It was easier to keep hating him than it was to forgive him.

She had to eventually forgive him, she realized that now. Not for him, but for her. Like chains shackling her to the past, she could no longer pollute her heart with bitterness, fear, distrust, or anger. She had to forgive him because hate was another way of holding on and she couldn't hold on much longer.

"Please," he whispered. "Forgive me."

She turned to look at him, the words of forgiveness on the tip of her tongue. Could she trust him not to hurt her again? Could she give him her heart and love him the way she longed to? How could she love again when she was terrified of falling? He took a step away from her and fell to his knees in front of her.

Her stomach dropped to her feet and she knew that determined look on his face. She wasn't going to like what he was about to do.

"Take up the spear and run it through my heart," he instructed.

Her jaw dropped, her eyes widened, and Akantha stared at him. Blood thundered in her ears and her heart raced in her chest. "What? Have you suddenly taken leave of your senses?"

He shook his head. "No. I don't want to live if there's no chance of earning your forgiveness."

She shook her head. The man had lost his mind. "No. I won't do it. I can't do it." She stepped away from him.

"Please," he begged.

"Why are you doing this?" she asked.

"I'd rather die, than live knowing you'll never forgive me. I love you, Akantha, with all of my heart and all of my soul. I always have and always will. Living without you isn't really living, and I'm tired of just existing. I want to be with you and I want you to love me. If I can't, I'd rather die than keep going through this long, torturous, empty existence without you."

"Damianos, please don't make me do this. Don't ask this of me." Her hands shook, her knees went weak, and her legs threatened to give out from under her. This latest attack in their war struck with surgical precision and had taken away her armor. Now all that was left was her surrender.

Why was he doing this? Couldn't he see she couldn't do what he asked? She lost Matheus and now she stood to lose him. He had backed her into a corner and was forcing her hand. She either had to do what she had been threatening to do for untold centuries or face truths she wasn't ready to face.

"I must," he insisted. "I'm tired of the games. I'm tired and weary down to my soul. Please, Akantha. If you truly hate me like you say, you won't hesitate to do it."

She stared at him. The bastard was forcing her hand and forcing her to admit her feelings for him. "Gods above and below help me, I can't. I can't kill you. There have been so many times I wanted to, but I can't do it." She knew why, but she didn't want to admit she still loved him. At least out loud. She was terrified to love him again. Their eyes met and locked. The breath stayed in her chest and the world slowed to a stop around them. Akantha couldn't move even if she wanted to.

He stared at her. "Admit that you love me." The world stuttered into motion with the sound of his voice.

She lowered her head and stared at spot on the floor.

"Admit it," he urged. "Or kill me now."

"I love you," she whispered.

"What scares you so?" he asked.

There was so much she wanted to say and was practically screaming on the inside, but the words would not come. He destroyed her once, she didn't want to risk him doing it again. "You," she whispered, not daring to say anything else.

"I promise you, Akantha, I will never hurt you again. I would die before I hurt you. May the gods strike me down and send me to Tartarus for all eternity if I hurt you again. My word, my love."

She looked at the outstretched hand. Her throat tightened, making it difficult to swallow, and butterflies fluttered in her stomach. His hand was a live viper ready to bite if she dared to reach out and touch it. Fear coiled around her and its cold tendrils squeezed her heart. Her mouth was full of cotton. A hand came up, shaking as it did, and she held it out. Her eyes returned to his and she held his gaze. Her feet moved forward and she felt her hand slide across his. A smile stretched his mouth and light danced in his brown eyes. His hand closed around hers.

Damianos rose and closed the small distance between them. He pulled her toward him and wrapped his arms around her, crushing her against his body. Her whole body shook and he cupped her cheek with a hand. "There's nothing to be scared of," he assured her. "I love you, and I will never hurt you." His lips brushed lightly across hers.

Akantha was still while he kissed her, not daring to move. He deepened the kiss and any remaining resistance inside of her broke into a million pieces.

CHAPTER THIRTY-TWO

LONDON, ENGLAND 1941

Akantha was up before the dawn could turn the grays and blacks of the room to color. Damianos still slept next to her, snoring not so softly. A hand rested possessively on her hip and she wondered if he thought she'd run away, even in his sleep. She yawned and knew she could use a few more hours of sleep, but she wouldn't sleep any longer. Her mind was already moving too fast to slow down enough to go back to sleep.

Her head was on his chest and she listened to the steady beating of his heart. The troubles of the outside world faded away in the steady rhythm, but her inner conflict remained. She didn't know what to do.

She turned her head and looked at his face. Sleep softened the hard planes and made him look younger. A slight smile turned up the corners of his mouth. She sighed deeply. She admitted she loved him, the words were out, and there was no going back. Admitting her feelings to him wasn't the worst thing to happen, but now she'd have to deal with the fallout. He'd want more than last night and she couldn't handle more right now, not with her heart in a million pieces. She had two options open to her.

She could stay and go through this war with him, and then—she didn't know exactly what would happen, but it would probably be spending years with him. They had spent a few decades together through their long lives, but she didn't know if she could do it right now. It may take her a decade or two to get over Matheus, but Damianos would soothe the wounds Matheus had inflicted upon her heart and soul, and there was a chance they could make each other smile.

The other option was to leave. She could walk away and give herself time for her wounded heart to heal in peace. He would track her down, it was inevitable as the changing tides, and make her face the repercussions of admitting her feelings. It could be a few years or a few decades, but he would find her. Their fates had been intertwined since the night she ran away from the temple and they always would be.

She pinched the bridge of her nose and sighed deeply. She had to make a decision before he woke. Once he was awake, there would be no resisting him. If she were going to leave, now would be the time to do it. She looked at his face, smiled, and dropped a kiss on his chin. He stirred and mumbled something unintelligible.

She smiled and dropped another kiss on his chin. "I love you," she whispered.

Damianos woke to the sun pouring in through the window and for a brief moment he was taken back to a small room in Athens. He smiled and he turned to find the space next to him empty. The lonely light of morning illuminated a slip of paper on the pillow next to his. He pulled himself up to a sitting position and looked around the empty room. She was gone and he wasn't in the least bit surprised. Her eyes had spoken volumes, telling him she would never stay. The spear still leaned against the wall in the corner where she had left it the previous day.

The words were out and she had admitted she loved him. There was no going back. He may not be able to be with her right now, but he would be one day. Even if it took decades. She was worth it. The gray-eyed woman had captured his heart the moment he laid eyes on her and no other woman would do. He loved her, thorns and all, and he knew he would never stop. Hindsight was 20/20 and looking back, not telling her the truth was the biggest mistake of his life.

He reached over and grabbed the note.

I trust you. I forgive you.

Damianos smiled. He would track her down as soon as this war was over. They had unfinished business and she wasn't going to get away from him that easily.

CHAPTER THIRTY-THREE

BUENOS AIRES, ARGENTINA 1945

The sun was hot and relentless, the air thick with humidity. A sea of people filled the marketplace deep in the heart of Buenos Aires and a cacophony of voices filled the air. The cafe was crowded, but Akantha sat alone at a small corner table outside. She sipped a cup of coffee as she waited for her SOE contact. The war was over, but ratlines allowed Nazis to escape Europe to South American countries. Tired of war-torn Europe and needing something to do, she volunteered to hunt down the cockroaches who had escaped. Staying busy behind enemy lines for the war helped her get past Matheus's death, but she hadn't been ready to settle down. She only wished she could have killed Himmler before the coward took his own life.

She glanced at her watch. Her contact was ten minutes late and counting. A firm believer in being punctual, she expected others to be punctual. She lifted the cup to her lips and paused. An all too familiar face greeted her.

"What are you doing here?" she asked, placing her cup on the table.

Damianos grinned and slid into the chair across from her. "Hello, Akantha."

Akantha sighed. Of all people to show up, it had to be him. "What are you doing here? How did you find me?"

"It's good to see you too." He smirked. He slid a manila folder across the table toward her. "I'm your contact."

"You're late," she grumbled and stared at the envelope, but didn't reach for it.

"Morrow sent me," Damianos explained and signaled for a waitress. "He suggested I assist the SOE."

Her eyes narrowed. "Why would he do that?" The Supernatural Police Department taking an interest in the mundane world was unusual. They policed and monitored the "weird world", as most called it.

A waitress arrived and took his order. Once she was gone, he continued. "He believes some of the cockroaches who fled are of concern."

"You mean—"

"Yes."

A heavy sigh escaped her. As if hunting down Nazis wasn't hard enough, some of them were supernatural types. Her job suddenly became a lot harder. "I suppose you're not here to just deliver the information."

He grinned. "Morrow and the SOE decided this was going to be a joint venture."

Of course it was, and she couldn't argue with it. Much. She thought she'd have a decade or two without having to face him and her confession. Now he was here, she had to work with him, and it was inevitable he would want to talk about it. "What are our instructions?"

"Bring them back for prosecution and justice."

"And if they resist?"

He shrugged, his heavy shoulders rolling with the motion.

"Extreme prejudice was mentioned." He reached across the table and took her hands. "This could be fun."

She didn't pull her hands away. "Fun?"

"Fun," he smiled. "You, me, an exotic setting, and some hunting. What isn't fun about that?" He didn't say what they were hunting. They were in a public setting after all.

She pulled a hand from his and picked up her cup. She took a long sip. "I guess time will tell if this turns out to be fun or not."

The waitress brought Damianos's coffee and set it down on the table. He thanked her with a smile and then picked up his cup with his free hand. His other hand still held hers. "It can't be worse than that trek across Asia we took."

She set her cup down and tapped the side with a fingertip. "I never asked, how did you end up working for Marco Polo?"

"Morrow," he answered. "Morrow wanted me to travel to Beijing to deliver something for him. He made all the arrangements." He smiled. "I volunteered to go when he was looking for someone."

"So you thought to just stop by and grab me?"

He smiled. "I didn't hear you objecting at the time."

She blinked and then laughed. "My husband at the time was rather upset to find you in my bed."

"I think he was even more upset when I ran my sword through him."

Akantha laughed again. "Yes, yes he was."

"What did you ever see in him?" he asked before taking a sip of his coffee.

"He was rich and had land," she said with a shrug. "It never hurt to add some more wealth and land to my assets. I still own those lands."

He shook his head, chuckling.

"You weren't any better," she said. "I know about all those wealthy ladies you suckered out of money."

He smiled. "They were willing to be suckered out of it too."

"I'm sure they were," she said dryly. His eyes gleamed with merriment over the rim of his cup. She couldn't remember the last time they laughed about something together. It almost made her forget the horrors of the recent war. Almost. She still woke from nightmares of the camps and Matheus.

"Did you get home?"

Akantha nodded. "I did. Just long enough to close the house."

"You closed the house? Where's the walking carpet?"

"It was time to move on," she said with a wave of her hand. "I was there since 1920. I'll go back in four or five decades." She smiled. "He's with a friend."

"Good. Before we get down to hunting business, we have other unfinished business to deal with."

The smile faded and all amusement drained out of her. "That can wait." She knew he'd bring it up sooner or later, she just wished it had been later. She wasn't ready to discuss this with him.

"No, it can't. I'm not going to spend our entire mission tiptoeing around the subject. We're going to talk about this now and get it all out in the open. You've had four years."

She expected him to show up much earlier than four years, but there had been a war raging. If she knew him, he had been out on the front lines. Akantha sighed and tried to pull her hand away. He squeezed, preventing her from doing it. "Fine. Talk."

"First, the spear is safe and in good hands. I gave it to—"

"I don't want to know who has it. As long as it's safe, that's all that matters."

He smiled. "It's safe."

"Good." She didn't doubt him. He had seen first-hand what the spear could do and knew he wanted it out of reach as much as she did.

"Now the other things."

She swallowed past the sudden lump her in throat and her hand became sweaty in his. She put her free hand on her lap so he wouldn't see it shake. "I don't know what there's to talk about. I said what I said and wrote what I wrote. There's nothing else to discuss."

Damianos smiled and took a sip of his coffee. He looked over at her and she looked away. "There's plenty to discuss."

"Such as?" She looked back at him.

"Us."

"There is no us."

"Precisely. That's the problem." He casually took another sip of coffee. Hers remained untouched.

"That's not a problem," she insisted.

He smiled at her stubbornness and the expected resistance. She never failed to disappoint him and she made living worthwhile. "It is from where I'm sitting."

"Change your seat."

Damianos laughed. "I have missed you." He brought her hand up and dropped a kiss on her knuckles. The thought of being reunited with her carried him through the past four years and the war. "Don't you ever get tired of being wrapped up in how things used to be?"

No answer.

He dropped another kiss on her knuckles. "Let's work on making new memories."

She remained quiet and he expected as much. She looked away. A faraway look appeared on her face and he knew she was processing his words. She looked at him and took a sip of her coffee. "Okay," she said, setting the cup on the table.

He blinked and the shook his head. "Did I just hear that correctly? You agreed without arguing?"

She rolled her eyes and sighed. "Yes."

He stared at her, the power of speech leaving him. He forced his mouth to move. "This is the first time in a very long time that you've ever done that."

She just looked at him, her mouth pressing into a thin line.

He smiled. "I'm not going to make you repeat things already said or written, but what I want from you is an honest chance. We love each other and it's time to move forward, not dwell on the past. Are you willing to give us an honest chance?" He picked up his cup and sipped, giving her a chance to respond. The coffee was better than any he had in the past six years. Now if he could find a bottle of good beer, he'd be set.

She looked away and he watched her as she mulled over his words. She never could look at him when it came to the subject of them. The noise of the marketplace filled in the silence between them. He sipped his coffee while he waited for her to speak. She looked back at him, placing her cup on the table. "Yes."

He blinked and then smiled. He brought her hand up and placed a light kiss on her knuckles. "I love you," he said. He didn't expect her to return the sentiment right now, but she would eventually. She squeezed his hand and smiled. He released her hand and slid the envelope closer to her. "Let's finish our coffee and start hunting."

THE END

Thank you for reading! Did you enjoy?

Please Add Your Review! And don't miss more books from City Owl Press

**Discover more from Sydney Ashcroft and Dani Nichols at
www.nicholsandashcroft.com**

Please sign up for the City Owl Press newsletter for chances to win special
subscriber-only contests and giveaways as well as receiving information on
upcoming releases and special excerpts.

All reviews are **welcome** and **appreciated**. Please consider leaving one on
your favorite social media and book buying sites.

For books in the world of romance and speculative fiction that embody
Innovation, Creativity, and Affordability, check out City Owl Press at
www.cityowlpress.com.

ACKNOWLEDGMENTS

I'd like to thank the following people for helping me on this incredible journey. Amber Duell for all those Sunday morning Panera writing sessions. I wish you still lived in Maine. Laurie MacAllister for the song, for the music to write to, and being one of the most awesome and funniest people on the planet. Shelly Lopez for your amazing editing and helping to get this cleaned up. To Jennifer Colvin for all those chats and for the beta read. Amanda and Tina for giving us the chance to make a dream come true. Lastly, to Goose for eighteen years of writing together, shenanigans, adventures, and tons of laughs. - Sydney

I want to thank Jaymee, Amanda, and Joshua for growing up and moving away from home. Gone are the days of last minute grocery shopping, extra laundry loads, and prowling the house looking for missing dishes. You left your mom with more stories to tell and free time to write them. Best kids ever! - Dani

ABOUT THE AUTHORS

SYDNEY ASHCROFT originally hails from Pennsylvania and is a die-hard Penn State fan, but moved to New England over twenty years ago and has never looked back. She currently resides in Maine along with her daughter, a beagle, a cane corso, and a foster beagle. During the day she works full time in the information technology field and writes by night. Tea, chocolate, and folk music fuel her through the day and writing sessions. When she's not writing or working, she enjoys spending time with her daughter and dogs, going to see live music, and plotting shenanigans with her co-author.

DANI NICHOLS is a first time author living in the California Central Valley, happily ensconced between the wine trails and the foothills. She's a career public servant who frequently bribes the cat off the laptop so she can write the kinds of stories she loves to read. Dani stocks up with travel experiences, coffee, Ben and Jerry's Peanut Butter Cup ice cream, and the occasional bottle of wine to fuel her literary escapes.

www.nicholsandashcroft.com

ABOUT THE PUBLISHER

City Owl Press is a cutting edge indie publishing company, bringing the world of romance and speculative fiction to discerning readers.

www.cityowlpress.com

CPSIA information can be obtained
at www.ICGtesting.com
Printed in the USA
FSHW01n1457070918
51959FS